Secret's Shadow

trouble. Cassidy McCabe has a special spot on my bookshelf. I anticipate her next adventure!" —T.J. MacGregor, author of *Mistress of the Bones*

Satan's Silence

"Matthews delivers another well-crafted page-turner. If you haven't discovered Cassidy and Starshine yet, pick up *Satan's Silence*. Begin reading it on a day when you have little else planned because once you start, you won't put it down until you reach the last page." — *Cats Magazine*

"Matthews has done an excellent job of creating an interesting and sympathetic character without becoming cloying or unrealisic—one who faces her fears and forges ahead. Fortunately, for the reader, this book is no struggle—just good, enjoyable reading." — *Mystery News*

"Alex Matthews delivers a good tale because of Cassidy's flaws and the author's superior writing ability."
— *Harriet Klausner, online reviewer*

"Both of these books are good reads and are out-of the-ordinary." — *Mysterious Women*

Secret's Shadow

Alex Matthews

Intrigue Press

Copyright © 1996 Alex Matthews

Printed and bound in the United States of America. All rights reserved. No part of this book may be reproduced or transmitted in any form
or by any means, electronic or mechanical, including photocopying, recording, or by an information storage and retrieval system—except by a
reviewer who may quote brief passages in a review to be printed in a
magazine or newspaper—without permissin in writing from the publisher.

For information, please contact Intrigue Press, P.O. Box 456, Angel
Fire, NM 87710, 505-377-3474.

ISBN 1-890768-03-0

First Printing 1996
First Paperback Printing 1998

This book is a work of fiction. Although Cassidy McCabe and the
author have many circumstances in common, none of the actions or events
is based on real events in the author's life. Names, characters, places and
incidents either are the product of the author's imagination or are used
fictitiously. Any resemblance to actual events or persons living or dead is
entirely coincidental. Although the author and publisher have made every
effort to ensure the accuracy and completeness of information contained in
this book, we assume no responsibility for errors, inaccuracies, omissions,
or any inconsistency herein. Any slights of people, places or organizations
are unintentional.

Grateful acknowledgment is made for permission to reprint the
following material:

A line from the comic strip *Sylvia* © 1995 by Nicole Hollander. Used
by permission. All rights reserved.

A line from the comic strip *Buckets* by Scott Stantis © 1995 by
Tribune Media Services Inc. Thanks to Mary Beth Pacer. Used by permission. All rights reserved.

Lyrics from "Good Morning Starshine" by James Rado, Gerome
Ragni, Galt MacDermot © 1966, 67, 68, 1970 James Rado, Gerome Ragni,
Galt MacDermot, Nat Shapiro and EMI U Catalog Inc. Thanks to Rose-
marie Gawelko. Used by permission. All rights reserved. Warner Bros.
Publications U.S. Inc., Miami, FL 33014

1

CAT

Cassidy McCabe zipped her rattletrap Toyota into the left hand slot of her garage and dodged around garden tools strewn along the wall. *Later than I thought. Should've left an hour ago.* She emerged from the dark garage into a yellow wash of street lights on Briar, breath quickening at the thought of what might await her on her answering machine.

She rattled down the door, scanning both the alley next to the garage and the street leading to her large corner house. Exhaust fumes and the shriek of sirens floated in from Austin Boulevard a half block to the east. Austin was the demarcation line between one of the highest crime ghettos of Chicago and her own middle-class, struggling-to-integrate suburb of Oak Park. Living so close to Austin, she was always careful. But careful had turned to vigilant since the calls began.

Across the street a woman hurried down Briar from the bus stop, shoulders hunched, one hand gripping a briefcase, the other jammed in the pocket of her corporate-type suit, pepper gun probably clenched in her fist. At the end of the block, a trio of black teenagers standing in the middle of the intersection exchanged high volume, belligerent "Fuck-you's."

A warm spring night, scattered cars parked on both sides of the street. She stepped into the shadow at the corner of the garage, checking quickly for occupants.

Don't be a baby. Only a couple of anonymous calls.

Jogging the ten yards from garage to gate, she allowed her mind to drift back over the evening. Another godawful Wednesday night dinner with her mother. *Thirty-seven, divorced, a therapist yourself and you still let her get under your skin.*

She sprinted through the gate toward the pool of light at her back door. Spotlighted by the bulb, a cat sat erect in the middle of the mat, watching her arrival with all the aplomb of an official delegation. As Cassidy climbed the steps, the cat undulated to the door and poked its nose into the crack.

"Sorry, your highness. Wrong house." She was turning the key when the ringing began. She bolted through her client waiting room, raced across the kitchen. Her hand grabbed for the wall phone, then wavered. *Might be him.* The machine could take it.

As the fourth ring faded, Cassidy started toward the

door to lock up. But the ringing resumed, drawing her back like a tractor beam to stare at the phone's sleek plastic surface. Chewing her lower lip, she leaned against the refrigerator and counted rings. Four, five, six. Why didn't the machine cut in? The second call followed the first so quickly the machine had not had time to reset itself. She picked at a loose end of tape across the corner of a Sylvia cartoon. Maybe the same caller redialing right away to harass her.

Your imagination's running away. You do occasionally receive calls that are not threats.

After nineteen rings it finally stopped. She took a deep breath, the tension in her neck and shoulders subsiding.

She turned to see the cat, who had slipped in with her, sniffing along the edge of the stove. Small, only a kitten, lean as a dollar bill. She heard her mother's tart voice: Never feed a stray. Once you feed them, you can't get rid of them.

"Hey you. Cat."

Enormous amber eyes looked up, ears and nose forming a tiny triangle, one ear orange, one ear black, small pink nose. White, with orange and black patches. A calico, so it had to be female.

"You picked the wrong person to schmooze. I don't even like cats." She pictured a shabby kitchen with cats on the counter, refrigerator, table, a stink that knocked you out when you walked in the door: the house of her best friend in childhood.

Inching back behind the curling seam in the linoleum, the cat flattened her ears, twitched the tip of her tail. Wide almond eyes seemed to say: I might be willing to overlook this irrational prejudice, but don't expect me to beg.

"I'm broke, I can't afford another mouth to feed. You wouldn't want to live with a cat hater anyway, would you?"

Mrump

"Oh, forget my mother." Ferreting a can of tuna out of the cabinet, she grabbed a used lunch plate from the counter, plopped food on it, and held it out to the cat. "It's not like I usually follow her advice or anything." The cat bumped its head against her hand. "Course I always live to regret it."

As the cat growled over the tuna, she rounded the oak cabinet which separated the kitchen from the client area, crossed the waiting room, and locked the back door. After shredding newspaper into a box, she left the cat scouring an empty plate, closed the swinging kitchen door, and went upstairs to her master bedroom. Flicking on the overhead, she crossed to her executive desk in the corner, eyes instantly drawn to the red light on the answering machine. Three blinks.

Stalling a little longer, she reprogrammed the controls so the first call would pick up on the fourth ring, subsequent calls on the first. One ring would be easier to resist.

Stop procrastinating.

She took a pen out of her ceramic-mug penholder and pushed playback.

"Seven-thirty. Thought you'd be here by now. I made that tuna casserole you always like so much, but it'll get soggy if it has to sit much longer."

Beep.

I'm never on time, she knows that. Tuna casserole—haven't liked it since I was ten years old.

"It's Maggie. Village board was really something. This gay rights debate—it's bringing all the insects out of the woodwork. Somebody actually said, 'If people choose to be ho-mo-sexual....' And here I always thought Oak Park was progressive. Oh, and by the way, remember the thing about John Carter getting sued? He just got served. Malpractice against therapists—it's going to be the scourge of the nineties."

Beep.

Gotta be hard for Maggie, listening to that bilge. And why'd she have to mention malpractice? I don't want to think about overdue bills.

"As I told you before, we need to locate your ex." The voice, cool and precise, like a voice on public radio. The instant she heard it, her heart began banging into her rib cage. "You're screening your calls, and it's beginning to annoy me. You parked your beige Toyota in the garage at ten-twenty-five. You walked in the door just as the phone started ringing and refused to pick up. We'd prefer not to hurt you, but if you don't start cooperating, we'll be forced to apply pressure."

Beep.

Oh shit. Worse than oh shit. Watching the house. Kevin, you jerk, you wanted the divorce. What've you done now?

Hugging herself tightly, she rocked up and down on her toes. Third time Public Radio Voice had called. Avoidance wasn't working.

Do something! Call the cops. Get help.

No you don't. No thrashing around. Can't find Kevin. Hasn't shown his face since the last time he tried to borrow money. This guy's scary. Too slick to get caught. Keep your mouth shut, lie low, and maybe he'll leave you alone.

Her eyes darted to the north window, then to the west, one on each side of her corner desk, the interior light creating glass surfaces as opaque as reflector sunglasses. She flipped the overhead off and looked down from the north window. A large maple sporting frilly new leaves obscured the view. She lowered the blinds.

From the west window her gaze swept a wide, well-lighted street, lined with arching trees. A few parked cars, a man walking a lab. *Nobody standing under a lamp post.* Large older homes, mostly dark now, tucked away for the night.

Everything looked ordinary, reassuring. She pictured her grandmother's bungalow, remembering how safe she'd felt growing up there, back when Oak Park still resembled Hemingway's village of wide lawns and narrow minds. All that had changed now. Late in the sixties, when the west side of Chicago turned black, block by block like dominoes, Oak Park found itself standing squarely in the path of a sociological steamroller. The narrow minds hightailed it out to the all-white land beyond O'Hare, leaving behind a band of resolute citizens determined to stop racial turnover at Austin Boulevard and transform their village into a racially, socially diverse community. Oak Park became a magnet for crusading types who saw the village as a sanctuary for modern urban refugees: minorities of all kinds, interracial families, Unitarians, gays, singles, the handicapped—you name it, a place for everyone.

Cassidy was a firm believer in Oak Park's reinvented

identity. But the problem was, the village represented a small, idealistic island surrounded by a sea of predators. It had no moats, no walls to keep out the bad guys.

Public Radio Voice was out there somewhere, but he wasn't likely to wave up at her. She lowered the blinds, did her entire yoga routine, not the usual three stretches and a flex, then climbed into her king-sized bed. After a long stretch of racing and churning, she finally fell asleep.

A small, furry body suddenly plopped on her face. She sat bolt upright. Fur flashed as the cat retreated to the foot of the bed.

"Oh no! Not you."

Two big eyes shone in the dark.

"What do you do, walk through walls?" *The kitchen door doesn't close tightly. It's not her fault.*

Cassidy lunged but the cat was faster. She leapt off the bed, white fur disappearing into darkness.

ॐ ॐ ॐ

She was in her childhood home. Her mother was in the kitchen making tuna casserole and Kevin was in the bedroom talking and laughing with some woman she didn't know. She was in the living room, deep in telepathic conversation with a calico cat perched on the mantle.

"He's coming," the cat said. "Forget Kevin and your mother. There's nothing you can do to save them. You've got to save yourself."

"Who's coming? I can't run off and leave Kevin and Mom."

"Too late. There's nothing you can do. He's coming."

"Who's coming?"

"The man with the voice."

She sensed a gigantic, shadowy figure at the door. His voice blared through a loudspeaker, enunciating with exaggerated precision. "If you are found hiding Kevin, you will be sent forth naked and alone, to sit on other people's doorsteps and beg for food."

Kevin and the woman laughed louder.

The smell of tuna casserole made her gag.

The cat opened her mouth and emitted a howl . . . the howl turning into a scream . . . the scream turning into her alarm.

2

RETURNING A CALL

She patted around the night stand until the alarm stopped squawking. Exerting great effort, she peeled up her lids. Another pair of eyes—eyes that had turned a warm, affectionate green—gazed into hers. The cat rumbled loudly, exhaling tuna-breath.

Remembering she had an early appointment, she rushed downstairs, hoping a hit of caffeine would clear her head. She gulped coffee and stood under a cold shower, trying to get the old synapses to start synapsing again.

As she brushed her teeth, she wondered why she'd agreed to see Ryan at eight instead of nine, her usual starting time. She dabbed on makeup. Although she hated to admit it, she tended to be overly accommodating with him, more so than with other clients.

ta ta ta

"Well . . . how's it going?" she asked.

"Not great." Ryan slumped back into the garage-sale black vinyl sofa.

His elegant blue suit contrasted incongruously with the black plastic tape she'd applied to holes in the seat where buttons were missing.

"What is it?" The coleus on her wicker table drooped. She'd forgotten to water it again.

"Everything." Wide windows stretched across two sides of the paneled room, flooding it with morning light. "Everything keeps getting worse."

Crossing her legs, she jiggled a sandaled foot. What did that say for her, after two years of therapy?

"This last week I've been going through something, only I don't know what. Just this panicky feeling, like I'm going down for the third time."

C'mon, brain, work. "No idea where it's coming from?"

As he fixed his eyes on the mustard carpet, Cassidy took inventory of physical signs of stress. His fine-boned face, normally youthful under gleaming, prematurely white hair, looked drawn, the cheeks too hollow, the creases too deep. A malignant exhaustion seemed to be consuming him from within. What was wrong? If only the wires in her head would connect up the way they were supposed to.

"Dammit." Lifeless blue eyes met hers. "Can't put my finger on it."

My brilliant clinical skills—a tad unwired as well. At least he doesn't seem to notice.

"Lately, I've been remembering things. Things I . . . regret."

"Want to tell me?"

His mouth quirked in a wry half smile. "Not really." She waited. "There was a woman. I let things get out of hand."

She didn't want to hear this.

A flicker of irony passed through his lackluster eyes. "It's damn hard to live with a woman who's all wrapped up in a delinquent kid from her first marriage. 'Poor Scott, you don't understand, he's just got this little problem with drugs.' Especially hard to live with, now that the old spark's gone out of the bedroom."

"So you've been regretting this woman. Anything else?"

"You're tough." The half smile again. "Oh, just the anger. Wish I could get rid of the anger. Sometimes it makes me do things, that's all."

The question 'What things?' formed in her mind, then drifted away.

He bent forward, arms resting on knees, hands dangling. "Did I tell you Luke's birthday's coming up tomorrow?"

"He's going to be . . . let's see . . . five, isn't it?"

He nodded. "Kristi and I are in total disagreement. No surprise, right? She wants to have a whoop-de-do birthday party on Sunday, invite all the relatives. I don't like it, but I let her have her way."

"Will Scott be there?" Kristi's nineteen-year-old son, Ryan's stepson.

He lifted his chin. "It wasn't total capitulation." Voice sardonic. "I told her she could go ahead with the party but only if Scott stayed away."

"Every time you talk about Scott, you radiate anger. I agree Kristi's too easy on him, but why do you care so much?"

"Suppose I had some kind of agenda for the kid when I married Kristi. He was just twelve then, already starting to get in trouble. Guess I wanted to be Spencer Tracy and save the wayward youth. Guess I'm really pissed off he didn't want to be saved."

"Sounds right." *I wouldn't like living with a punk either.*

"Okay, I've got insight and I'm still pissed. Why can't anything be easy?" He grinned, and even in the haggard face the grin was pretty dazzling. *Shame he had to play rescuer.*

"Speaking of pissed," he continued, "I actually tried to call Zach this week. Why is it that talking about Scott reminds me of my little brother?"

"Why do you think?"

"Zachary did some of the same things when he was in high school."

"What else?"

"Don't know. Guess I wanted to fix Zach, and he resisted me too, just like Scott."

"So . . . you called him." She fidgeted in her beige director's chair, crossing and uncrossing her legs.

"Started thinking how long it's been since we talked and got the urge to try again. I never know when to quit. But true to form, he didn't get back to me. Guess that tells me what I need to know."

Her clock chimed on the hour. Ryan handed her a check and set an appointment for next week. She couldn't find her calendar but knew that Ryan's session was one she wouldn't forget.

He took a step toward the door, then turned to face her. "Funny thing. I was thinking about something else and this dream I had last night popped into my head." He looked at his watch. "Five minutes more?"

"Sure." *Hand on the doorknob, that's when they drop the bomb. Oh, and by the way, decided to leave my wife, run off with a topless dancer.*

He sat back down, eyes staring out the window, hands planted on knees. "Attic of my mother's house. Just an old attic, filled with boxes, kind of spooky. Luke there by himself, wearing a party hat with a big five on it. Party noises from down below. I was invisible, sort of like a ghost. Couldn't do anything except watch. Miniature live animals in boxes, zoo animals, only they didn't really seem to be part of it. Just there.

"Then a strange thing happened." His eyes, more focused and alert now, glanced briefly at hers. "Know how I've talked about not being able to feel the way I should about Luke? I mean, I love him and all, but it's always been so remote. Couldn't get over being mad that Kristi went ahead and got pregnant after promising not to. Anyway, I gradually started feeling what he was feeling—sadness, loneliness. Then a kind of scared feeling, like something bad was about to happen. One part had his feelings, another part had my own—this desperate urge to grab him up and protect him." His voice took on an edge. "But I couldn't do anything. I was only this ghost."

He sat forward, legs brushing the wicker coffee table. "Both of us started hearing footsteps. Coming up the stairs, getting louder and louder. Mixing in with our heart beats. Luke was absolutely terrified. I could feel his terror. And I had this horrible sense of helplessness. Then this huge shadowy shape came through the door. Couldn't make myself look at the face. Didn't want to see who it was." Abruptly, he stood up. "That was it. I woke up, heart pounding, sweat pouring down my face."

"I think we need to take some extra time and talk about it."

He glanced at his watch again. "I'm already late for community relations. Raging controversy over whether it's okay for police to stop black teens on the street. We'll have to put it on hold."

❧   ❧   ❧

After Ryan left, Cassidy checked out windows, searching for Public Radio Voice. The house was visible from so many angles—street in front, street on the side, alley in back. Standing at her dining room window, she noticed a young man in shabby jeans at the door of the house across the street. He circled the building, hopped on a motorcycle and rumbled off. Neighbors kept a close watch, scrutinized for suspicious activity, counted on each other to bring down a swarm of police at the slightest sign of trouble. Everybody she knew had had their brush with crime, from stolen bikes to burglaries. People who loved the village accepted it as the price you paid to be an Oak Parker: sort of like the hazing students endured to be a Greek, only the reward was more worthwhile.

At lunchtime, she noticed a green sedan with tinted windows tucked behind a van——looked like a Mercedes but she couldn't be sure. *Why tinted windows? Something to hide?*

At the end of the day, exhausted from sleeplessness and anxiety, Cassidy couldn't stand being cooped up one minute longer. She took out the bike Kevin had given her twelve years ago, the only time he ever remembered her birthday. A ping on every rotation, the transmission was permanently frozen, she loved it anyway, just as she would love an ancient relative suffering the infirmities of old age.

A soft, luminous evening, near the end of May. As she pedaled around Oak Park, spring air and trees bursting with new leaves lifted her spirits. She passed a frivolous Victorian, gingerbread newly painted in intricate detail; a stalwart, brick Georgian; a prim, ladylike Queen Anne, fronted with the raw wood of a new porch going up. A lawn mower whirred, the scent of freshly cut grass tickled her nose. She pedaled hard to escape the frenetic screech of a boom box, slowed for the chunka, chunka, chunka of a basketball. An elderly couple——black woman, white man——holding hands as they ascended the library steps brought a soft curve to her lips.

After an hour's ride, she made a quick stop at the supermarket, then headed home. Walking into the kitchen, grocery bag in hand, she looked around for the cat. From the top of the cartoon-plastered refrigerator, the small calico eyed her warily. She plunked the bag on the counter, carried the smelly box of newspaper out to the garbage, then returned to find the cat on the linoleum countertop poking her head into the plastic bag.

She pulled a Dutch oven with missing handle out of the cupboard. "Gift from Mom." Taking a package of litter from the grocery bag, she poured an inch into the pan. "Now don't get the wrong idea. Don't think this means you've won me over." She set the Dutch oven on the floor and the cat jumped down to sniff it.

She dumped out three cat food cans and dished up some food, hastily putting the bowl on the floor to prevent the cat from springing back onto the counter. "You need to understand, this is only a temporary reprieve. Just thought I'd check to see if anybody's looking to adopt a cat. Which seems unlikely, so don't get your hopes up. No takers by next week, it's off to the humane society."

As she went through her nightly routine in the bathroom, the cat perched next to the sink, swatting at the water from the faucet, leaving muddy prints across the vanity, toilet and tub. Cassidy moved on into her bedroom and tossed aside the satin comforter, then climbed into the king-sized bed left behind by Kevin—motto in life: Bigger is Better—and picked up a half-read mystery. Propping front paws on Cassidy's chest, the cat extended a pink nose and delicately brushed her lips.

Cassidy jerked away. "No sense of boundaries."

She was struggling to keep her eyes open till the end of the chapter when the phone rang. She dropped the book, instantly alert. Public Radio Voice?

The machine clicked and whirred. She heard a familiar male voice: "This is Ryan. Give me a call soon as you can."

Beep.

After ten. *Not tonight. Can't do anything more tonight.* But what if it's important? Maybe she should call back now. He hadn't said urgent and most things could wait until morning. Probably just wanted to reschedule. And anyway, she didn't want to be too accommodating.

She finished the chapter and turned off the light.

ze ze ze

Early the next morning she called Ryan's house and left a message on his machine. At midmorning she called his office and left a message with his secretary. That evening she sat down at her desk and tried again. This time the phone was answered by a woman, voice sounding shaky. *Must be the wife, Kristi.* Cassidy asked for Ryan. A long pause followed, voices coming through in the background. She picked up the wine bottle she kept on her desk to collect loose change and rattled the coins.

Finally, a man's voice came on the line. "You mind telling me who this is?" His tone curt, almost angry.

"Cassidy McCabe. I'm returning Ryan's call." A knot was forming in her stomach. "Is something wrong?"

Another long pause. Her hand tightened on the receiver. She could hear voices again, only this time they were muffled, his hand over the mouthpiece. Sounded like arguing.

The man's voice returned. "The therapist, right?"

"Uh . . . I can't . . . "

"I know, confidentiality. Doesn't matter, your name's in the note. I'm Zach, Ryan's brother."

"Zach? Well," she took a deep breath, "is there some reason Ryan can't talk to me?"

"Yeah, there's a reason." Another pause. "Shit, what I'm trying to tell you, and I don't know any way to say it except to say it, is . . . Ryan's dead."

3

MEETING THE FAMILY

For a long moment everything stopped—a pause button pushed in her brain. "What? It doesn't seem possible. I just saw . . . he just . . . How could he . . . ?" She grabbed a pen out of the ceramic mug.

"How could he?" Zach repeated. "By putting a gun to his head and pulling the trigger, that's how."

"Oh shit. Oh no, I'm so sorry . . . " Biting her lip to stop the words, she stabbed the pen into an unopened envelope, jabbing again and again until the point broke, leaking a bead of ink. She rubbed the edge of her hand across the envelope, smearing ink over the pile of papers on her desk. "I'm saying all the wrong things."

"Nobody knows what to say."

"When did it happen?"

"Some time last night. Study over the garage. Kristi found him."

"This must be so awful. For Kristi, for you. Everyone."

"Awful for you? Loss of that weekly check, I mean?"

"What?" She missed a beat. "What's awful is that Ryan . . . " She wiped her hand across her lap, leaving a trail of blurred ink on her mauve skirt.

"C'mon, you're just the therapist. You see him an hour a week and collect your money. What does . . . did he mean to you?"

Her hand clutched the phone even tighter. "I don't think this is a good time to talk. You're probably pretty . . . overwhelmed right now."

"Don't tell me how I'm feeling. I'm not your client, Ryan was. Helluva lot of good it did him."

"I don't know what to say. I can understand why you'd be angry."

"Therapists are always so fucking understanding. Why didn't you fix it? Fix him. Stop him from offing himself."

"Wish I had an answer."

"So do I." He sighed. "Sorry, I shouldn't have sounded off like that. I don't mean to dump on you."

"I'm sure you've got your hands full. Maybe we can talk some other time."

"Right." He hung up.

She glanced down at the blue smear on her cotton skirt. *Stupid,* her mother would say. *You've ruined your favorite skirt.* So many losses. Heaviness settled over her.

Sick to her stomach, weighed down by the leaden feeling in her body, she wandered downstairs and out to the enclosed front porch where she dropped onto a wicker couch. As the sunset faded, a mild breeze jangled the wind chimes hanging from her eaves. Images flickered in her head. Ryan's blood-soaked body crumpled over his desk. Ryan, brimming with vitality the first time she'd seen him. Ryan, ghost-like in an attic with his five-year-old son. She heard his voice saying, " . . . like I'm going down for the third time."

But not suicidal. Can't believe he was suicidal.

The cat jumped into her lap and she absently stroked silky fur. Atop a scarred picnic bench in front of the couch were a half-filled coffee mug and a wadded-up napkin.

"How could I have missed it—even if I was less than alert?" The cat pricked her ears. "Three years as a therapist, and I've always picked up on the signals, always known in my gut when someone was really at risk." The calico reared her head, fixing her eyes on a fly and jumping to the floor as it disappeared out the window. "I've always been scared somebody'd suicide on me. But not Ryan—never Ryan. Just can't believe he'd do it."

The cat leapt onto the picnic bench, grabbed up the napkin and scuttled off. A minute later she was back cuddling on Cassidy's chest.

What if it wasn't? What if he died . . . some other way?

There you go, getting tangled up in "What-if's" again.

But what if it wasn't?

The cat purred and licked her cheek.

ə ə ə

The following day, Saturday, the local weekly appeared on her front steps. She plunked onto the wicker couch and skimmed the front page: "Anti-tax Group Opposes Police Hirings." *I must be the only Oak Parker not on some kind of crusade.* Tenant's rights, historical preservation, save the elms, put a cul-de-sac at the end of my block.

As she flipped pages, a name caught her eye: "Martin Lawrence Proposes Homeless Shelter." Ryan's uncle, on half the committees in town. She turned to the obituaries. "Ryan Hollister, 43, died Thursday at home . . . survived by . . . Art Director at Lomax and Stratton Advertising, Inc . . . visitation will begin Saturday at Wilcox Funeral Home."

She headed for her office, pulled Ryan's file and dropped into her director's chair. "Age three, father died. Eight months later, mother remarried. Hated stepfather. Age four, stepbrother Zach born. Caretaker for Zach. Age twelve, stepfather left."

Her session notes were spotty, some no more than brief phrases. "More conflict. Anger goes on and on. Where's it all coming from?" *What's that mean?* Through the window above the taped-up sofa she watched a robin light on the branch of a small tree as she tried to remember what her comment had referred to.

"Depression worse, zoo, attic, fifth birthday, child at risk." This final note was fresh in her mind, but it now seemed more of a commentary on the jumble in her head than anything else. *Couldn't think straight. Damn cat screwed up my sleep.* If she hadn't let the cat in, if she'd gotten a decent night's sleep, would she have handled the session differently?

If she'd been at her best, would she have seen the suicide coming? Or would she still have this overwhelming sense he didn't do it.

ఈ ఈ ఈ

That afternoon she edged into a long, narrow room, her eyes flitting away from the casket at the far end. Taking a deep breath, she pushed back the feeling of heaviness and flattened herself against the wall, overwhelmed by the mob of darkly clothed bodies, cloying mix of flowers and perfume, low-pitched hum of voices. Subdued lighting gave her a sense of unreality, as if she'd stepped out of the bright sunlight of day into an artificially lit movie set, where, any minute now, a director would step forward to say "Cut," and Ryan would climb out of the casket, face expressing impatience, hands brushing his elegant suit.

She scanned the crowd for familiar faces. Oak Park was such a small townish kind of place, she seldom left her house without running into client or friend. But this group seemed outside her usual sphere—old blood, old money, families who lived in Oak Park estates or architecturally significant houses and never worried about their insurance bills. Not all the wide lawns belonged to narrow minds. Many, in fact, belonged to shameless Doopers— Dear Old Oak Parkers— who'd pitched in to save Oak Park from the ghettoization that had decimated the west side of Chicago.

Standing near the casket were an older man and woman with a look about them——aristocratic angle to the face, lean pliancy to the body—that reminded her of Ryan. Must be Mildred and Martin Lawrence, the mother and uncle. Martin, family patriarch and protector, leaned solicitously in toward his sister, while Mildred, indomitable queen mother, held herself straight as a plumb line.

A tall, sandy haired man clapped a hand on the uncle's shoulder. Zachary? Cassidy studied the broad, clean-cut face, high forehead and widely spaced eyes. Not the brother, she decided. At least a decade older than the under-forty Zach.

Cassidy's eyes settled on a willowy figure at the center of a knot of men. Ryan's wife Kristi. Masses of unbridled, crinkly hair springing out rampantly around a deeply tanned face. Quicksilver features registering one emotion after another, a computerized, endless-loop sign, from sadness to frustration, frustration to outrage, on and on. *What is it about her?* And then she had it. *Sexy.* An innate sexiness emanating from an internal electricity totally separate from curve of body, style of clothing, performance in bed.

So that's it. Why he'd never leave. Why he couldn't stand losing his sex drive when she got pregnant.

Cassidy abruptly became aware of how others must see her: short, slender, a decent figure if you wanted to be flattering. A face Kevin had lyrically called heart-shaped, but by any objective standard would be deemed narrow—gaunt, even, when she was at her worst. Shoulder-length auburn hair that was way overdue for a cut. Watching Kristi, she felt like the *before* photo in a makeover ad.

Cassidy tried to pick out other family members. She wondered how Luke was doing. *Shit, he woke up on his fifth birthday and his father was dead.* She looked for the stepson Scott and the brother Zach but without success.

If Ryan didn't kill himself, who did? Maybe somebody in this very room.

Imagination's running wild again.

Sensing movement on her right, she glanced around at a man standing beside her, back to the wall, washed-out Coke bottle eyes darting at her face, then swooping back over the crowd. "Don't know why I'm here," he muttered.

No one else within earshot; he must be talking to her. She felt mildly embarrassed, the feeling she got when schizophrenics talked to her on the street. But she also had an urge to connect, disliking the sense of dangling out there all alone.

"You a friend of Ryan's?" she asked.

"Never friends." The words bitterly emphatic. "Fact is, the real reason I'm here is to celebrate."

"Celebrate?" Her voice was incredulous, thinly layered with disgust. She took a closer look at the deeply lined, swarthy face under a wiry crop of jet black hair. Older than she'd first thought, at least sixty. The hair—she could see now it was dyed—had thrown her off.

"You wanna know why?" He turned, slouching against the wall, directing watery eyes at her forehead. His camel suit, nap worn at knees and elbows, hung loosely on his slight frame. " 'Cause Ryan fucked me over, that's why."

Don't want to hear this. She ought to turn her back. But some perverse need to listen, even to nasty, improbable bits of gossip, sucked her in.

"You wanna know what happened?" Narrow, heavily-lidded eyes slid around, avoiding hers. His wrinkled face seemed asymmetrical, the two sides not quite belonging together, the left side mocking the right. "Here's how it went down. I'm a free lance producer, see. That is, I produce commercials, all kinds of TV spots, hired by ad agencies. But awhile back, work started drying up. I went a year, nothing happening. I got to the point I was pretty desperate. Then this guy I know let it slip that an agency exec was spreading rumors I'd screwed up a major project." His loose mouth stretched into a wide grimace, then snapped back like a rubber band.

Cassidy edged away from him. "Did you? Screw up a major project?"

"Nah, nothing like that. One thing I know is production. Anyway, I figured it had to be Ryan. The asshole," he jerked his head in the direction of the casket, "had a personal grudge going way back, so I could believe he'd started spreading lies as a way to get even. Except it's hard to believe anybody could wait that long . . . " His voice trailed off into a mumble.

"Sounds pretty flimsy to me. All you've got is second hand rumors."

He stared down at her feet, one side of his face brooding over his grievance, other side parodying his sense of tragedy.

She started to walk away but he gripped her arm to stop her. "Oh, he did it all right. That's just the kind of thing he'd do." He dropped his hand. "I went to his office, begged him to get me some work. He played innocent, denied knowing anything about it. But I could tell."

Cassidy felt a slight prickle along the back of her neck. Maybe he was crazier than she'd realized. She took a small step backwards.

"Only good thing," he continued, one side of his face lighting up, "is a couple weeks after we talked, the shithead went and offed himself."

Therapists need an off-button. What is it about my face that telegraphs to all the flakes—here's a sucker who'll put up with you? "I think it's time to be on my way," Cassidy said through clenched teeth.

A hurt look came into the faded eyes. "I didn't mean to bore you." He pushed away from the wall. "Oh, well. What can you expect?" He extended a frail hand. "Name's Jerry. You're a good listener. Thanks for taking the time."

She shook his hand and he shambled off. *Just pretending to be put upon. Real reason you listened to that drivel, you're avoiding what comes next.*

She turned toward the flower-thronged casket at the front of the room. Bile rose in her throat. She swallowed and started her legs moving.

Halfway across the room, the woman she'd guessed to be Kristi stepped in front of her. "I know who ... You're Cassidy McCabe, aren't you?" The sign on her face flashed hatred.

"That's right." Cassidy stepped back as the woman moved in on her.

"What're you doing here?"

"I wanted to say good-bye."

"Who do you ... I think you've got a lot of nerve."

"I don't know what you mean."

"Flaunting yourself in front of me like this."

"Ryan was important to me." Cassidy's mouth went dry. "I needed to say good-bye."

"Important to you?" Her voice rose shrilly. "What about me? He was a fucking lot more . . . You ruined my marriage and then you got him so depressed . . . I mean, if it hadn't been for you, he wouldn't have . . . "

Jealous he talked to me instead of her.

Cassidy straightened her shoulders. "Oh no. You're not going to get away with that. I know this is horrible for you and I'm sorry, but I didn't cause your problems."

"Everything got worse after he started seeing . . . We would've been okay, but you got him so worked up over the past . . . He never let anything go, he just went further and further . . . and I couldn't reach him, no matter how hard I tried it just kept getting . . . And now he's dead."

Tears spilled out of Kristi's big green eyes, leaving bruised, mascara-smudged pockets.

Cassidy was dimly aware that people were gathering around them. Stepping out of the circle, a tall, white-haired man, the one she'd identified as Martin Lawrence, came up behind Kristi and put his hand on her shoulder.

"Take it easy, my dear."

Kristi rubbed tears away with the back of her hand, blurring purple blotches into long streaks. "She shouldn't be . . . She's just making it worse."

"This whole ordeal's been entirely too much for you," he soothed. "Maybe you should ask Zachary to take you home."

He looked at Cassidy. "I'm sorry about this. We appreciate your coming but this has been extremely difficult for all of us, and I think Kristi here has exceeded her limit in the last few days. Sometimes people hit a breaking point, as I'm sure you realize."

"That's not true," Kristi cried. "Well, maybe I shouldn't have been so ... But I meant every ... " Her face shifted to despair.

"I know it's been hard," Cassidy said to the older man. He responded with a courtly little nod, reminding her of Ryan.

She addressed Kristi, whose exhausted face looked like a smeared palette, colors all running together. "I'm sorry, really I am. I never meant to hurt you."

Forcing herself not to hurry, she made her way to the door.

ɜɐ ɜɐ ɜɐ

The next day, Sunday, the weather turned hot and muggy, a taste of August in May. Chicago springs were notoriously fickle. You could go to bed in an ice storm and wake up to a heat wave.

The hot, sticky air made her feel like wilted lettuce, too listless to ride her bike, too preoccupied to read, too restless to dig dandelions in the yard. The cat knocked a geranium off a living room shelf and she couldn't even work up the energy to yell at her.

The phone rang late in the afternoon and she picked up in the kitchen. The caller introduced herself in a clipped voice as Mildred Lawrence. "That little scene at the funeral parlor was most unfortunate."

She calling to apologize? Cassidy leaned against the doorframe between kitchen and dining room, scuffing the toe of her tennis shoe against mottled gray linoleum.

"That's all right. I certainly understand why Kristi . . . Ryan's wife, that is . . . would be upset."

"Ryan's widow."

"Oh, right." A pause. "Well, Mrs. Lawrence, what can I do for you?"

"She's a widow because Ryan—my son—is dead."

Cassidy waited, staring at a Cathy cartoon taped to the refrigerator. She read the words over and over but nothing registered.

"And the family believes he might not have died like that—this terrible thing might not have happened—if he'd had a therapist doing the job properly."

Oh shit. Here it comes. "I'm sorry you feel that way."

"I'm sorry Ryan's gone," the woman snapped. "I'm sorry he was the victim of incompetence. Or worse."

"Just what did you call to say?" Cassidy managed a reassuringly firm tone.

"I hope you're not planning to cause any further distress by making an inappropriate appearance at the funeral."

"Mrs. Lawrence, I certainly will not attend the funeral if I'm not wanted." *Wild horses couldn't drag me.* "I do want to say, however, that it often happens that families of a suicide need to find a scapegoat in order to defend against their own pain and guilt."

"'Families of a suicide?' And how do therapists defend? By quoting textbooks?"

Oh boy. I really had that one coming. "I'm sorry, I

shouldn't have said that."

"I also called to do you a little favor. Thought I'd give you some advance notice so you can start shopping for your attorney. Papers will be served quite soon."

Cassidy's hand tightened into a fist, nails digging into her palm. "You're suing."

"We have an excellent case for malpractice. Ryan left a little note, you see, telling us about the impact of his therapy."

Cassidy thanked her for the warning and hung up.

Oh shit, why didn't I pay that insurance bill? How am I going to get an attorney without a retainer?

Don't panic. The legal system moves at glacial speed. You'll think of something. And if you don't, Public Radio Voice may turn it into a non-problem before it ever gets to court.

ò& ò& ò&

As darkness settled, Cassidy realized she'd forgotten to eat all day, so she put together a salad. Throughout the afternoon, the air had grown increasingly oppressive. As she sat at the dining room table reluctantly stuffing veggies into her mouth, drops of sweat fell from her chin onto her plate. The cat jumped onto the table and eyed her warily, waiting for the usual swatting and shooing. When Cassidy failed to respond, the cat edged close enough to snag a chunk of celery off the plate. She took a lick, gave Cassidy a disgusted look, then poked at it until she knocked it off the table, clearly proud of her success in getting rid of it.

After dinner Cassidy left her plate with scraps of lettuce, blobs of watery dressing on the table. *Slovenly*, her mother would call it. Even though Cassidy had deliberately chosen not to be what her mother wanted, she secretly suspected herself to be the bearer of a defective housekeeping gene, a flaw disqualifying her as wife and mother.

She dragged out to the front porch, carrying a glass and jug of Carlo Rossi. The enclosed porch, a narrow room running the width of the house, contained a mismatch of wicker and plastic furniture, as well as boxes and other odd bits she couldn't figure out what to do with. A hot wind was whipping up, clattering the wind chimes that hung from the eaves. She sank onto the wicker couch, poured a glass of wine, and set the jug on the weathered picnic bench she used as a table. A fleeting whiff of rain offered a preview of coming attractions.

This is not a good idea, said the voice in her head in charge of proper behavior.

When Kevin had left, during those early months when the pain was so acute she could hardly hold her body upright, she had slipped into the habit of drinking a glass of wine or two—or was it three or four?—before bed. Then, as the hurt subsided, she had gotten a grip and vowed never to fall into that kind of drinking again.

A glass of wine won't hurt. This has been a one-hundred percent godawful, shitty day, said the voice that wanted her to feel better.

She took a large swallow and watched the heat lightning. Prancing along the rim of the wicker frame, the cat swatted at a strand of hair and stuck her nose in Cassidy's ear. Halfway through the glass, the rain began beating down.

From Austin Boulevard sirens screamed in all directions, keening off into the distance, howling toward her. Shootings, police chases, ambulances careening to the hospital. Gazing through the downpour into a gloomy swath of light from the lamp post, she watched as a small station wagon pulled up in front and a man got out.

She tensed, ready to run inside and lock the door. *Stop!* commanded the part that was fiercely angry at being bullied by thugs. *Running away won't help. He'll just come back later.*

Get inside and call the police! screamed the other, more practical voice.

Before she could decide, a bulky, rain-coated figure was standing in front of the screen door looking in.

4

A VISIT

"Hello."

Jumping up, she positioned herself on the other side of the screen door. "Yes?"

"Zachary Moran. The one you talked to—"

"Oh," she swallowed. "I didn't expect . . . I thought it was somebody else."

"Out of context." A smile in the voice.

"Right. You're the—let's see—fourth member of the family I've encountered in the last two days. Do Kristi and your mother think I'm so stupid I just don't get it? Or you here to serve papers?"

He laughed. "I'm no emissary from the family. Fact is, they're not overly fond of me either."

"Oh. Well, what then?" She pressed tightly against the

door, holding it closed.

"You said you wanted to talk about it later. What happened to Ryan, I mean. So I thought I'd take you up on it."

Nobody says the word—suicide. "Did I say that?"

"You know, this rain is really coming down. How about if I come inside where it's dry, and we can talk about whether or not we want to talk."

This is not a good idea. Ryan's whole family is after me like a pack of wolves after a rabbit. "I still don't know what there is to talk about."

"I promise, I'm not a rapist or axe murderer. Regardless of what Ryan may have said."

"Well . . . " She couldn't think of a good reason not to, so she opened the door and stood aside.

"That's better." He tossed his raincoat over a chair. The light on the porch, filtering through the living room window, was too dim to afford a good look at his features, but he was clearly shorter and more solidly built than Ryan, not fat but on the stocky side. He wore generic tennis shoes, faded jeans and a black tee shirt inscribed with the word, "Heineken."

"So," he said, settling on the wicker couch next to the spot where she'd been sitting, "what I had in mind was discussing some of my thoughts and feelings about this thing with Ryan." His voice was detached, uninvolved, even when talking about the brother he was about to bury. Laconic, as if everything were a joke.

"Why do I feel like I'm being set up?" Crossing her arms, she leaned against the doorframe.

"I don't know. Why?"

"Maybe because most people don't sit down with a stranger and talk about their feelings. Sounds to me like your idea of bait to use on a therapist."

Hands behind head, he stretched out his legs, letting go with a rumbly laugh. "You're not going to be easy, I can see that. What can I do to prove I'm not out to get you? I really just want to talk about Ryan."

"Why me? Why not Kristi or your mother?"

"What's that you're drinking there? Could you maybe spare a glass for a rain-soaked visitor?"

"Carlo Rossi. I doubt it's up to your standard."

"Hey, I'm living off a reporter's salary. None of the family money's blowing my way."

"Wait here, I'll get another glass."

When she returned, he was jiggling his fingers on the floor in front of the cat, who was stalking his hand.

"Nice cat."

She handed him a wine glass, then removed a stack of magazines from a molded plastic chair and sat opposite him on the other side of the bench. After filling his glass, she thunked the jug down on the floor next to the magazines.

"Why do I want to talk to you? Because you know more about Ryan than just about anybody. I need to understand what happened. If I could come up with a reason—if I knew why he did it—maybe I could believe it."

"You know I can't tell you anything." *Even if I had anything to tell.*

The cat, who was grabbing at Zach's shoelace, succeeded in untying it.

"Pretty clever." He leaned forward, locking eyes with

the cat. "What other tricks do you do?"

"She's a one-cat wrecking crew."

"Cats are fun. They keep you humble." She jumped into his lap.

"I've got all the humility I can stand right now."

"What's her name?" The cat propped herself on his chest and gazed affectionately into his face, purring loudly.

Traitor. "Since I don't plan to keep her, she doesn't have a name," Cassidy said, an edge to her voice. "I don't like cats."

"How can anybody not like cats?"

"You like cats so much, why don't you take her?"

"Wouldn't be any good at it. I'm almost never home. People keep giving me plants, I don't know why. Guess they think I should be more domestic or something. Anyway, the plants always die." He held up his glass. "How about a refill?"

She hesitated. Maybe she should tell him to go home. Then she handed him the jug.

"Where's your glass?" he asked.

No more wine for you. It's obvious you've got to stay on your toes with this guy. Wind howled, rain pelted the porch roof. She held out her glass and he poured.

"Now," he said, setting the jug on the picnic bench between them, "getting back to Ryan. In retrospect, did you see any sign at all that this was coming?"

Her lungs pumped faster. "You sure you're not here to serve me papers?"

"Evidently you still think I'm trying to set you up."

"That sounded like entrapment to me."

"Since you keep talking about papers, I gather you know Queen Mildred's going to sue."

"She called to tell me about it."

"Mom can be mean as hell. Everyone—that is, mostly Mom and Kristi—have convinced themselves it's all your fault. I was pretty rough with you on the phone, but that's because I overreacted to the note. After I calmed down, I realized blaming the whole thing on you is a crock."

"What's in the note?"

He tilted his head, eying her speculatively. "You sure you want to hear this?"

You most definitely do not. "Tell me."

"What it said was, talking in therapy made Ryan more depressed. Maybe if he'd never met you he could've snapped out of it on his own, but too late now. All because of therapy. Something like that."

"Oh Lord! So why wouldn't you blame me?"

"I don't think any therapist has that kind of power. I tried to talk Ryan out of going into therapy but he never took anything I had to say seriously."

"You're really down on therapy."

"Mildred made me see a shrink when I was in high school. To say it didn't help any would be charitable."

"So, the reason you're not blaming me is, you can't imagine any therapist having enough influence to precipitate a suicide. Is that it?"

"I'm just not in favor of seeing a therapist to handle problems. I think people are better off dealing with things on their own."

"One of those cowboy types, huh?" She poked the

magazines with her toe, sending several of them sliding across the floor.

"At the same time, I also think Ryan always knew what he was doing. I can't believe he'd have stayed with it for two years unless you were competent and the therapy was helping. Given that, it doesn't sound right to me that Ryan could've been suicidal without you picking up on it."

What's he doing, reading my mind? "Even competent therapists sometimes miss signals."

"You think that's what happened? Did you miss the signals?"

"Talk about entrapment." She gazed into her nearly empty glass. "I don't know . . . I can't figure it out. But to answer your question—no, I don't think that was it." Tears stung the back of her eyelids. "I don't think I missed the signals."

"Well, then . . . "

"Are you saying what I think you're saying?"

"Let's assume you're right." Lowering his head, Zach spoke tentatively, as if thinking aloud. "Let's assume he wasn't thinking about it beforehand. If that's the case, something must've happened to make him suddenly decide. Something he didn't put in the note. Or—and this is what I really think—it wasn't suicide."

Narrowing her eyes, she caught her lip between her teeth. *So I'm not the only one.*

Zach lifted his head and met her eyes. "I just can't make myself believe he offed himself."

The cat leapt off Zach's lap and stretched, extending her forepaws and raising her rump. The tree at the corner of the house groaned. Rain lashed the screened windows, coming through and splattering her back.

"What about the note?" she asked.

"If there weren't any note, if he'd simply been found with a bullet in his head, would you've guessed suicide?"

"Not Ryan. Never."

"You know, when we were kids, there was this guy in Ryan's class who took his father's gun and blew out his brains. Ryan kept going on about how awful it was for the mother to find the body, and how if the kid wanted to waste himself, he could've found a better way to do it. He even sneaked over and looked in the room before they cleaned it up. He kept describing that scene, I think he must've had nightmares about it."

"You really think somebody else pulled the trigger?"

"And another thing. Ryan hated growing up without a father. He never would've done this to Luke, I'm sure of it."

"The note was in his handwriting, wasn't it?"

"Maybe somebody forced him to write it, I don't know. Right now, all I've got is this strong gut feeling he didn't do it."

"You going to the police?"

"Already did." He waved a dismissive hand.

"And?"

"They went through the motions. Heard me out and said they'd look into it. But the guy I was telling my story to kept glancing at his watch."

"Why not give them a chance?"

"Cop as much as said he thought I was just another crank inventing a murder that didn't exist. I made the mistake of telling him I'd neglected to return Ryan's call a few days before, and he made a big deal out of the guilt factor."

"So, what're you going to do?"

"Right now, I'm going to see if I can beg a cup of coffee off you. We've killed about half a jug of wine and I'm not thinking too straight."

"I could use some myself. Stay here, I'll bring it out."

As she opened the front door, he got up to follow her inside. "If you don't mind, I'll just tag along. I like to see people's houses."

She raised her brows. "Not big on waiting for invitations, are you?"

"Working as a reporter's liberated me from all my early socialization."

She led him through the living room, decorated at minimal expense with jaunty, colorful posters and wall hangings from Pier I. Then through the dining room, past the remnants of dinner on the table—which she grimaced at but refused to apologize for—-and on into the kitchen.

He stopped in front of the refrigerator to read the cartoons she had taped up. "This is a great house. Oak Park's full of these wonderful old places."

"These wonderful old places kill you with maintenance."

She measured out coffee, poured water into the coffee-maker. Rain had blown in through the open window, leaving spots on the clean dishes in the drainer. Rinsing them off, she glanced through the window of the neighbor's kitchen, a couple of yards' distance from hers, where a clump of kids in assorted sizes and colors was hanging out. The couple next door had adopted several children of different races— Cassidy could never remember how many. Whenever she saw them en masse, she was reminded of a Beneton ad.

"You live in this big house all by yourself? How many bedrooms?"

"Three." *What is this, twenty questions?* The coffee-maker gurgled, filling the kitchen with the strong aroma of fresh coffee.

He wandered around the oak cabinet and into the waiting room. "This where you see clients? How do you like working at home?"

"Love it." As the coffee dripped, she leaned back against the counter, arms crossed in irritation.

"Mind if I look at your office?" He opened the door, switched on the light. "Nice. Homey feel."

"I suppose so," she said sharply as she poured coffee.

"Sorry 'bout that." Closing the door, he came over to stand in front of her. "I have this rotten curiosity—sometimes it gets the best of me. You're pissed off, I don't blame you." He shook his head. "I've just been . . . off kilter since it happened."

She handed him a mug, then added cream and sugar to hers. As they sipped coffee, she observed his countenance under the light. Ryan's fair-skinned, blue-eyed face had been all fine lines and angles, the face of a thoroughbred. Zach's dark-haired, deeply bronzed face was smoother and rounder, fairly nondescript, with humorous eyes and a fast mouth. Easy going, but it didn't give away any secrets.

"I lost a brother and I've got my own load of guilt. But

with all this talk about suing, it must be even worse for you."
His smoky gray eyes looked into hers. "You probably miss
him more than I do."

She blinked in surprise. She wasn't used to people
noticing her feelings. *Don't think I like this.* "Who's the
therapist here?" She laughed shakily. "You trying to turn the
tables on me or what?"

They finished their coffee and returned to the porch. His
raincoat, draped over a chair, had developed odd, squirmy
bulges. The cat stuck her head out.

"She trying to get me to take her home? You must've
put her up to it."

The cat crawled out from under the coat, thrust her head
into one of the pockets and emerged with something in her
mouth. Jumping down, she dropped her booty on the floor.
A red pistachio. She began bapping and scooting it around
the porch.

He put on his coat, then turned to face her. "So, you
going to help me with this?"

5

PAYING BILLS

"What?"

"You and I have to find out what really happened to Ryan."

"You must be crazy." Taking a step back, she crossed her arms over her chest.

"We're the only ones with any motivation to do it. My family's perfectly satisfied to put the blame on you. The police are happy to call it a suicide." He rested his hands lightly on her shoulders. "But you and I each have our own reason for wanting to know if he really did it himself—or somebody did it for him."

If we prove it wasn't suicide, I get out of being sued. And out of feeling guilty the rest of my life. "I don't know how to investigate a murder." She swallowed. "Besides, it sounds dangerous. And I'm a coward."

"That's okay. I know what to do." His tone breezy, as if it were some kind of game.

"So what do you need me for?"

"I know about investigating. But you've got information about Ryan no one else does."

"This is not a good idea."

"I'll call tomorrow and we can talk about getting started."

❧ ❧ ❧

Sunday night's rain washed away the heat, and Monday morning the air was crisp and cool. From her bedroom window, Cassidy sighed over the grass in her yard, which appeared to have grown two inches overnight and the bright yellow dandelions that had popped out all over. *At least in Oak Park dandelions are politically correct.* The lawn in front of Village Hall had been covered with them ever since they passed the pesticide ban.

Dandelions are the least of your worries. Time to face up, kiddo. She planted herself in front of her paper-littered desk and began searching for the malpractice insurance bill. The heap of unopened mail, unpaid bills, unread journals made her stomach sink. *Hopeless. If you get sued, that'll be the end of you.*

The cat pranced into the bedroom, hopping in an odd, sideways motion, then made a sudden high leap, jackknifed, and grabbed her tail.

Cassidy propped chin on hand. "You're distracting me," she said. "C'mon, distract me some more."

As if on cue, the cat jumped onto the desk and rubbed her face against Cassidy's cheek, purring fervently.

"If I run out of money, you and I can go sit together on some other doorstep."

The cat bapped an unopened envelope onto the floor.

"You're telling me to dump them all and just forget it. You don't know how tempting that is."

She organized the clutter into three piles: to-be-read, to-be-filed and to-be-paid, then took her checkbook out of the drawer, a pen out of the pink ceramic mug and began writing checks.

"Kevin, I hate you." The cat curled up on the to-be-paid stack, scattering several bills across the top of the desk. "It's all his fault, you know. I'm not personally a deadbeat, and I wouldn't be in this jam if he hadn't neglected to pay taxes, back when we were married."

She rubbed her finger over the chipped corner of the desk, remembering the day she and Kevin had struggled to carry this behemoth upstairs. She dropped her end, and when they finally had it in place against the bedroom wall, she'd felt sick about marring Kevin's prize—this elegant, inlaid, satiny desk, presented to him by his new employer in celebration of his having accepted a job selling securities.

Kevin had tilted her chin, telling her he would rub the chipped corner for luck, and whenever he did, would see her bonnie, bright smile cheering him on. Then he'd swept her up and carried her outside, she pretending to fight, to the hammock hidden away in the bushes and made love to her under the stars.

The cat fished a rubber band out from under a brochure

and raced out of the bedroom, stolen prize in her mouth. "And besides," Cassidy yelled after her, "I've almost managed to dig myself out. If it weren't for this damn suit, I'd have everything paid off in another year."

The phone rang. She remembered Zach saying he'd call. Probably it would be better if she didn't answer. Probably it would be better if the phone company disconnected her. People like her shouldn't have a telephone. It only got them into trouble.

"Hello?" It was her mother, wanting to drop by with leftover lasagna for lunch. Cassidy was too distracted to think of an excuse. Besides, she liked her mother's lasagna.

She hung up, wondering if Zach really would call. Maybe he'd been drunker than he seemed. Maybe the whole idea—the non-suicide conspiracy theory—was merely a boozy flight of fancy concocted to allow them both to wriggle free from guilt.

She placed a call to Honor Teasdale, a psychologist she saw occasionally for supervision. "I've got a case—had a case—that's really bothering me. I need some professional feedback." She made an appointment to drive out to Honor's house on Tuesday.

She located the final notice for her malpractice insurance, dated three months earlier, and called the company to inquire about the possibility of reinstating it so she'd be covered against the suit. The answer she got was exactly the one she expected.

ia ia ia

Her mother stood next to the stove, dish in hand. An

inch shorter than Cassidy's five-two, she had the kind of shape a personal ad might describe as "Rubinesque," permed gray hair worn in an old-lady style, and a face that settled most comfortably into an expression of disapproval. She'd been wearing sensible shoes since she was twenty, and she still signed "Mrs. Helen McCabe" even though her husband had walked out on her thirty-two years ago. As Cassidy came through the doorway, she said, "What's that I smell?"

"I don't smell anything." Cassidy hooked a thumb into her jeans' waistband and shifted her weight to one hip.

"I picked up on it soon as I walked in the door." She sniffed the air. "Have you got a cat?"

"Well, not exactly. That is, I'm not keeping her—just letting her stay until I find a home."

Her mother shook her head. "It's not that easy to get people to take cats. I'm afraid you'll get stuck with it."

"I was talking to someone just last night who'll probably adopt her."

"It's not good for your clients to smell cat box when they walk in the door, Cass. Besides, it's expensive to keep animals. You can't afford it."

"It'll only be a few days." She took the dish from her mother's hands. "This looks wonderful. The house'll smell great after we've nuked it."

The two women made salad, heated lasagna, and sat down at the teak table. Swallowing a mouthful of thick red sauce and stringy mozzarella, Cassidy gazed into crystalline sunlight pouring through wide, uncovered dining room windows.

When they finished, her mother said, "I talked to your grandmother yesterday."

Cassidy smiled fondly. "How is Gran?"

"She hasn't heard from you lately."

"I know," she sighed. "I ought to call more often."

"You've always been her favorite."

"It's just that she has a different relationship with me than with you."

Cassidy pushed her plate back and plopped her elbows on the table.

"I suppose it's because you're the granddaughter. There's always friction between mothers and daughters."

Or maybe it's because you leeched off her all those years after Dad left.

"I just can't understand why you won't let her help out," her mother continued. "God knows you need it, and all the money's going to be yours someday, anyway."

Unclenching her teeth, Cassidy said, "Mom, we've been over this a dozen times. I don't want Gran's help, all right?"

One of us has to be able to stand on her own two feet. If I could get us out of scrapes all those years I lived with Kevin, I'll be able to think of something now.

"You never would accept help from anybody. I can remember when you were two years old and you kept tripping over your shoelaces and wouldn't let me tie them for you."

Grinning, Cassidy said in a childlike voice, "I can do it myself."

"Only you couldn't." Her eyes misted. "Do you know

what it was like for me? Never able to give my little girl a hand when she needed it?"

Cassidy patted her mother's arm. "I know, Mom. I always was prickly and hard to get close to. I can't help it, that's just how I am, and I'm sorry it's so frustrating for you."

"And so unreasonable." Her mother pulled her arm away. "You won't accept money from your grandmother." Her mouth pursed. "And you won't let me move in with you, even though you've got this big house, and if I were giving you what I pay for rent we'd both be better off."

Sitting up straighter, Cassidy planted the flat of her hand firmly on the table. "Mom, that's enough. We're not going to discuss it."

Helen McCabe heaved a huge sigh. "Have it your own way. You always do."

᲻Ჰ   ᲻Ჰ   ᲻Ჰ

When she finished seeing clients for the night, Cassidy went upstairs to find three messages on the machine.

"It's Maggie. How come I haven't heard from you? We're past due for our monthly lunch. Give me a call, you hermit."

Beep.

Maggie'll expect me to fill her in on everything. I just can't face it.

"My name's Judy Mihalik. I've got a friend who says you're very good and I'd like to schedule an appointment." She gave her number and hung up.

Beep.

At least my reputation isn't totally ruined yet.

"Zach here. I've got some ideas I want to bounce off you."

Beep.

This is not a good idea. The more I listen to him, the more susceptible I get.

At ten-thirty she was sitting up in bed wearing the old "Springsteen" tee shirt Kevin had left behind, book in lap, toes wiggling under the sheet to tease the cat. The phone rang and she ignored it. The machine went through its usual routine and a voice came out of the box. "This is Zach. Pick it up."

Trudging over to the desk, she pushed the stop button. "All right, I give. What do you want?"

"Why didn't you call me back?" he demanded.

"Because I keep telling myself this whole idea is nuts. Yes, I'd like to believe it wasn't suicide. But I can't see myself stalking a murderer."

"Obviously, I can't force you. I'm going to dig into Ryan's death. I could use your help, but if you don't want to I'll go it alone."

I should get out of this right now. She chewed on her lower lip. *But what if your gut's right?* Don't worry, Zach can handle it. *But maybe you do know some things he doesn't.*

"Okay," she said in a small voice. "I'm in. Where do we start?"

6

SUPERVISION

"Kristi."

"Oh no," she groaned. "I can't talk to her. You'll have to tackle her on your own."

"Because of that little contretemps at the wake?"

"That and the fact she wants to sue my ass into bankruptcy." Cassidy tapped a short, burgundy fingernail against the green bottle on the desk. She collected loose change in the bottle hoping to save enough to take Maggie out for her birthday. "Not only do I not want to talk to her, but I have reason to believe she doesn't want to talk to me. Other than to verbally scratch my eyes out."

"Kristi's on the emotional side, I grant you. But other than that, she's okay."

"You said Kristi and your mother are convinced it's all

my fault."

"I did say that, didn't I?" His voice breezy.

How unreasonable to think what you said yesterday has anything to do with today.

"Mom's a real hardass but Kristi's easy. We get along okay."

Cassidy pictured Kristi with her innate sexiness. *I'll just bet you two get along okay.* She thought fast. "Wait a minute. I just remembered somebody who sounds like an actual suspect. There's this crazy guy named Jerry who came to the wake to celebrate." She recounted everything he'd told her. "Why not start with him?"

"Gotta be Kristi. We need to find out what all happened the night Ryan died."

"But Jerry had a motive."

"C'mon McCabe. Stop making excuses."

Cassidy ran her tongue around the inside of her teeth. She asked, "What's my role in all this? Tell me again why you need me there."

"As a reporter, I've learned it's impossible to get a good interview unless I know one helluva lot about my subject beforehand. Ryan and I haven't talked much of late. I've got the cliff notes—you've got the details. You'll pick up on things I miss. Trust me. Together we'll make a helluva of a team."

"She can't talk to me. We're legal adversaries." Cassidy swiveled her chair away from the desk and propped her feet on the cold radiator beneath the open window. Not a whisper of wind. Heat lay in the room like a smothering blanket, making it difficult to breathe.

"You haven't got the papers yet. Anyway, Kristi's willing to overlook the legal issues."

Overlook? Kristi's not the one being sued. You can't talk to her—you'll leave yourself wide open.

What's important here? A man died and all you're concerned with is your own ass.

"Fact is," Zach continued, "I've already got a meeting set up for Tuesday night. Course I had to sweeten the pot a little, but I thought I'd discuss that with you on the way over."

"Discuss? You just make decisions and order me around. Tell me now."

"When one spouse goes into therapy," Zach said hesitantly, feeling his way, "the other develops an avid curiosity about what's getting said in the privacy of the therapist's office . . ."

"Oh no. Don't ask me to reveal anything confidential."

" . . . so I thought, if you were to offer Kristi maybe just a summary, just a few general comments, she might find the prospect irresistible."

"You know I can't do that."

"I don't see this as compromising you that much. No juicy details. Just a few superficial remarks. Besides, therapists violate confidentiality all the time, you know that."

"Not when they're being sued."

"You still think I'm trying to set you up?"

"What does it look like?"

"Stop being paranoid. I'm not interested in your malpractice problems. If I had any influence with my mother whatsoever, I'd get the suit dropped. You end up out on the street, I'll take you in. Your cat, too."

She pictured Ryan's face, her chest tightening. "It doesn't seem right—"

"Ryan's dead. It can't possibly hurt him now. And think about Kristi, what it's like for her." Zach's voice dropped a notch. "It's bad enough she had to find his body, brains splattered all over the wall. Imagine what it'd be like to have your husband waste himself and never know for sure—how he felt about you, how much you might've contributed to it."

She agreed Zach could pick her up Tuesday at eight.

🍂 🍂 🍂

She tossed the burgundy satin comforter onto the floor and lay down under the sheet. In an effort to save money, she'd refrained from turning on the room air conditioner, hoping open windows would suffice, but the unmoving air was so thick it felt like she was drowning in humidity. When she closed her eyes, a technicolor movie of Ryan's suicide started up in her head.

She got out of bed and groped her way down the enclosed, L-shaped staircase to the living room, leaving the lights off so she couldn't be seen through the windows.

"Here, kitty, kitty," she called, wandering through the house. Eventually she located the unresponsive cat sprawled out on the wicker couch, all four legs sticking up in the air. Snatching her up, Cassidy carried the squirming, scratching feline upstairs, her claws creating bloody tracks across bare skin scantily covered by the extra large tee-shirt. Barely hanging on until she made it into the bedroom, Cassidy dropped the cat on her bed. She shut the door, closed the windows and turned on the air conditioner.

"Long as I'm headed into bankruptcy anyway, what's another five dollars on my electric bill?"

Pulling herself into a tight little bundle at the foot of the bed, the cat glared up at her.

"I should be entitled to something in return for buying cat food, changing kitty litter— which, I assure you, is no treat—and providing Your Highness with a soft bed."

The cat turned her back and stared at the door.

"How is it that I always get into these nonreciprocal relationships?"

She returned to bed and gingerly closed her eyes, hoping the images of Ryan's death would not replay themselves. Minutes later, she felt a small body curl up against her back. A comforting rumble gradually lulled her to sleep.

ᏒᏃ   ᏒᏃ   ᏒᏃ

"Last Saturday was our anniversary. A year since our first date. We planned a really special evening. I was going to cook, and he kept saying he had a little surprise, he was going to make it the best night ever." Carla had china blue eyes and golden, cotton-candy hair curling around her face. She was forty-one, but usually it didn't show, her petite body and sprightly manner stripping years off her age. Today the deceit worked in the opposite direction, adding instead of subtracting. Her misery, visible in the slackness of her body, the heavy lines and sagging muscles of her face, made her seem old.

Carla's eyes filled. Cassidy pulled a Kleenex box out

from under the coleus leaves and pushed it across the wicker table toward her client. Pale light slanted across the black sofa, showing up tiny pieces of foam that had worked their way through cracks in the vinyl and scattered across the seat like bread crumbs.

"Friday night I stayed up late cleaning. Got up early Saturday so I could work out. I always worry about my stomach pooching. At my age . . . well, you know." Grimacing, she pressed a hand with slender, outspread fingers across her slightly rounded stomach.

"He was supposed to come at seven. So I shopped, then spent hours fixing this really incredible meal. I went all out, all his favorites. And then, he just didn't come. I waited and waited. Tried calling his house but no answer. I was imagining something terrible had happened, that he was in an accident or dead or . . . But that wasn't it. He just decided not to come."

"What a terrible night. Must've been one of the longest you've ever lived through." Listening to Carla brought up Cassidy's old anger at men who could care less how much they hurt the women who loved them. *His name Kevin?* she wondered.

A sudden noise from the waiting room outside the office distracted her. She sat up straighter. *What was that? Back door opening?* Clients usually rang the bell. She listened intently but could hear nothing beyond the radio she played in the background to muffle voices. *Some say love . . . is like a razor . . .* Really a noise? Or her mind playing tricks?

She felt an urge to excuse herself and take a look. *Stop*

being ridiculous. Since the cat had arrived, she often heard unexplainable noises.

She forced her attention back to Carla, pushing the thought of an intruder out of her mind.

"I can't understand it." Carla leaned forward, arms folded across her stomach as if the pain were physical. "Jim was so enthusiastic. Kept hinting about a surprise. I actually thought . . . " Her voice dropped. "I hate to admit it but I thought maybe it was a ring, that he was going to give me an engagement ring." Her bewildered eyes met Cassidy's. "Why would anyone do a thing like that?"

When the session was over, Cassidy conducted a walk-through inspection. She found paw prints leading across the kitchen counter, through the dining room and over to the coleus on the living room shelf, the location of a rather thorough dig, but no evidence of an intruder. Cassidy hoped the cat had not decided to water the plant as part of her foray into gardening. *If you don't chill out, you will get paranoid. Just like Zach said.*

After lunch she peeked through windows checking the streets. No cars with darkened windows. It had rained during the night, and the brisk air sparkled with crystalline light like freshly washed windows. She sprinted to the garage, trying not to notice the fresh crop of dandelions that had sprouted on her lawn. She got out her Toyota and began the hour's trek to Woodridge, where her supervisor Honor Teasdale lived. She needed to be home before six, when her evening sessions began, but she had plenty of time. Setting her own hours was one of the perks of private practice. She had the flexibility and time to do whatever she wanted, except she never had any money to do it with.

She drove south on I-294 through a wide band of upscale new developments—the executive corridor they called it. Looking at palatial houses on flat parcels of treeless land made her appreciate Oak Park's rootedness, its every-body-knows-everybody sense of community even more.

Exiting from the tollroad onto a four lane highway, she glimpsed a green sedan turning onto the ramp just as she was leaving it. Tightening her hands on the wheel, she pressed down slightly on the accelerator. This far out, traffic was light, towns infrequent. She checked the rearview mirror again. A green Mercedes was rapidly closing the gap between them. Although realizing she could never outrun the other vehicle, she could not stop herself from pushing the old Toyota to its top speed of eighty. Moments later, the Mercedes had moved into a position such that, from the reflection in her mirror, it appeared to be right on top of her back bumper.

She clutched the steering wheel and kept her eyes straight ahead, praying her lane would stay empty, the Mercedes would have a blowout, she could refrain from doing the Mafia's job for them by running her car off the road herself. Sweat dripped from her forehead into her eyes, obscuring her vision. She careened over a curving, hilly route, past wooded fields and farmland, and finally sighted a cluster of buildings in the distance. She gradually lightened her foot on the gas, bracing herself for impact, expecting the Mercedes to mow her down. She allowed herself another glance in the mirror. The other car had dropped back a few feet. She tapped the brake. By the time she passed a sign indicating she had crossed over the border into Carter's Creek, she had the speed down to forty. She saw a painted board up ahead announcing Mary's Diner. When she reached the entrance, she swerved into the parking lot and screeched to a stop.

The Mercedes continued on down the highway. She sat shaking behind the wheel, waiting to see if it would double back. After ten minutes, she went into the diner rest room and threw water on her face, then took a stool at the counter and gulped down a Coke.

He's just playing with you. He's not ready to do anything yet.

Except give me a coronary. In which case he'll never find out that everything I know about Kevin adds up to a big, fat zero.

ta ta ta

"So," Honor said in her husky contralto, "what do you want to work on?" The retired psychologist's iron gray hair was piled loosely above an angular face punctuated by a large, hawkish nose. Her flowing black pantsuit was looped with heavy silver jewelry.

"That's a tough question." Sipping mint tea, Cassidy gazed through the front window at an expanse of grassland. "First, what to do about all this guilt? And the other thing— my intuition says it wasn't suicide, but I keep wondering if I might be convincing myself just to keep from feeling guilty."

"What specifically do you feel guilty about?"

"If Ryan really was suicidal, I should've recognized it

and sent him for a psychiatric eval. Also, in that last session when he told me he was feeling more depressed, I should've checked for suicidal impulses. And what bothers me most, I should've taken his call that night."

"Three things you neglected, and it's possible not doing them contributed to a suicide—if it was a suicide."

Slumping back into the cushions of the low-slung, contemporary armchair, Cassidy felt the tension ease away.

"When you've punished yourself enough, you'll let go of it."

Cassidy nodded.

"What kind of person was he?" Clinking her teacup down on the glass coffeetable, Honor rested thin, liver-spotted hands in her lap.

"Ryan tended to be overresponsible—no surprise, considering he was parenticized from an early age. As eldest son of a powerful family, he carried a heavy load of expectations, but seemed able to meet them without much difficulty. Given all this, he still managed to be pretty much of a nice guy—generally loved and admired by the people around him. Despite his need to be a superstar, he was able to maintain a high degree of sensitivity." Cassidy swallowed, pushing down the rush of pain that had risen in her throat. "Even though his wife turned his whole life upside down by bringing a punk teenage stepson into the marriage and then getting pregnant with Luke, he refused to walk out on her."

"What else?"

"What do you mean?"

"You've cited a lot of strengths. What about the weaknesses?"

"Well, I don't know . . . I can't think of any."

"What do you suppose might be stopping you?"

Chewing on her lower lip, Cassidy watched a small country schoolbus stop at the corner to disgorge a bunch of kids. She felt confused, couldn't focus on the question.

Honor leaned slightly forward, chains clanking. Cassidy caught a whiff of musk. "Any chance it's connected with your father? Or Kevin?"

"You think I'm idealizing Ryan? Because the men in my life have always been so irresponsible?"

"What do you think?"

"What's frustrating is, I'll always wonder. Maybe I could've prevented a suicide if I'd been able to see Ryan without the rose-colored glasses."

"Back to the guilt, huh? Maybe guilt feels better right now than grief. Could be your instincts are right and it wasn't a suicide."

"I hope I'm not just fooling myself."

"What about the brother? What's he like?"

"Another one of those irresponsible men. Can't even keep his plants from dying."

ﺏ ﺏ ﺏ

She opened the back door and stepped inside, then paused. What was wrong? The cat, who usually greeted her, was nowhere in sight. *Getting complacent. Thinks I'm such a softie I won't get rid of her, so she's sleeping on the job.*

She had only half an hour to grab a bite to eat and get ready for her six o'clock client. No time to hunt for a malingering feline. But it bothered her, the cat not having made an appearance. She checked the front porch. "Kitty, kitty." She looked in her bedroom, the second bedroom, the upstairs bathroom, behind the shower curtain, down the basement.

She's not about to show her face until she's good and ready. Or maybe she got out somehow. If she's gone, good riddance.

"Here, kitty, kitty." She continued opening doors and peering into the corners of closets. Finally, as she was standing in front of the refrigerator trying to think about dinner, she heard a plaintive cry.

7

KRISTI'S STORY

"Where are you, dammit?" She checked all the bottom cabinets, frantically trying to locate the source of the sound.

Maiooow! Loud and demanding.

She opened her office door and the cat bolted out. Purring riotously, she rubbed against Cassidy's legs, then raced back into the office, picked up something and carried it around the oak divider and into the kitchen. Dropping her treasure, she swatted it into a corner next to the stove. Cassidy caught her breath. A red pistachio.

She stared at the cat, trying to remember if she might have inadvertently shut her in the office. When she'd closed the door after Carla, the cat had not been in the room. She distinctly remembered what a chore it'd been at lunch, fending off the hovering cat as she crept closer and closer to

Cassidy's tuna salad.

She rushed inside, opened the middle drawer of her corner filing cabinet and took out the folder marked "Ryan Hollister." Nothing missing. She wandered into the kitchen and watched the cat chase her prize across gray linoleum so worn down the pattern was almost indistinct, eventually losing it under the curling seam. Nearly six. She ought to eat even though the thought of food made her wince. All too often her stomach had embarrassed her by sudden loud rumblings just as clients were getting into their deepest feelings.

She opened the refrigerator and gazed vacantly inside, stomach knotted, mind fixed on the pistachio question. Was this the same pistachio the cat had stolen from Zach's pocket Sunday night? If she could find the first pistachio on the porch, she'd have her answer.

She searched under magazines, behind boxes, between cushions on the couch. No pistachio. But a small, red nut could disappear any number of places. She could not rid herself of the idea that the first pistachio was still on the porch and the office pistachio a second, brought into the house while she was gone.

࿒ ࿒ ࿒

Having finished with her six o'clock client, Cassidy stood in front of her floor-length bedroom mirror trying to talk herself into an off-hand, who-cares attitude toward the meeting with Kristi. She noted her auburn hair, in need of a cut; her lavender blouse, wrinkled and sweaty from the drive to Woodridge; her black skirt, matted with cat hair.

Ryan had commented more than once on Kristi's taste for expensive clothing, her impeccable sense of style.

Cassidy shuffled through outfits hanging in her closet, the majority purchased at a resale shop. After changing into a purple sundress, she attacked her hair. The attempt to inflict order on her unruly mop proving futile, she went downstairs to wait on the porch for Zach.

It was nearly eight and the pale remaining daylight was fading into a cool dusk when she settled onto the wicker couch. She had miscalculated and was ready early. She picked up the magazines scattered across the floor, copies of *Family Circle* and *Woman's Day* her mother had foisted on her. The only time she ever opened them was when everything in her life went awry. She ought to find some other place to keep them. She didn't want Zach getting the wrong idea—that she cooked or something.

A sleek black sedan, driving slowly, turned down Hazel. There was something about it she didn't like. It moved out of her line of vision toward the cul-de-sac at the end of the block. She took a deep breath. *You're overreacting. You're not required to worry unless it's a green Mercedes with tinted windows.* Moments later it reappeared, heading back the way it had come. It stopped in front of her house. She couldn't see the driver through the passenger side window but had a clear view of the empty square where the front license plate belonged. The man who lived across the street strolled into his yard and the black sedan glided away.

When Zach pulled up in his gray Datsun wagon, a matronly car of a certain age, Cassidy stayed put on the couch. As he approached, she realized she was acting like a helpless female going on a date, a courting ritual she despised. *Who do you think you are, your mother? What happened to your principles?*

He opened the screen door and stepped onto the porch. The cat leapt onto a chair and adoringly stretched out her nose to snuffle his hand. He scratched the top of her head.

"Name her yet?"

"I'm not keeping her, I told you."

He pulled a pistachio out of his jeans pocket and flipped it onto the floor. The cat dived after it as though it were filet mignon. Cassidy's mouth tightened.

"You could call her Pistachio."

"I can restrain myself from making bad puns about nuts, but just barely." She stood and reached for her bag. "Let's go."

➚ ➚ ➚

A golden-hued child lunged across the dim hallway and tackled Zach around the knees.

"Take it easy," Zach yelled. "You better watch out. I'm gonna get you." He pried Luke off his leg and threw him over his shoulder. With the boy giggling and kicking all the way, Zach carried the child into a brown-toned, walnut and leather living room where he lowered him onto the burgundy oriental and pinned him to the floor. "I'm gonna hold you down 'til you stop screaming."

As she waited in the hall, Cassidy wondered what it was like for a five-year-old to grow up in a house with dark paneling, heavy furniture and subdued lighting. Obviously, he was not as chastened by his surroundings as she was.

Squealing with laughter, Luke demanded that Zach let him go.

Kristi stopped beside Cassidy. Her face showed tenderness. "Luke's crazy about him. It's really helped, having Zach come by. Kept him from thinking so much about . . ."

Kristi wore a white tennis dress that showed off her soft curves and long tan legs. But the dark, crinkly hair frizzed around her face, looking like it had gone untouched by a comb for days. Her eyes were bleary; her whole body drooped. The internal electricity was subdued, as though she were going through a brownout.

Cassidy struggled to hold on to her anger, but it was no use. She kept putting herself in Kristi's place, imagining what it would be like to explain to a son a father's suicide. "It must be so hard to talk to him about what happened."

Kristi shrugged, her face shifting to pain. "I'm not handling it very . . . He doesn't really understand. I can't seem to stop breaking down in front of him. Anyway, let's go on back to the sun room. Zach can come along when he gets Luke settled down."

Kristi led the way to a lime and watermelon room. Two sides had glass walls through which silhouettes of trees and a deep blue, twilight sky could be seen. Rows of plants lining the walls made Cassidy feel like she'd stepped into a jungle. *Probably kills off the extras by giving them to Zach.*

A pitcher of iced tea, a bottle of wine and an assortment of crystal stemware were waiting for them on a circular glass table. Circumventing a large toy pick-up with a couple of Heinekens cans in the bed, Kristi offered her a drink. Cassidy accepted a glass of iced tea and eased into a floral wicker armchair, one of a matched set in front of a large-screen television.

Kristi opened the Cabernet Sauvignon and was filling her own glass when Zach hobbled in. He had a beer in his hand and Luke wrapped around his leg.

"Did you know there's a monkey loose in the house?" Zach asked, putting his beer on the table.

Luke emitted a shrill, high-pitched chatter. Even with his face scrunched up, Cassidy could discern delicately etched features in a creamy circle of skin framed by smooth, white-blond hair. A frenetic version of a Hallmark Cupid.

"This is no kid. This is a monkey. Just a noisy, rowdy, little monkey." Zach swooped down, yanked the boy off his leg and held him at arm's length. "We may have to put him in a cage to quiet him down."

Luke yelled louder, flailing his arms in an attempt to grab Zach again.

Kristi dropped into the wicker loveseat and leaned forward to tap her son on the shoulder. "Now Luke, Mommy wants to talk."

Luke ignored her.

Tossing a child-sized shirt off the seat of the other chair, Zach sat down and grasped the boy's arms firmly. "All right, that's enough." His voice serious now. "Isn't it about your bedtime?"

"No!"

"We've been kind of lax about bedtime lately," Kristi licked a drop of wine from the corner of her mouth.

"Tell you what," Zach said. "You go put your pj's on right now, I'll come up later and we can play one game."

"I wanna play now," he whined.

"Later."

Luke threw him a sulky look and stomped out of the room.

"He's doing okay," Zach said to Kristi.

Tears welled up in her wide green eyes. "I can't understand it. How could a man with a beautiful child like ... "

"Did you see any sign at all that this was coming? Any warning signals?" Cassidy asked. "I mean, did he seem to be making any special arrangements? Talking about what to do when he was gone?"

Kristi gazed at the ceiling for several moments, then shook her head. "Nothing. You know, what I keep thinking about is ... " Her eyes filled again. "I keep wondering how he felt about ... if all that fighting ... I mean, we didn't fight that much ... But still, I can't get it out of my mind." She tugged on a strand of hair, stuck the end in her mouth.

Cassidy reached over and placed her hand on top of Kristi's, which was clenching and unclenching in her lap. "He didn't kill himself because there were problems in the marriage."

"Then why? Why would he do it?"

Cassidy shrugged helplessly. "He was angry because you got pregnant with Luke when he didn't want children. But he never stopped loving you."

The creases in Kristi's face softened. "I couldn't see any reason not to have a baby."

"Kristi," Zach said, "would you mind telling us about the night it happened? I know it's hard to talk about, but Cassidy'd like to hear the details."

She looked stricken. "I can't stand to even . . . "

"I know," he murmured. "But we really need to hear it."

She sighed deeply. "Well, I suppose . . . Let's see, it's hard to think." She paused. "All week long he seemed, I don't know, kind of moody, distracted. He was like that so . . . He did a lot of, you know, brooding."

"What happened that night?" Cassidy prompted.

"We didn't really talk until dinner. That's when we worked out the final details for the party."

"Luke's birthday party?"

"We were trying to decide how . . . We bought this new play equipment, you see, but it was . . . We didn't want to put it together ahead of time. So we were trying to decide about . . . And Ryan'd made plans to play golf in the morning with a friend. I wasn't too happy about that." Her hands fluttered vaguely.

"Just the two of you at dinner?" Zach asked.

Kristi's face flashed anxiety, then covered it instantly with innocence. "No, Scott was . . . He was the one who finally came up with a plan. He volunteered to get up at the crack of dawn on Sunday and . . . Ryan was surprised. Sometimes they don't get along so . . . But that night he said the kid was being pretty decent."

"That reminds me," Zach interrupted. "Where is Scott? I was surprised I didn't see him at the funeral."

Kristi's expression softened into concern. "The morning I found him, Ryan I mean, I was so . . . I went into Scott's room and woke him up and then he went into Ryan's study. Most people don't realize it, but he really is a sensitive . . . Anyway, he felt like he had to get away, so he flew off to stay with his father for awhile."

"I can see how the whole thing'd be pretty devastating for a kid who's only nineteen." Cassidy sipped bitter iced tea, the taste of tea bags that had steeped too long.

Kristi nodded.

"So . . . why don't you go on with what you were saying," Zach urged.

"Where was I?"

Zach tossed his beer can into the back of the red and yellow toy pick-up. "You were telling us about dinner,"

"Oh yes . . . we finished dinner and Scott went . . . Ryan had some work to do. Said he might be late and not to wait up. I just watched television and went to bed."

"One other thing," Zach said. "Did Ryan keep a gun in the study?"

Kristi looked startled. "No, I didn't think . . . I never went into . . . It was off limits." Her eyes darted to Cassidy. "I hate to say it, but there were lots of things I didn't . . . I mean, I'd been feeling kind of, you know, shut out ever since Luke was born."

After further talking which failed to bring up any new information, Zach suggested they say good night to Luke. The three of them trouped up the wide staircase, down the hall to an open doorway, and into a brightly patterned, red, white and blue bedroom bearing the perfect look of a designer room. As well as the chaotic look of a Toys "R" Us explosion.

Before they got inside the door, Luke lunged again.

"I only play with guys, not monkeys." Zach struggled to keep himself upright. "So, which is it gonna be?"

Letting go of Zach, Luke pulled himself up tall. "Let's play Pictionary."

Adorable. A bright, spunky, beautiful little boy. If only—

As Luke searched through piles of toys, Kristi explained, "Zach gave it to him and he's always crazy to find someone to play it with."

Leaving Zach to do the bedtime routine, the two women retreated to the sunroom. Darkness pressed in on glass walls, the brass lamp over the table creating a pool of light in the middle of the room. Kristi picked up the wine bottle and filled her glass to the rim, her movements jittery and abrupt. "Sure you won't join me?"

"Well . . . all right."

Kristi poured another glass. "I didn't want Ryan to be, you know, in therapy. I didn't like it that someone else . . . especially another woman . . . "

Cassidy nodded. "It's hard to have the man you love talking to somebody else."

Kristi blinked back tears. "I'm afraid he made me sound like . . . He thought I cared more about the children than— But I loved him more than anybody."

ta ta ta

"Dinosaur!" Zach yelled.

"That's not all," Luke taunted.

"He's doing something. Dancing."

"That's not all," Luke repeated.

"What else? The name of the dance? You need the name?"

The bell rang.

"You lose," Luke crowed. "The hokey pokey. It was dinosaur doing the hokey pokey."

"Okay guys." Kristi leaned against the doorframe. "Time to give it up."

Cassidy followed her into the room. "I've really got to get going."

Luke jumped up, knocking over his chair. "C'mon, Mom. Five more minutes, just five more."

"Nope," Zach said. "Time to quit. It's already a bunch past your bedtime."

"He can't get enough of that game," Kristi commented. "He's always showing me pictures."

Zach gave the boy a bear hug and tucked him into bed. When Luke was settled, Kristi walked her visitors to the door. As they parted, Kristi took both of Cassidy's hands in hers. "I'm really glad Zach talked me into . . . I wanted to be mad but now I can't."

"Does that mean we don't have to fight it out in court?"

Dropping Cassidy's hands, Kristi raised her own to her throat. "I wish I . . . I don't really want . . . There's nothing I can do."

When they were in the car, Cassidy said, "You know, it's funny. I'm feeling the same way. Like I should be angry, we should be enemies. But I can't muster the energy for it anymore. Even if she does sue."

Zach took her to Clancy's. Although just beyond the border of Chardonnay-and-brie Oak Park, it was many more social strata away. The interior was dark and comfortably shabby. A handful of patrons were hunched over mugs of domestic beer. Zach guided her to a table in the corner.

When they were seated, he asked, "What do you think?"

Cassidy gazed at the waitress, a plump woman around sixty-five wearing runover tennis shoes and a black polyester dress with a gathered waist that emphasized her girth. "She's lying," Cassidy replied.

8

CLOAK AND DAGGER

Zach nodded. "I agree."

The waitress approached, eyes black and snappy, mouth wide and good natured. "What'll it be, folks?"

Cassidy said, "White wine."

Zach said, "Jack Daniels and soda."

"Jack's good." The plump, roughly reddened face gave him an approving nod. "Folks go out, they should treat themselves. Drink the good stuff." She turned to go.

"Wait, I've changed my mind." Cassidy was suddenly famished. "I'll have what he ordered. And a side of onion rings."

"That's the spirit. None of that wimpy wine. Go for a real drink." The waitress jotted it down and left.

"The reason I'm so sure she's lying," Cassidy continued, "is Ryan was over the limit with Scott. That bit about good old Scott solving the play equipment problem just doesn't ring true. It'd be easier for me to imagine that hoodlum selling dope to little kids on a playground than putting his brother's jungle gym together."

"What about the visit to the ex? She lying about that too?"

"If he's not with his father, where is he?"

"Good question. Far as I know, Scott hasn't been seen since Ryan died."

The waitress brought their order. "Nice to see a young lady like you order some real food for a change, 'stead of them green salads hold the dressing. Everything tastes good has grease in it. So forget about grease." She planted her hands on ample hips. "I say, eating should be fun. People should enjoy their food. And you," she looked pointedly at Cassidy, "don't have to worry. You could stand to put some meat on."

Cassidy stuffed onion rings into her mouth. "If I decide I need fattening up, you can play Jewish mother."

"Jewish mother," she snorted. "I like that. I'd make a helluva Jewish mother."

When the waitress was gone, Zach said, "You don't need fattening. You're just right the way you are."

She looked up, startled.

"Just because we're partners in crime solving doesn't mean I can't look. You're pleasant to look at, you know. Even though you don't seem to be aware of it."

"Don't say things like that. Now I'll feel self-conscious."

"Okay, we'll talk about Scott. Seems to me, the next thing to do is, call his father and find out if he's really there."

"Right. You happen to know the father's name?" Cassidy wiped grease off her chin.

"Now I do. Couple of times I offered to watch Luke while Kristi was out, which gave me the chance to poke around some. I came across a letter from her ex. Fortunately, it had a return address." Zach took a large swallow, rattled the ice cubes and plunked the glass down on the rough wooden table.

"You went through Kristi's things?"

"Ryan's and Kristi's. Nothing in his stuff seemed much use, though."

"You mean, you've been making yourself available on the pretense of helping—but your real agenda was to snoop?"

"Hey, watch the hostility, shrink. I really was able to give her a hand. And I also took advantage of opportunities as they became available."

"I can't believe you'd violate your sister-in-law's privacy like that. You don't seem to feel the least bit bad about it, either."

Zach's eyes narrowed. "Actually, I'm rather proud of myself. We need to get hold of Scott's father, and because of my farsightedness, we can do it. In case you've forgotten, we have a mission here. Our mission is to play detective and discover what really happened to Ryan. What detectives do is snoop."

License to snoop. Suppose that also makes it all right to go through my files. Glaring, she tipped up her glass to finish her drink. "It's late. I've got to get home."

"One more thing. Did Ryan ever mention owning a gun?"

"Not a word." Cassidy wadded her napkin into a tight ball and began jiggling it in one hand.

"The gun bothers me. I don't know that we ever talked about it specifically, but I would've pegged Ryan as anti-handgun. Especially considering it's illegal to own guns in Oak Park."

"Maybe you could check with the police and find out if it's registered."

"I already did, and it isn't. But that doesn't mean anything. There are unregistered guns all over the place."

She placed the napkin in the ashtray, then laid her hand palm down on the table. "Well, I agree with you that Ryan didn't seem the type. Although, when people start thinking about suicide, they sometimes go to great lengths to set it up. So maybe, if Ryan really did kill himself, getting the gun was part of the plan. Maybe he acquired the gun recently with the sole purpose of . . . " Noticing that Zach was regarding her oddly, she left the sentence unfinished.

"It's amazing how you do that," he said.

"What?"

"Go from normal person to therapist in the blink of an eye. It's sort of like watching Clark Kent pop out of a phone booth in his Superman costume."

༄ ༄ ༄

After working late Wednesday night, she left her air conditioned office to face sticky heat throughout the rest of the house. She trudged up graying oak stairs, the cat darting in front and doubling back to trip her. As she dragged into the bedroom, the cat plopped down just outside the doorway, cold amber eyes seeming to say, "Doors are an affront to cats. I want this door open."

"Tough luck." Cassidy closed the door in her face, then turned on the window air conditioner.

The cat wailed.

She opened the door. The cat minced up to the door sill and sprawled across it. Cassidy nudged her into the bedroom and banged the door shut. As the cat stared resentfully at the slab of oak standing in the way of freedom, she crossed to her desk and pushed *play* on the answering machine.

"Zach here. Call me."

He answered right away. "I talked to Scott's dad. He's got no idea where the kid is. Says Scott spent a couple of weeks with him last summer and his new wife couldn't stand it."

"So Kristi's lying."

"Next step, find out where he is and what he's been up to."

"Seems like a tough assignment. I have the impression a kid like Scott could just disappear into the drug culture."

"I've got some ideas. Why don't we get together and do some brainstorming on this one?"

Why don't we not get together and just admit we don't know what we're doing?

Zach's terse voice clipped along. "How about I buy dinner on Friday night? You can order the biggest item on the menu and take home enough for three meals. How's that for an offer you can't refuse?"

How does he know I'm so broke, a free meal's almost irresistible?

"Well . . . I guess. But I'm buying my own."

"Those feminists sure have made life hard on you gals."

๏ะ ๏ะ ๏ะ

The next morning her doorbell rang while she was in session with Frank, a man whose wife had recently moved out. Tears streaming down his face, he was in the middle of describing what she'd said as she packed to leave. The doorbell rang again. Struggling to keep her attention on the man's story, Cassidy tried to think of an empathic comment. The bell rang insistently. She finally stopped hoping it would go away and excused herself to answer.

A bald man wearing a sports jacket was standing at her back door. "You Cassidy McCabe?"

She nodded.

He handed her a business envelope, turned, and left. The embossed return address said, *Lawrence, Rutherford and Hall.* Not until the session was over did she open the envelope. The legalese inside made no sense to her.

You don't have to read it to know what it means. It means you fucked up and you're going to lose everything.

Four weeks before the answer's due. If we come up with a murderer, they can't sue.

Don't count on it.

The cat jumped onto the counter and Cassidy absently scratched behind her ear. "You and I may end up out on the street yet." She saw herself sitting on a park bench with the cat perched on her shoulder doing therapy for a bag lady.

❧ ❧ ❧

Around noon on Friday, Cassidy opened the refrigerator and searched through plastic containers storing contents of unknown origin, finally locating one last carton of yogurt. She leaned back against the counter, planning to reread her favorite Sylvia cartoons while she ate. The cat, who appeared out of nowhere whenever she was in the kitchen, leapt onto the counter and began cooing and coaxing about the yogurt. Cassidy placed the lid under the cat's nose, sticky side up. The cat took a lick, then knocked it to the floor, sticky side down.

"Let's do lunch again sometime—maybe in the next decade."

The phone rang.

"Hi, gorgeous." Kevin's rich voice triggered a jolt of excitement which, in the next instant, flipped over into panic.

Propping herself in the doorway between the kitchen and dining room, Cassidy tried to stop the racing in her mind. "You've done it to me again."

"Now, babe, take it easy. You have this unfortunate tendency to always expect the worst."

"Only where you're concerned."

"Let's not bicker, love. We have to talk."

"Why is it that, hearing those words out of your mouth sends my anxiety level soaring?"

"C'mon, babycakes. You can't tell me you haven't missed our little chats." The warmth in his voice almost melted her defenses. "Wish I could talk longer, but we really have to get down to business. We need to meet in person—best make it this afternoon, oh, say about one-fifteen. What I want you to do is, park your car in the lot behind Walgreen's on Lake Street, then walk in the back entrance, straight through and out the front door. I'll be waiting in a green Jag parked right in front."

Her breath caught. Her hand tightened on the phone. "We don't really need all this cloak and dagger, do we?" She sucked in air. "Tell me it's not that bad."

"Are you kidding?" He hung up.

Cassidy slowly replaced the receiver. "You notice," she said morosely, turning to the cat, "the total lack of any *Will-you? Would-you-be-willing? Is-it-okay-with-you?* Along with the absence of any *Pleases, Thank-yous, Sorrys-for-fucking-up-your-life.* None of these words exist in Kevin's vocabulary. Of course he assumes I'll go running to the rescue. Why wouldn't he? God knows I've done it enough times in the past."

Still seated on the counter, the cat began washing her tail.

"So . . . what should I do?"

The cat refused to make eye contact.

"You think I should say, *Forget you, Kevin. This is not my problem.*" She sighed deeply. "I wish I could. If I could do that, I'd know for sure the thousands I've spent on therapy weren't wasted."

The cat flattened her ears, twitched the tip of her tail.

"You don't approve. You think I should forsake all others and devote my life to taking care of you."

ð ð ð

At one p.m. she walked out the back door into steamy afternoon heat. Halting on the porch, she checked up and down the street. No sign of the Mercedes. A few parked cars but all appeared unoccupied. Playing in her neighbor's yard was a bunch of kids representing so many races it could've been a subcommittee of the U.N. Strolling past her gate, a sixtyish Hispanic man walked his toy collie, pooper scooper, as required by village ordinance, in hand. He tipped his straw hat and murmured the usual fluid, indistinct greeting. Across the street an elderly lady in frilly pink dress weeded her tulips.

This is not a good idea. The cat's right. You should go inside and stop answering the phone and wait until Public Radio Voice finds Kevin on his own.

Taking a deep breath, she raced to the garage, backed out and headed west on Briar. Halfway down the next block she slowed for a half dozen older teens, full-grown vertically but unfilled-out in shoulders and chest, skin tones ranging from deep mahogany to light oak. They had fanned out across the street and were slowly advancing on her Toyota with a "fuck-you-honky" insolence expressed in each defiant, swaggering step. She crawled forward. Although recognizing this as a form of ritualized teen bravado she'd encountered before, it nonetheless heightened her already pumped-up adrenalin. When she was close enough, almost, to graze kneecaps with fenders, the line split, allowing just enough space for her car to pass through.

On the short drive to Walgreen's, she checked her

rearview mirror a dozen times. Twice she glimpsed a sleek black sedan, but Kevin's paranoia aside, she had no reason to think it was following her. She pulled into the lot and parked. No black car. No green Mercedes.

Just as she was walking into the store's rear entrance, she glanced back over her shoulder. A black car had pulled into the handicapped spot closest to the entrance. The driver's door was opening.

9

KEVIN

Cassidy bolted through the aisles of the store, nearly tripping over a small child who darted past her. When she got to the front door, she stopped and swiveled around. A tall man in a suit had just come through the back door and was running toward her. *Stop!* ordered the proper behavior voice. *Take a good look. Memorize his face.* But she couldn't force herself to do it. Her glance ricocheted away as though his image burned her eyes. Panic fluttered in her chest. She gulped air, trying to fill lungs that were moving too fast to let oxygen in.

She burst out of the store and into a wall of heat. Lunging toward the green blur directly in front of her, she saw the back door fly open and arms reach out to pull her inside. She put one foot on the car frame, then felt herself dragged forward and into Kevin's lap. He pulled the door shut and the car jerked forward.

Disentangling herself, she twisted around to look out the rear window. A tall, sinewy man stood just outside Walgreen's. He appeared meticulously groomed, not a hair out of place despite his dash through the store, with a lightly tanned face wearing a winner's smile. He looked exactly like her image of FBI agents on television. Their eyes met momentarily, then the car swerved, she tilted sideways against the door, and he was gone. "Shit!" She turned to face Kevin. "You've done it to me again. Now he thinks I know where you are."

Kevin grinned his adorable, lopsided grin, touched a finger lightly to her lips, and in a phony Irish brogue, said, "Now, darlin', dinna work yourself up. It's Kevin himself who's here to take care of you. So dinna worry your bonny wee head." He winked and dropped his hand casually onto her thigh.

"Take your bonny wee hand off my leg or I'll slug you."

Chuckling, Kevin removed his hand. "See what I told you, Philly? She's always punching me, slugging me. Any excuse to get her hands on my body."

Cassidy focused for the first time on the driver, whose round, fleshy face under a deeply receding hairline had glanced back with a smile.

"Phil Stoch. Don't tell me you're still hanging around with this character."

"Hey, the two of us are partners. Friends for life, right buddy?" Kevin said, speaking for him.

"Where're we headed, anyway? How can you be sure

it's safe?"

"What's this? Not enough cloak and dagger to suit you?"

"Don't worry," Phil said in a soft, deferential voice. "Nobody can get to us through you."

"Oh great. That helps a lot." She peered out the window intently. No black cars in sight. Moving as far away from Kevin as possible, she concentrated on slowing down her breathing.

Several miles out of Oak Park, Phil turned off the main highway into a forest preserve. He drove down a narrow, twisting road, then pulled onto a secluded dirt track and parked.

"C'mon." Kevin grabbed her hand, pulling her out behind him. Phil shuffled around to the back of the car, weighted down by a heavy paunch that was larger every time Cassidy saw him. He unlocked the trunk and removed a picnic basket and a tall plastic container.

Kevin said, "Chez Paul's a little out of the question just now, but we did come up with this creative alternative." He was tall and big boned, with broad shoulders, slim hips, and an easy, graceful way of moving. His bronze hair, nearly the same color as his tanned face, was short and loosely curled, giving him the ruffled, breezy look of a man who'd just stepped off the bow of a ship.

Reaching a clearing back in the woods, Phil opened the basket and withdrew three fluted champagne glasses and a red blanket, which he laid out on the ground. Kevin dropped cross-legged onto the blanket, while Phil lumbered into a squat, put hands on the ground for balance, then clumsily eased himself down. "C'mon, babe. Sit." Kevin opened the plastic container and took out a bottle of Dom Perignon.

Cassidy paused at the edge of the blanket, considering whether she wanted to participate in Kevin's little piece of theater. Phil, who'd happily accepted the role of Kevin's gopher for at least ten of his thirty-five years, was clearly loving every minute of it. He looked as excited as a kid getting Michael Jordan's autograph, sitting there with a glass in each chubby hand, his puppy eyes watching Kevin deftly work the cork loose.

"C'mon, darlin'. Sit down and join us in a glass of champagne."

She lowered herself onto the blanket, accepted a glass from Kevin, allowed him to fill it. When he raised his glass, the other two followed suit. They clinked glasses.

"To love, money and the good life," Kevin boomed.

"To giving it all you've got," Phil echoed.

"To staying alive," Cassidy threw in.

She took a sip and held it in her mouth, savoring the burst of bubbles on her tongue. "Such expensive taste. Of course, I knew that already."

His eyes crinkled. His mouth slipped sideways into that adorable smile. Every time she saw him, it hit her again, like being punched in the stomach, why she'd fallen for him all those years ago.

She lifted her chin. "So . . . what's all this about? Or, maybe a better question, what do you want?"

Kevin shook his head. "Sure and it's a shame that one so lovely should be so cynical." His fingers traced the bones in the back of her hand, which was resting on her knee.

"It's money, of course. But I can't imagine why you might think I'd have any. Or if I did, why I'd give it to you."

"Well . . . as a matter of fact, you do have money. Or, to put it another way, access to money. You have your grandmother. And the house."

Angry words buzzed in her head, enabling her to break loose from his tractor beam. Clenching her teeth to stop them, she reminded herself that she needed to dig up all the dirt before verbally punching him out. "That's true," she replied mildly.

"As to the second part, why you might want to help—it's just possible you might prefer to avoid having to arrange my funeral. It's also possible you might like to protect your mother and grandmother from a similar inconvenience. Anything happened to you, I expect they'd take it pretty hard."

"Just say it straight. Remember—this is me you're talking to. It won't do you any good to be cute."

"Okay, here it is. I made the mistake of borrowing money from some thugs. Fifty grand, to be exact. When I borrowed the money, I gave them a copy of an old title to the house that has both our names on it, so they think the house is their collateral. Therefore, they expect you to make good on the loan if I'm not able to."

"Oh, Kevin, how could you! No—don't even answer that. Let me ask this instead—why not sell the Jag, for starters?"

He beamed his lopsided grin at her. "I'd be happy to—if the title were in my name."

Cassidy redirected her glare to Phil. "Whose?"

Phil's apologetic brown eyes slipped away from hers. "Belongs to his girlfriend." He jerked his head in Kevin's direction. "Actually, an ex-girlfriend. She threw him out, but he had the keys to her place. And she's in Europe, so . . . "

Kevin shot him a look and he stopped.

Cassidy shook her head. "Phil, you disappoint me. After all these years, you're still letting him pull the strings. Remember the time he talked you into that phony accident scam? And the time he nearly got you arrested for faking furnace repairs? Don't you ever learn?"

Phil had his head lowered so all she could see was the round top, bisected by a hairline that had receded to the crown. One half was shiny pink scalp, the other nappy brown hair. "Yeah, but this one sounded so good."

Looking up, he gave her a sheepish smile.

Only reason you're pissed at Phil is, you've let Kevin do the same thing so to you so many times.

"Tell her the whole story." Kevin tipped the bottle in her direction, but she put her hand over her glass. "Maybe if she hears all of it, she'll find it in that hard heart of hers to be more charitable."

"About time somebody was charitable," Phil muttered. "The mob sure don't seem inclined to be."

"We put together this telemarketing scheme," Kevin said in the enthusiastic tone that set alarm bells ringing in her head. "What we were doing, actually, was collecting money for worthy causes. You wouldn't believe how much people will contribute. Why, they just write out checks and stick them in the mail. And those checks really add up."

She twirled the glass stem between her fingers. "Bet I

know what charity you were collecting for, too."

Kevin pulled his brows together in mock indignation. "Matter of fact, one of the causes I'd planned to donate to is the Cassidy-Back-Taxes fund. Unfortunately, the venture was cut short before I'd accumulated sufficient cash flow."

Phil rubbed at a coffee stain on his orange shirt front. "State's attorney closed us down."

"You got arrested?"

"Not exactly," Phil continued. "But we had to fork over all the money we'd collected. And that's what we'd earmarked for paying off the mob."

She cocked her head at Kevin. "You still haven't said how you happened to borrow money in the first place."

"Can't open a business without cash," he replied. "We had to rent the office, do some remodeling, get the phones put in. Amazing how fast you run up fifty big ones."

10

PINEAPPLE AND PEANUT BUTTER CUPS

"So now the mob's after you to collect," Cassidy said dryly. "Well, that's an interesting story. But I don't feel any charitable impulses racing from my hard heart to my soft head."

"C'mon, babe," Kevin said in his warmest, most enticing tone. "I can't believe you'd stand by and let me be killed. Could you honestly live with yourself if I got wasted because you refused to give me a hand when I needed it?"

"You don't want a hand—you want fifty-thousand dollars."

"Uh, not exactly," Phil interrupted. "It's up to sixty-five, what with the interest and all."

"Save the blandishments for your girlfriend." Cassidy laid the glass down carefully on the blanket. "From the looks of that Jag, her hand's a lot closer to sixty-five thou than mine."

Refusing to meet her eyes, Phil picked blades of grass and piled them up in front of him. "She won't do anything. She's too pissed. Besides, you're in this too. You're the one they know how to find, not us."

Kevin shot him a look that clearly said *shut up.*

"So I should help. Because you put my life on the line."

Kevin reached over and took her hand. She did not respond, but neither did she withdraw. "Why don't you get out of here," he said to Phil, who obediently rolled to his hands and knees, struggled to his feet, picked up the basket and ambled back to the car.

"Listen, love, I know we've been joking around, but this is no laughing matter. You really should think about getting the money from your grandmother. Remember how much she liked me? She always said I made her feel like a girl again. Think how she'd hate it if I got killed because you refused to ask for help."

"The day you walked out on me, Gran said, 'Thank God that two-timing fucker is out of your life.' "

He lifted her hand and lightly kissed each of her fingertips.

"Kevin, you and I have had this same conversation at least a hundred times. I will not go to Gran for money. She practically supported Mom and me when I was growing up, and she deserves to hang onto the money she's got. There's no way of knowing how much it may cost to take care of her when she starts to fail."

"But this is different. I don't think you quite understand who we're dealing with here. This is not some plot out of one of those mysteries you're always reading. These guys have ways of finding people. They kill as easily as you'd grind out a butt. Don't let me down, babe."

She held his gaze, thinking that he was as good as ever at making a pitch. When she finally saw the waver of doubt she was looking for, she asked, "Are you done?"

His hand slid up her arm. "Not quite." He inched up to her shoulder and caressed the back of her neck the way she'd always loved. He shifted around so his face hovered over hers. She closed her eyes as his lips came down, moving slowly and gently, eliciting from her mouth an automatic, deeply ingrained response. After the meltdown was complete, he broke the contact and pulled away.

Allowing herself a small sigh, she opened her eyes. "You always were a good kisser." She stood up.

He stood up also. "Is that all?"

"You didn't expect me to change my mind over a kiss, did you? You're not *that* good."

"What the hell, it was worth a try. You know, I always did like screwing you." Stepping back, he looked at her with genuine curiosity. "If you knew you weren't going to give in, why the encouragement?"

"I didn't exactly . . . Oh, well, maybe a little. I just wanted to see if the old fireworks were still there."

"Were they?"

She thought about it for a couple of beats. "To some

extent . . . Yes, I'd have to say they were. But not as much as before. They no longer turn my brain to mush. My brain is still telling me to say no."

After getting dropped off in front of Walgreen's, she walked inside and checked to see if the man—she assumed it was Public Radio Voice—was still around. No suits anywhere in the store. She proceeded to the candy aisle and snatched up a bag of bite-sized Reese's Peanut Butter Cups. When she got inside her car, she tore open the plastic bag, unwrapped a chocolate cup, and bit it in half. She ate two more, chewing slowly to make them last, then licked the chocolate from her fingers, stuffed the bag in her purse, and drove home.

🐾 🐾 🐾

Joints stiff, hands cold, Cassidy wandered into the house, dropping her purse on a chair as she passed through the waiting room and on into the kitchen. *This can't really be happening. Kevin won't really be killed.* The cat wriggled between her legs, nearly tripping her, then pounced onto the washed-out green countertop and spoke in an imperative tone.

"You hungry again?"

Mrorw! The cat nuzzled her hand, knocking the milk carton lid Cassidy'd forgotten to replace when she put milk in her coffee down to the floor.

Cassidy took a can out of the cupboard, opened it halfway, then realized she had grabbed the wrong one. "Would you consider pineapple in lieu of cat food?" she asked.

Mrow.

"Guess it's pineapple for me. Pineapple and peanut butter cups, what a winner."

The cat cleaned her plate, grabbed up the plastic lid and zoomed out of sight.

Her mouth dry, the back of her neck a cement post, she poured ice water and went out to the porch, even though it felt like stepping into an oven with late afternoon sun pouring through the windows. Across the street a young mother sat on the front steps of a gabled brick house overseeing three little kids bouncing in and out of a wading pool. The tallest, a boy similar in size and coloring to Luke, filled a bucket with water, ran up to a smaller girl in a blue sunsuit, and threw it at her.

The phone rang, her four-thirty client saying she'd be an hour late. As she hung the receiver on the kitchen wall, Cassidy remembered that Zach was supposed to pick her up at six. Now she'd be in session until six-thirty. She couldn't reach him, so she taped up a note asking him to wait on the porch.

ta ta ta

"If I could just get something going with Andy, I'd stop seeing Roger. For real this time." Michelle's childlike face under a mop of dark, curly hair scrunched in frustration.

"I don't think it works that way," Cassidy said.

"I've been trying to break off with Roger ever since I found out he's married but I'm never able to stick with it," Michelle was a softly plump, twenty-six-year-old with round face, full pouty lips, and throaty, Debra Winger voice.

"You can't develop any kind of intimacy with Andy when you're hiding this intense part of your life."

Michelle thrust out her lower lip. "That's what Roger did. He made sure I was hooked before he told me about the little wifey who's out of town all the time."

"You want to treat Andy the same way Roger treated you?"

"Stop making me feel guilty, all right?" Looking at Cassidy from under her brows, she quirked her mouth in a sly smile that said, *don't be angry.*

Straightening the Kleenex box on the wicker table, Cassidy met Michelle's dark brown eyes. "I know you don't mean to hurt anybody. The problem is, whenever somebody comes along who's a decent guy and available, bells just don't go off."

Nodding glumly, Michelle picked at a loose end of plastic tape.

"If what you wanted to do was likely to work, there'd be no harm. But unfortunately, you can't hold out on Andy and develop a relationship at the same time. Relationships require honesty."

≈ ≈ ≈

After the session, Cassidy's mood was lighter. Easier to focus on someone else's troubles than her own. As she headed toward the porch where she expected to find Zach, she became aware of a nattering of distant voices. She cocked her head, getting a fix on where they were coming from, then dashed upstairs.

"Hi." Zach was sprawled across her bed, shoes off,

remote control in hand, cat bundled onto his chest.

"Three people killed in an apartment building fire in Cicero ... " The television image of flames billowing out of a low rise building briefly distracted her.

"You go through my medicine chest yet?"

"I wanted to see the six o'clock news. Ready for dinner?"

"You know, I don't much like people wandering into my bedroom."

"You have a real thing about privacy, don't you? I came upstairs because I couldn't find a TV anywhere else."

"You ever hear of impulse control?"

The phone rang. She took a step towards it, then jerked around to look at Zach. *Don't answer. Get him out of here.*

The machine clicked on. Zach sat up straighter. The cat disappeared.

"How come you're not answering? You think it's your boyfriend and you don't want him catching you with another guy in the bedroom?"

"No, of course not. I don't . . . " Whirling around, she started searching frantically for the stop button.

"I watched you drive off with Kevin this afternoon after your clumsy attempt to evade me." A precise, colorless voice issued from the machine. She gulped air, breathing too fast. "I've been much too patient waiting for you to divulge his hiding place. You're nearly out of time. If you don't stop this childish game soon, we'll end it our own way. An ending I promise will not be to your liking."

Beep.

11

PIZZA

Zach had twisted around to sit on the edge of the bed facing her. "What was that all about?"

"Six casualties resulted from today's four-car pileup on Lake Shore Drive."

"Strictly my problem." *That's right—get belligerent. Sure to help.*

"Come off it, Cassidy."

"In other news, ex-mayor Jane Byrne held a press conference this afternoon to ... "

"Shut off the goddamned television, will you?"

Zach pointed the remote control at the screen and a woman's face dissolved in mid-sentence. "Now sit down and tell me what this is all about."

"There's no reason to get into it."

"Just sit down."

She pulled out her desk chair and plopped into it.

"Okay. Now, somebody who sounds like a Mafia guy wants you to tell him where somebody named Kevin is. Who's Kevin, anyway?"

Her forehead knotted, her mouth drew into a deep frown, letting him know what she thought of his questions. "Kevin's my ex. This is none of your business."

He waited, the way she did in therapy when the client stonewalled.

"Kevin borrowed money from the mob and Public Radio Voice—that's my harassing caller—keeps trying to get me to tell them where he is, only I don't know where he is, and I wouldn't tell if I did. At least, I don't think I would."

"He said he saw you and Kevin together."

"Kevin didn't tell me where he's staying."

"You've been getting threatening phone calls? Why the hell didn't you tell me?"

"Why should I? I hardly know you." *For all I know, you broke into my house and went through my files. And left a pistachio for the cat.*

"It just so happens I don't want to come over here some day and find you at the bottom of the basement steps with your skull caved in. I happen to like you. And your cat."

"Well . . . that's nice. But I don't see what good it does for you to know about the mess I'm in." Twisting around to stare into fading daylight at the window, she chewed on her bottom lip.

"What is it you're not saying?"

She told him about the meeting with Kevin and the

pressure to borrow money from her grandmother.

"What're you planning to do?"

She raised her hands in a gesture of helplessness.

"You talked to the police?"

"I keep thinking about it, but I don't know if that'd make it better or worse. Guess I'm afraid if the police get into it, *they*, whoever *they* are, will find out and come after me even faster."

He nodded. "The mob's got informants all over the place."

"So . . . " Turning her head away, she looked out the window again.

"So, what *are* you going to do?"

She snapped her head around. "I *told* you, I don't know. Ignore it, I guess. I can't think of anything else."

"Chrissake, you're acting like this is some kind of TV movie. If this guy really is a member of the mob—and there's no reason to think he isn't—you've got to take this seriously. Why not borrow the money? The bank, your family, whatever."

She considered what he was saying. But even as she tried to see it objectively, she could feel the back of her neck turning into a concrete post again. She crossed her arms over her chest. "No."

"Shit. You're being very difficult, you know that?"

"That's not true. I've given in on everything else."

"Buddy of mine at the paper covers the mob. I'll see if he can find out who's behind this. Maybe he's got some clout, I don't know."

The concrete in her neck started to soften. "It's just that

. . . I don't like having other people bail me out."

"You're the therapist, you want to do all the fixing. Well . . . since we don't have any immediate solutions, what say we table Public Radio Voice for now and get something to eat. But if you don't let me buy dinner, I swear I'll go to your grandmother myself."

"Okay, you can pay."

He took her to a neighborhood pizza place called Al's. They slid into a dark wooden booth with initial-carved table. He ordered the pepperoni special and a pitcher. They bounced around ideas for locating Scott, finally deciding that Zach would "borrow" a photo of the teenager from Kristi's house and show it to some narcs he knew. Then Zach, who worked for the *Chicago Post*, chided her for not subscribing to a daily paper, and Cassidy counterattacked by blasting the media for intrusiveness and sensationalism.

Feeling stuffed and having run out of subjects to disagree on, Zach had the pizza remains wrapped, insisting Cassidy take possession of the doggie bag. He drove back and parked in front of her house.

"Wait," he said as she turned to open the door. Pulling her gently toward him, he rubbed the back of his hand against her cheek. "I like talking to you. You don't let me get away with anything." He moved to face her. "I keep wondering what you'd taste like." He licked the corner of her mouth, then kissed her. "Mmm. Not bad."

It was not a great kiss, not one to go down in history, but pleasant enough. To stop herself from moving her mouth back against his, she ducked her head and pushed away from him. "Pizza," she said. "I taste like pizza."

"I like pizza."

"We've both had enough for one night." She shoved the door open and jumped out.

"Wait for me." He opened his door.

"No!" She was surprised at the urgency in her voice. "If you walk me to the door, it'll seem like a date. I've got enough problems as it is, and I don't want to have to worry about whether we're partners in crime-solving or dating or who knows what. So stay in the car. Please."

This is weird. I haven't kissed anybody in three years, and here I've just kissed two men in the same day. And it may be another three years before I do it again.

ta   ta   ta

"Jim called," Carla said, shifting her clear blue eyes away from Cassidy's. "Just when I'd stopped crying myself to sleep at night, wouldn't you know it?"

"How'd you feel about hearing from him after he stood you up a couple of weeks ago?" The way Carla's mouth turned up softly at the corners when she mentioned his name gave Cassidy her answer.

"I know, I should've been pissed." Carla sighed deeply. "I'm not s'posed to feel happy that he called, right?"

"When it comes to feelings, there aren't any shoulds." Cassidy noticed the coleus on the wicker table was looking pathetic again. She reminded herself to water it after the session.

"You always say that. But from the expression on your face, I get the idea you disapprove of my wanting to talk to him."

Cassidy gave her a straight look. "I understand you're really hooked. Of course you want him to call. I'm just worried he'll do it to you again."

"Me too." Carla brushed a tangle of fine gold curls back from her face.

"So, what'd he say about the no-show he pulled on your anniversary?"

"Nothing."

"Nothing?"

Carla's pastel fingernail traced the slanting line of sunlight across the vinyl seat. "I know I should've confronted him. I shouldn't have let him get away with pretending it never happened."

"So, what *did* you say?"

"I made a big deal about going out with a bunch of friends that Saturday night. Acted like I'd had a wonderful time without him. Said we went skinny dipping and watched the sun come up, then we all had breakfast at this really cool restaurant."

Cassidy's voice turned comforting. "You didn't want him to know how much he hurt you."

She nodded miserably. "I feel so stupid. He knows it was all a lie but I can't bring myself to admit it. Now I can't even bitch him out for standing me up."

After the session, Cassidy continued thinking about how people some times invented stories, only to feel trapped in their lies later. Carla would be happy to have some graceful way of taking her fabrication back. Perhaps the same was true of Kristi.

She called Zach, got his machine and left a message.

She was downstairs feeding the cat when the phone rang. She answered and a professional male voice said, "Cassidy McCabe, please."

"This is she."

"My name's Tony Chiparo. I've been told you're a good therapist and . . . I need to see someone." A hint of embarrassment.

"Evidently someone gave you my name. Would you mind telling me who referred you?"

"I'm sorry to seem rushed, but somebody's going to show up in my office any minute now. I'd like to set the appointment first, fill in the details later."

"What would be a good time?"

"Look, I know this is short notice, but I'm going out of town Wednesday and it's really important I see you before I leave. Could you do me a big favor and squeeze me in tomorrow night at nine?"

Eight was her usual her cut-off. "I'd rather make it earlier. How about—"

"Can't get there any earlier. I'll be working down to the wire. I realize I'm imposing but this is really urgent."

What could be so critical? A muscle twitched in her eyelid. Something's not right. *Don't be paranoid. He sounds professional. In some kind of crisis. You've had plenty of people demand instant appointments when their life goes up for grabs. Besides, you need the money.*

"All right, tomorrow at nine." Where was her calendar—upstairs or in the office? "But first I need your phone number, and I'll have to give you directions—"

"Don't worry, I can find you. Oops—someone's coming. See you tomorrow."

12

DEATH WISH

The cat, who had scarfed down her food while Cassidy was on the phone, was now squirming around, showing her tummy in paroxysms of delight over having been fed.

"On the rare occasions I happen to buy food you approve of, you act like an orgiastic nymphet."

The cat suddenly sprang onto the counter, then bounded to the top of the refrigerator. Enormous amber eyes stared down.

"So, you think he's all right? Everything could be legit. I mean, maybe he's embarrassed at calling a therapist, afraid someone'll hear him on the phone. He might've been so uptight he didn't even notice he wasn't answering any questions. In fact, he seemed so nervous he probably won't show."

Despite the words, the creepy sensation she'd been feeling in her stomach since hanging up the phone did not go away.

ⓢ ⓢ ⓢ

Zach did not get back to her that night.

Tuesday morning as she drank her coffee on the porch, fragments of past sessions popped into her head. Ryan, frustrated: "We were so close. Now, he never calls. And half the time when I leave messages, he doesn't get back."

Ryan, critical: "Good education. The family behind him. But all he wants to do is hang out in bars and chase women." Ryan, disappointed: "Used to think he'd settle down once he got all the running around out of his system. He lived with one woman for several years. Then he just walked out."

Zach called at noon and she picked up in the kitchen.

Where were you last night? "I've been thinking the best bet might be another crack at Kristi. I'm guessing if we confront her with what we know already, we can get the truth." Stretching the telephone cord, she crossed the kitchen and leaned against the counter next to the refrigerator.

"You've got a point. At least we know where she is."

They set a time to meet.

"There's another thing." Zach's voice took on the tense clip he used when he was about to say something she didn't want to hear. "You keep your back door unlocked, don't you? Clients just ring the bell and walk in."

"Right." She ripped a yellowed Calvin and Hobbes off the refrigerator door, wadded it up and lobbed it at the cat.

"I don't think that's too smart."

"I don't think it makes much difference." *I think you walked through a locked door yourself.* "No lock's going to keep out a hit man."

"Maybe not, but it'd slow him down. You ought to keep both doors locked all the time."

"Can't. I'd have to interrupt sessions to let clients in." She struck the cat's rump with a Sylvia cartoon crumpled into a marble-sized ball. The cat, who'd been stalking the first missile, leapt straight up.

"What's the matter with you? You keep refusing to do anything. You have a death wish or something?"

"I have to do what's best for my clients. I can't afford to let this mess in my personal life interfere with my work as a therapist." *Can't afford to screw up again.*

"You can be very pigheaded, you know that? If you won't lock up when clients are scheduled, you could at least do it when you don't have sessions. Promise me you'll do that?"

"I don't know . . . I suppose I could."

"That a promise?"

"Yes. Okay." *Maybe. I'll think about it.*

She hung up. Opening the refrigerator, she looked inside, then banged the door closed again. She went to the coat closet, took down her purse and got out the bag of peanut butter cups. Grabbing a handful, she stood in front of the sink staring into the kitchen next door as she slowly chewed.

She was not used to anybody showing concern or trying to take care of her. It didn't feel right. She didn't like it.

ॐ ॐ ॐ

At ten to nine she was upstairs in her desk chair, cat in lap, hoping that Tony Chiparo would blow off his appointment. The more she thought about it, the more she realized the mistake of letting a stranger in her house who'd refused to give out any information. But what could she do? She felt too stupid to call the police. She could never let her mother know what she'd done. If she told Zach, he'd just yell at her some more.

She could, of course, lock her doors, turn off the lights, and sit with her hand on the phone, ready to dial nine-one-one. But she was a therapist and she'd agreed to see a client who appeared to be in crisis. To break that commitment would violate everything she believed in.

At five to nine the doorbell rang. She jumped slightly; the cat sprang down and disappeared. The creepy feeling returned, twice as strong.

Don't go down. It's crazy to see this weirdo alone in your house.

What's the alternative? Hiding under the bed?

As she descended the stairs and passed through the living room, she was aware that blackness outside the closed windows had sealed in the rooms like gigantic black tape, imprisoning her along with the curt man waiting for her at the other end of the house. She trudged past her second hand, paisley blue sofa, moving along with a nobody-home-inside feeling. As though watching herself from some other place, she was aware of the grim, taut cast to her features, her stiff-legged gait.

Time took on a slow motion quality as she continued her trek on into the dining room. At a once-removed level, she noted the musty smell of the rooms, the syrupy feel of humid air, the staccato click of sandaled heels on hardwood floors.

Turning into the kitchen, she picked up a muted strain of music, her waiting room radio playing in the background. "Stand by me," a male singer throbbed to the accompaniment of a heavy beat. She traversed the length of the kitchen, then came around the cabinet room divider.

Tony Chiparo was standing, hands in the pockets of pleated-front, black pants, gazing at the bulletin board on the wall next to her back door. She had a momentary sense of having seen him before that blinked and was gone. As he turned toward her, she felt an instant wave of relief. He had the clean-cut, boyish face and tall, trim body of someone she'd expect to see playing the good guy on a made-for-TV movie. He took a step in her direction, eyes narrowing, hands on hips.

"You must be Tony Chiparo." She stopped in front of him, extending her hand.

For an instant, he stood absolutely still, a freeze frame. He did not lean forward. His hand did not respond to hers. She had a feeling of impenetrability, like standing in the presence of a wall. Then his mouth, which she now saw was too full-lipped and sensuous to quite fit with her first impression of boyishness, slid into an expression that could only be called a sneer, and her blood suddenly ran cold. Small, dazzling-white teeth, an orthodontist's pride, showed between his rounded lips.

Belatedly, his manicured hand reached for hers. He held it a moment too long, she experiencing a flutter of panic at the sense of entrapment. She pulled her hand sharply away. Taking a step backward, she raised her eyes to his. That was when she knew her instinct when he first called had been right. His widely spaced, brassy eyes held exactly the same look she'd seen in the cat's eyes an instant before her claw flashed.

What the hell am I going to do? She crossed arms over her chest. "Let's level with each other, shall we? What's the agenda here?"

He smirked nastily. "Correct me if I'm wrong, but I believe I have an appointment, Ms. McCabe."

"All right." She turned on her heel, opened the office door and flicked on the overhead, soft light that usually seemed cozy but tonight felt shadowy, almost menacing. She marched inside and he followed, stepping in too close. When she stopped next to her chair, he was standing over her, only inches away. A subtle mixture of scents, wine and expensive cologne and something else—something sexual—made her stomach turn over.

She drew back. "Sit over there." She pointed to the patched-up sofa opposite her chair. He waited a beat, then moved around the wicker table, brushed foam crumbles off the seat and lowered himself onto black vinyl. She closed the door, then took her place in the director's chair. With Chiparo across from her and wide windows on two sides wrapped snugly in darkness, the space seemed suffocatingly small. She breathed shallowly, feeling as if there were not enough oxygen for both of them. Earlier, she had closed the windows against chilly night air. Now, she had an urge to throw them open, but oppressive blackness pushing against glass stopped her.

Chiparo leaned lazily back and fastened his feline eyes on her. She crossed her legs, shifted, crossed them the other way. She made herself stop fidgeting and look up. He hadn't moved. He was still watching, his light eyes reminding her of reflective sun glasses. She got no sense of connection with him at all. His eyes came at her like laser beams, giving nothing in return.

"Well," she said, trying to get the squeak out of her voice. "Have you ever seen a therapist before?"

The well groomed head gave a curt shake.

"You have any questions about therapy? Or me?"

He remained motionless. They sat without talking for a full, agonizing minute. His mirrored eyes never wavered. He had thick, sandy hair brushed across a broad forehead, and colorless, nearly invisible lashes. She had first placed him at around forty, but now that she looked more closely, she noted a crinkling at the eyes, a fleshiness in the jowls that nudged her estimate upwards.

She moved her eyes past his head to the opaque black rectangle behind him. A radio voice from the other side of the wall burbled, "Good morning starshine, the world says hello . . . " *My God, what's going on here? If this turns out to be as bad as I think it is, there may not be any more good mornings for me.* "You twinkle above us, we twinkle below . . . "

"So . . . what is it you want to talk about?" *Shit.* Why couldn't she keep her voice steady? Not a good idea to let this jungle cat know she was afraid.

He lifted one shoulder in a casual shrug. Another long silence, seeming to drag on and on and on, ten minutes at least, although the numbers on her digital clock changed only once.

"Maybe you're feeling like you made a mistake and you don't really want to talk to a therapist after all. If you'd like to leave, that'll be okay. I don't mind."

A slow smile. "I haven't the slightest intention of leaving," he said in his metallic voice.

"Well, then, you'll have to talk to me."

He pulled a pack of Camels out of the pocket of his crisp cotton shirt, tapped one out and slid it in his mouth.

She had a sudden image of a Joey-Camel head stuck on Chiparo's body, which got a giggle started in her throat. Swallowing hard, she took three long, slow breaths.

"I'm sorry . . . I know sitting in a therapist's office can be stressful . . . I don't want to make it harder for you . . . I don't usually let people smoke . . . If you want to smoke, it really would be okay if you went outside . . . you could come back inside when you're through."

His eyes, which had the same metallic quality as his voice, continued to bore into her with their laserlike beams. He slowly took out a matchbook, broke off a match and struck it. He held the flame out in front of him until it burned halfway down, then touched it to the end of his cigarette. Inhaling deeply, he blew the smoke in her direction. He waved out the match and dropped it on the mustard carpet.

She gazed at the floor where the match had fallen, studying dark, rorschach-shaped splotches, the residue of ancient spills. "Oh, well . . . " She looked up. "I don't have any ashtrays in here. Let me get you an ashtray."

She bolted out of her chair. *Slow down. Do not run.* She walked stiffly into the kitchen, opened one of the cabinets and stared at the dishes inside.

This is your chance. Just keep moving until you're out the front door.

I can't let him see how scared I am.

Don't be stupid. He knows how scared you are. Now just get out of here.

I can't let him scare me out of my own house.

You should be scared. It's healthy to be scared of scary people.

She contemplated the dishes. Deciding between a saucer and bowl was too much for her. She shifted her weight from one foot to the other, chewed on one cheek. Finally she grabbed the saucer, dragged herself back into the office and placed it on the small wicker table in front of him. Keeping her gaze on the carpet, she sat down. When she looked up, his eyes were still fastened on her face. It seemed that he hadn't missed a thing, that his stare had penetrated the wall with the power of x-ray vision, maintaining its hold regardless of where she went. She forced herself to lean back in her chair and fold her hands in her lap.

He puffed on his cigarette. She watched the ash lengthen. When it was nearly an inch long, he flicked it onto the carpet and rubbed it in with his foot.

His brassy, cat eyes pinned her down. She concentrated on breathing slowly. Her foot jiggled. Her hands worked at each other in her lap.

The phone rang in the kitchen and she felt a desperate urge to jump up and answer it. She counted the rings: one, two, three, four. The ringing stopped. The answering machine had taken it.

It was hard to find a place to rest her eyes. She could not maintain eye contact. She could not allow her gaze to touch any part of him, nor could she tolerate staring at the black window behind his head. She tried to keep her eyes away from the clock, which seemed to have stopped altogether. Her eyes refused to obey.

The piercing whoop-whoop-whoop of sirens came and went, rising until they seemed to be racing into her back yard, falling as they zoomed away. They wove in and out of the music from the waiting room, a repeating refrain, a high-pitched constant in the background noise of her life.

She struggled with her thoughts, trying to focus on her breathing, to make herself take long, slow breaths, but she couldn't stay with it. Her attention bounced all over. She created worst case scenarios, the creep sitting across from her in the starring role. She wondered why Chiparo was here instead of Public Radio Voice. She invented conversations, reaming Kevin out for having sicced Chiparo on her in the first place. What was this predatory creature going to do when the session was over? Would Zack really take her cat?

The clock chimed. Her eyes zoomed in on it, even though she knew only half an hour had passed. Nine-thirty. Ten minutes to go.

Her hand darted out uncontrollably to straighten the Kleenex box, pluck a dead leaf from the coleus. Her back ached. Her arms itched. No matter how hard she tried, she couldn't get enough air into her chest.

Another millennium passed, and her eyes, with a will of their own, sprang back to the clock. This time the face displayed the magic numbers: nine-forty. Forty minutes of torture was enough.

She took a deep breath. "Session's over."

"I was under the impression your sessions ran an hour."

"Forty minutes. You'll have to leave now."

His sensuous mouth twisted into a loose smirk. "Don't you want to set another appointment?"

She stood up. *Make him pay for the session,* a manic voice shrilled in her head. She clenched her teeth to keep the hysteria from bubbling out.

He rose also and stood facing her across the low table. Everything stopped—-time, sound, movement. She was a living statue, part of a grotesque diorama. *This is it. Moment of truth. You should've run out when you had the chance.*

13

ANOTHER VERSION

He turned and took a step toward the door. Two more agonizing steps and he was on the other side of the office doorway. She followed, watching his back as he continued toward the outside door. He opened it, then turned to gaze at her another long moment. "I had no idea therapy could be so amusing." His voice chimed lightly like a brass bell.

Her breath escaped with a whoosh. She ran to the door and locked it. Dashing back into her office, she turned off the interior light to unseal the room. Instantly, the thick blackness behind the window lifted and the street lights revealed a dusky view of the yard and curb. He got into a car and drove away. She pounded the window, mad that she was too ignorant to identify makes of cars, too scared to run out and get his license.

Scurrying to the front door, she checked the lock, then sprinted up the stairs. Her thoughts raced. A huge pressure lay on her chest. She darted into the bedroom, startling the cat, and grabbed the phone.

She dialed nine-one-one, then slammed down the receiver before the call could be answered. This wasn't an emergency. She dialed directory assistance for the nonemergency number, dialed that, then hung up again. *What am I going to say? A strange client wouldn't talk and I got scared? The police probably think anybody who sees a therapist is a weirdo anyway.*

She paced the narrow space in the middle of her bedroom, hugging herself.

Got to talk to somebody. Kevin. If only she knew where he was. Her mother would be no help at all—worse than no help. Her friends would have no idea what she was talking about. She remembered her grandmother holding her when she was small. Her grandmother was too old now. But she had to find somebody.

She flipped through her Rolodex, found a number, dialed it. *He won't be home. He'll be out screwing around.*

Zach picked up on the first ring.

She felt an urge to hang up. She hesitated. If she waited long enough, he would do it. Finally, in a small voice, "It's me. Cassidy."

"You don't sound like yourself."

"I don't know why I called. There's nothing you can do anyway and there really isn't any point in talking about it, but, uh, you see, I got scared, and for a moment there I thought I had to talk to somebody, but now I can see it won't do any good and I can handle it myself."

"It's okay. I'm glad you called."

"I'm afraid I'm going to sound like one of those fruit-cakes who's always seeing rapists under her bed."

"What happened?"

She took a deep breath and told him about Tony Chi-paro.

"I'm coming over."

"No, don't. I'll be all right."

"You're not all right. You're scared shitless. Which is exactly what you ought to be."

"I don't want you to come."

"I'm not trying to hit on you. I'll sleep on the couch."

"This guy had every opportunity to hurt me and he didn't. That means they're not going to do anything right now." *Not tonight. Maybe tomorrow.*

"You just went through a really rough time. Anybody else you could stay with?"

"You trying to do role reversal again? You're not the therapist, I am."

"Okay, okay." A pause. "It's making me mad as hell, the way you refuse to protect yourself. And besides that, if you hadn't been scared out of your gourd tonight, it's my guess I never would've heard about Chiparo."

She didn't answer.

"Am I right?"

"I suppose."

"What's the matter with you? You feel guilty about Ryan so you're setting yourself up to get whacked?"

"You make a lousy therapist."

"What then?"

"Two things. First, I *can't stand* to be pushed around. Second, nothing you're telling me to do will make any difference. If anybody could truly protect me from these thugs, I'd be talking to that person like crazy. But I don't want to make a big deal out of this and talk it to death unless it'll do some good."

"I want a promise that the next time anything happens, you'll tell me."

"Why? What will you do?"

"Just because, and I don't know. Now, will you promise?"

The small voice again. "I don't like to make promises unless I'm sure I'm going to keep them."

"You don't think you'd keep this one?"

"I doubt it."

"Goddammit!" He slammed down the phone.

Cassidy curled up in the middle of her neatly made king-sized bed and buried her face in her arms. Tears started leaking onto the satin comforter. Her nose ran and she wiped it on her arm. She gasped for air, the gasps turning into long, convulsive sobs. Much later, when she'd cried herself out, the cat jumped up and pushed its nose into the crack between her arm and her face. A rough tongue scraped her cheek. Rolling over, she opened her eyes and saw a tiny triangle with moistly gleaming eyes.

ಜ ಜ ಜ

Cassidy was listening to Frank, the man whose wife had left him, describe his first encounter with a singles group.

He'd just gotten to the part where a grandmotherly woman put the make on him when the phone rang once, then stopped. It reminded her that a message had gone on the machine during the session with Chiparo, and she hadn't played it yet.

When Frank's session ended, she went upstairs and pushed the playback button.

"At this moment," a whispery voice said, "you're sitting in your office with a man who calls himself Chiparo." A lot of static. *Car phone?* "He's there to ensure your cooperation. One session with this 'client' ought to make it clear just how vulnerable you are. So keep this in mind, should the urge to go to the police come over you. Some secrets are better left alone. If you get stupid enough to talk out of turn, we'll know about it and be there before you can hang up the phone."

Beep.

That's odd . . . sounded like a different voice. A whisperer who wants to make sure I don't talk. So he sends the silent hulk to stare me down.

"This is Zach. You wanted to have a go at cracking Kristi's story, so I set up a meeting for the three of us Wednesday at eight-thirty. It'll be interesting to see you in action, shrink."

She pushed the erase button, then instantly regretted it. She should've replayed the whisperer's message to compare it with the others. After all the calls from Public Radio Voice, why someone else now? Maybe her old buddy had laryngitis. Maybe he'd been fired. Or—better yet—come to a more dire ending. Life insurance for hitmen must be sky high.

Voice was not the only difference. This time, the focus was on keeping her mouth shut. Had Zach's pal at the paper asked too many questions? The whisperer had warned that if she talked, *they* would find out.

She remembered the message from Public Radio Voice in which he described what she was wearing, what she'd been doing. Was someone right now peering in her window? Were they picking up her phone calls, bugging her conversations with the cat? Rationally, she knew the mob could not be omniscient. And yet, the possibility they'd found out so quickly about the first time she'd talked to Zach made her feel exposed, as though they really did see everything—like Tony Chiparo with his x-ray eyes. She wondered if they knew already that she'd again confided in Zach just last night.

ᴥ ᴥ ᴥ

"Cass, hi, good to see you." Holding a wineglass in one hand, Kristi opened the screen door with the other. She wore a turquoise playsuit that looked especially vibrant next to her bronze skin and dark, crinkly hair. Her face appeared rested, but her eyes were veined with fine red lines.

Cassidy forced a smile. Kristi seemed genuinely glad to see her, but only because she didn't know what was on the agenda. *Chiparo may be a jungle cat, but you're a weasel. A weasel in therapist's clothing.*

"Did I tell you," Kristi chattered as she led them through the shadowy hall, "that I decided to drop out of Village Players for a . . . I thought I could keep my part—I was Laura in 'The Glass Menagerie'—but it was too ..." They trouped past somber, earth-toned rooms with closed drapes, and into the sunroom. Dark shapes of trees beyond the glass walls were melting into a black backdrop. Brown, crackly leaves had turned up on a number of the plants lining the walls.

They crossed over to the table, past the red and yellow toy pickup which was now overflowing with beer cans. Kristi gestured toward a half empty bottle of Cabernet Sauvignon and Cassidy accepted without hesitation. Kristi poured her a glass, then topped off her own. A faint sour smell hung in the air. Kristi plopped down on the loveseat and Cassidy perched on the edge of the wicker chair. To-night, the television was running with the sound off. Cassidy tore her eyes away from cars careening through city streets and glanced at Zach, hoping he didn't really intend to sit back and watch her play shrink.

Zach said, "I'm going for a beer."

"I'm surprised he made it this far without getting tack-led," Cassidy remarked. "Luke must not be himself today."

Kristi's chameleon face shifted to concern. "Actually, he's not. The last few days, he's been moping ... I guess it's natural, at least that's what his teacher says."

"Teacher?"

"He goes to Montessori. Mrs. Kowalski—she's been there so long she actually had Ryan and Zach—tells me she's seeing signs of ... " Kristi's eyes filled. "It bothers him when I . . . He pats my hair and says, 'Don't cry, Mommy.' "

"I found him." Zach walked in carrying two beers and a squealing, piggyback Luke. Dropping to his knees, he dumped the boy on the Navajo rug. Luke stopped thrashing and Zach let go. Cassidy watched the boy closely. It made her heart ache to think what he was going through.

Luke jumped up and came over to stand in front of her. His blue eyes were large and solemn, without the shine she'd noticed last time. "Are you Zach's girlfriend?" he demanded, a disapproving edge to his voice.

"No, I'm not. Not at all. We're just friends." *Shut up. You're overdoing it.*

He seemed to relax. Glancing at Zach, who was sitting across from Cassidy, he said, "She's kinda pretty. But not as pretty as Mom."

Kristi laughed, a bright tinkling sound like wind chimes. "You're just prejudiced." She leaned forward to tousle his hair. "Cass is pretty too, but in a different way. She's more . . . she's got a quieter, steadier look to her. Not so . . . flashy."

Not so sexy. I'm as plain as peanut butter next to her.

"What am I gonna do with you, kid?" Zach laughed. "You're too young to be thinking about such things."

"I see kissing and hugging and . . . " he made a disgusted face, "mushy stuff on TV all the time."

"Tell you a secret," Zach stage-whispered. "I keep trying to get her to go out with me but she won't. Acts like I'm Clark Kent, she's Lois Lane."

As everyone turned to look, Cassidy felt her face getting hot.

Luke patted his uncle on the arm. "That's all right. You can find somebody better. I'll help."

After removing Luke from center stage and sending

him to his room, Zach tossed his empty can onto the pile around the truck and popped open his second. He turned to Kristi, "We've got something we need to talk about."

Kristi's green eyes widened. She reminded Cassidy of a startled rabbit, twitchy with adrenalin.

Zach continued, "Scott didn't go to his father's. He disappeared after Ryan died, hasn't been seen since."

Kristi's eyes snapped back and forth, darting from Cassidy to Zach. She breathed rapidly through slightly parted, colorless lips. "I can't talk to . . . Mildred said not to talk because of the malpractice . . . "

Goddamn lawsuit. Ryan's dead and all anybody cares about is money.

Zach said, his voice tougher than she'd heard before, "It's either us or the police. Now, where'd Scott go?"

"I thought he was with . . . I didn't mean to . . . Scott's really a, you know, good kid, but people sort of get the wrong . . . "

"Of course he's a good kid," Cassidy soothed. "You're just trying to protect him. That's what a good mother does, protect her children."

Kristi's bronze face shifted to tenderness. "Good kid." She tugged at a strand of hair.

Cassidy tilted her head and moved forward in her chair to mirror Kristi. "Wouldn't you like to tell us what happened? People always feel better when they talk."

"Can't." She jumped up and clutched the wine bottle, pouring the remaining half-inch into her glass. "I have to get more wine."

Zach started to get up but Cassidy motioned him to stay

where he was. "Let's wait till after you tell us." Cassidy rose and eased Kristi back into her chair.

Kristi held the goblet in both hands and raised it to her mouth, not drinking, just resting the glass against her lips. "What would happen if he . . . if he, you know . . . "

Cassidy asked, "You mean, if it was Scott who fired the gun?"

She nodded.

"He'd be arrested," Zach replied. "But with a good attorney, he might not do much jail time."

Kristi shook her tangled thatch violently. "I can't do that. If I tell you about . . . then I'll be the one . . . it'll be my fault."

Cassidy knelt in front of her. Removing the glass and setting it on the rug, she took both Kristi's hands in hers. Her voice was gentle. "I know you're scared. You want what's best for Scott, and sometimes it's hard to know what that is."

Kristi nodded.

"But you can't keep this a secret. You have to tell, because it's killing you. And because, if Scott gets away with it, it'll be the worst thing that could happen. Worse even than jail."

Kristi jerked her hands out of Cassidy's. "You're just saying that to get around . . . Nothing could be worse than jail. I know what happens to kids when they get sent away." Horror flitted across her face.

Cassidy got up and resettled across from her. She let some time go by as she relaxed back into the chair, clasping her hands loosely in her lap. "You're right—jail can be a bad experience. I suppose you think if you don't tell, nobody'll ever know, and Scott won't have to go to prison."

"There's nothing to tell." Kristi's voice came out thin and cracked. She refused to meet Cassidy's eyes.

"But you do know you're enabling him, don't you?"

"No!" She shook her head, put her hands over her ears. "I'm protecting him, you said so yourself."

"Enablement's protecting kids from consequences." Cassidy's tone was conversational, as if it were purely theoretical. "When people act out, if nothing bad happens, they do it again and they do it worse. A lot of mothers don't realize that the most important thing a parent needs to do—the most loving thing—is let them take their knocks."

Kristi dropped her hands, turned to stare at the television. The screen showed a cop shooting a man wearing a ski mask. She looked back at Cassidy. "Maybe about other things, not this."

"If he doesn't feel the pain, he'll just keep on the way he's going."

"I don't want to see him hurt," Kristi whispered.

"When I was in school," Cassidy said, making the story up as she went along, "I did a study of criminals who had three or more convictions. Ninety-eight percent said the first time they committed a serious crime, they got away with it, and that's what made them feel invincible, made them want to do it again. Most said if they'd been arrested the first time, they probably would've stopped."

Cassidy crossed over and knelt again, resting her hands on Kristi's knees. "If you don't tell, if he gets away with this, it's almost certain he'll do something worse."

Kristi moaned, her chest rising and falling in double time.

She going to hyperventilate on me? Locking eyes, Cassidy started taking deep breathes and Kristi gradually followed her lead.

"Tell us what happened."

"What happened . . ." Guilt flowed across Kristi's face. "I can't just start with that night. It doesn't make sense unless you understand that Ryan was always on his . . . Sometimes I thought the way Ryan yelled and tormented— It seemed like he was persecuting . . . I should've done something but I was afraid . . . Anyway, that whole last week, all Ryan could talk about was, he finally had proof."

"Proof of what?" Zach asked.

"Proof Scott was dealing. He used to ransack . . . He'd tear through everything, mess things up, take things. Sometimes he'd . . . Anyway, Friday evening Scott stormed in and said he wasn't going to put up with it any longer. He said if Ryan went through his stuff one more time he'd . . . he'd . . ."

"Kill him?" Cassidy's knees were sore from pressing against the rough texture of the rug but she didn't want to distract Kristi by moving.

Kristi nodded. "There was a big fight. They both sounded so . . . violent. Then Scott stormed out and Ryan got very cold and mean. He said . . . he told me he was going to turn Scott in to the police now that he had proof."

Cassidy gritted her teeth. *C'mon now. Big bad Ryan picking on poor little dope dealer.*

Kristi's eyes filled. Hunching inward, she shrank back

in the loveseat. "I begged him not to. I pleaded, I did everything . . . " Her face tightened with hatred. "He was hard and cold as . . . said he was going to turn him in Saturday morning and I should just shut up about . . . It was my, you know, fault. Ryan was destroying him, turning him into this kid I didn't even . . . I should've left Ryan years ago. Anyway, there wasn't anything I could do, so I went out to the health club for a couple of hours. And then I . . . " she looked down. "I don't want to talk about . . . " Her voice was barely audible. "I was so mad. So I picked up this young guy at the health club and we went out to . . . well, that isn't important."

Cassidy squeezed her hand reassuringly, but at the same time dropped her eyes so Kristi wouldn't see the skepticism in them. *Ryan's the bad guy because he wouldn't let the kid smoke dope and deal.*

"It was dawn when . . . I was so loaded I just fell into—I woke up the next morning with Luke climbing all over me. I was confused because . . . I told Luke to go find Daddy because Mommy wanted to sleep. He said Daddy wasn't home and then I started to really wake up . . . I was afraid. I thought maybe he'd left me." She stared straight ahead, remembering the fear. Her eyes welled up again.

Cassidy prompted, "What did you do?"

"I looked in the garage, and when I saw his car was there, I felt . . . But then I saw this brownish smudge on one of the steps . . . the stairs in back of the garage going up to—the brown stuff looked like a bloody footprint and I panicked. It took every ounce of will power I had to make myself go up those stairs and open the . . . " Blanching, her face shifted to horror.

"You don't have to tell us what you saw," Cassidy said.

"I won't. I won't talk about it. I took one look and went running . . . I didn't scream or anything. I didn't want to upset Luke. I was shrieking inside and acting normal on the outside. It was weird." Tears spilled over and dribbled down her slack face.

"You were wonderful," Cassidy murmured.

"But all the time, inside my head, I kept remembering Scott yelling out those, well . . . threats. Anyway, as soon as I got Luke settled, I ran into Scott's bedroom . . . " Again she stared off into space.

"Kristi, come back here," Cassidy said firmly.

Kristi looked disoriented.

"Don't relive it. Just step back from your memory— step way back—that's right—-and summarize what happened."

Kristi refocused on Cassidy. "Okay." She paused, then spoke in a distant voice. "Scott was sprawled across the bed . . . his jeans on the floor . . . This is the bad part."

"Take a deep breath," Cassidy instructed.

"There was blood . . . bloodstains on the jeans, and it looked like a big wad of money half in, half out . . . like he'd stuffed it in his pocket in a hurry. He got up slowly like he does when he's high. I waved the money in his face and screamed 'where did you get it?' And he grabbed the money away from me and said, 'none of your fucking business.' Then he put on the bloody jeans and left."

A moment of silence.

"That all?" Zach asked.

"He was walking out the door and he . . . he said, 'I got it from . . . from the dickhead.' "

14

THE DATE

Kristi clenched her arms across her stomach and rocked slightly. Zach headed for the kitchen to fetch another bottle of wine. Cassidy got up from the floor and wrapped her arms around Kristi.

"What have I done?" Kristi moaned.

"It was the right thing."

Pushing her away, Kristi stood up, a fierce look on her face. "Don't you dare . . . How can you begin to know? You don't even have children."

, After Kristi calmed down, she explained that Scott had often forged Ryan's handwriting and she feared the suicide note was his doing—that he'd blamed the therapy because she herself had been against it. They reassured Kristi again, extracting a promise that she'd go with Zach to the police.

Before leaving, they stopped in Luke's room to say good night. He was hunched over his table, seeming smaller, the sound and fury gone out of him.

"See what I did?" He held up three sketches.

Cassidy was struck by his emerging talent for carica- ture. He had managed to emphasize some essential feature in each face: Zach's high forehead and heavy eyebrows; Kristi's abundant, corkscrew hair; her own wide mouth and pointed chin.

He was the kind of kid she used to dream about. She wanted desperately to hug him, to fold him in her arms and take him home. But she had no rights here. She'd interfered enough already.

᠃ ᠃ ᠃

"You ever want to change professions," Zach said, pulling away from the curb, "there's a place for you in investigation. You were so good, I hardly had to play bad cop at all."

Just what I always wanted to do: break people down . . . pretend to be their friend . . . manipulate so they lower their guard.

"Hey, why so quiet? It doesn't seem right when you don't snap back at me."

"I don't feel so great about what we just did, okay?" She began digging in her purse, looking for the plastic bag.

"You taken up smoking or something?"

Finding the bag, she grabbed the last handful of candy. "Want a peanut butter cup?" She placed a Reese's in his outstretched hand. "You can only have one. Unless you want to stop so I can get some more." She unwrapped the remaining pieces, bit them neatly in half, and consumed them slowly.

She licked her fingers. "When I was a kid and Mom was working me over with guilt, I'd buy a bag of Reese's and go down to the basement and sit in a special corner near the furnace where it was warm. If I didn't gobble them down, if I ate slowly, I could make them last for hours."

"When I was a kid," Zach said, "and Ryan was giving me a hard time, I'd steal cigarettes out of Mildred's purse and sneak up in the attic and smoke."

"Did Ryan give you a hard time?"

"Are you kidding? He was four years older and had the kind of ego'd make Johnny Carson seem like a modest man. He thought I was a little punk who didn't know shit. You can bet your therapist's license he gave me a hard time."

"Therapists don't have licenses." *He probably was a little punk. Probably deserved it.* She paused, realizing she was splitting hairs. Social workers had licenses, but there was no generic *therapist* license. "Where're we going?"

"Thought we'd hit Clancy's again. Now you've finished off the peanut butter cups, you may not need a drink, but I do. Want me to stop somewhere so you can replenish your stash?"

"No. A drink'll do."

They sat at the same table as before. The pudgy waitress in the black dress and tennis shoes hurried over.

"I remember you folks. You're the one said I could be her Jewish mother. Chuckled 'bout that all night, I did."

Cassidy grinned. "I didn't think it was all that funny."

"Well, honey, around here you don't 'xactly have Joan Rivers for the competition."

They ordered Jack Daniels and soda, then sipped in preoccupied silence. When the waitress checked back, Zach ordered a second round without consulting her. Cassidy's first impulse was to protest his peremptory decision making, but on second thought, decided to let him get away with it. She really did want that second drink.

Zach emptied half his glass in one swallow. "Why is it I don't feel more excited about what we did tonight?"

"I'm not thrilled either. I keep running the whole scenario through my mind—Scott shooting Ryan, forging a suicide note, going back to his room and collapsing—and it just doesn't work. I can't see Ryan letting some drugged out kid blow him away. Or Scott having the presence of mind to write the note."

Zach turned his glass round and round, making wet circles on the dark wood. "I've been trying to convince myself it could've been Scott, but you're right. There are too many holes."

"How could a kid so high he didn't do anything to cover his tracks be sharp enough to get the note right, so it came out sounding like Ryan?"

"Now that you mention it, I doubt Scott could've written it under any circumstances. The articulation was exactly like Ryan, not at all like Scott."

"So . . . " Cassidy caught herself making circles with her glass the same way Zach was. "Scott didn't do it." She flexed her shoulders, releasing the tension. "This is weird. Here we're right back to the beginning as far as suspects go, and I'm actually feeling better. I still have my malpractice suit to face, plus feel guilty for the rest of my life. But at least we don't have to shove a round-peg Scott into a square-hole murder."

"Just because we haven't thought of any other suspects doesn't mean they don't exist. However, I can't think about it any more tonight."

"I keep going over what Kristi said about Ryan," Cassidy persisted. "About his tormenting Scott and making her life so miserable. She must be exaggerating. That's not how I see Ryan at all."

"All you ever heard was Ryan's side of it."

"I got the impression you weren't around enough to come up with an unbiased account yourself."

"When Ryan and Kristi were first married, I used to drop by fairly often. I was still trying to keep up our relationship back then. But the way he acted with Scott, and Kristi too sometimes, reminded me so much of how he used to treat me, I decided I really didn't like my brother very much. So I stopped making myself available."

Cassidy's jaw tightened. *If you blame the other guy, you don't have to feel guilty.*

"The reason I'd held on so long was, Ryan was the only person in the whole family I had any connection with. Mildred didn't know I was alive except to bitch me out. My old man was a joke. Martin was always busy doing *the Queen's* bidding. Letting go of Ryan meant not having any family at all."

Zach finished his drink, rattled the ice cubes and thumped the glass down on the dark wood. "But you know what? I came to the conclusion that families suck and I'm just as well off without one."

       ಶ ಶ ಶ

When the Datsun pulled up in front of her house, she opened the door but Zach took hold of her arm and stopped her from jumping out.

"There you go again. You're practically out the door before the car's stopped running."

"I don't want to take any chances."

"On what?"

She didn't answer.

"How about inviting me in? I haven't had any quality time with your cat lately. That poor animal is likely to get a complex from being called 'cat.' It's like naming somebody John Doe."

"I don't think so. About coming in, that is." She kept her face turned toward the door. "Why'd you tell Luke you've been trying to get me to go out with you?"

"I wanted to see what you look like when you blush. Besides, it's true."

"You haven't asked me out."

"I am now. I'd like you to come with me when I do Day in Our Village this Sunday. Have you ever been to it before?"

"Sure. Lots of times."

"Okay, then you know it's perfectly harmless. So, I'd like you to go around the village with me and eat brats and listen to music and get your face painted. I'd like you to be my date."

"Why?"

"Goddammit, Cass. Do you always interrogate guys when they ask you on a date?"

"Guys don't ask me on dates."

"You don't let anybody get close enough. Okay, I want to go out with you because you're cute and you've got nice boobs and sometimes you're fairly smart. And because you're a pain in the ass and I'm a sucker for punishment. Now, will you go?"

This is not a good idea. You promised yourself that next time you'd look for someone stable and dull who paid all his bills before the first of the month.

She jumped out of the car, then turned back and said, "See you at one on Sunday."

☙ ☙ ☙

Thursday morning Cassidy and the cat stood on the landing at the bottom of the basement steps, checking out the one-handled dutch oven. The cat sniffed, then pawed the floor around the pan, apparently trying to dig through the concrete.

Holding her breath, Cassidy planted her hands on her hips. "I know it stinks. You don't have to tell me it ought to be buried."

The cat diligently continued her scraping.

"Stop trying to make me feel guilty." She dumped the litter in a trash bag, spilling nearly half onto the floor.

"You're very demanding, you know that? You want new litter every week. You won't let me get away with scooping out the chunks and leaving the same stuff sit.

You're such a princess, I don't know why I put up with you."

She refilled the pan, turning her head away to avoid the dust billowing up as she poured. The cat, who had watched each step with fascination, leapt in the moment she finished and rolled around in delight.

"You're disgusting. Now you'll have dust and litter all over and I'll probably forget and touch you. Yuck."

Having finished her gleeful display, the cat turned herself right side up, dug a hole, and put the litter to its proper use. Cassidy swept up. The doorbell rang.

Jerking upright, she glanced at her watch. Almost eleven. Had she forgotten an appointment? She was so preoccupied nowadays. The problem with working at home was, every now and then she got caught with her professional persona askew.

The bell rang two more times. Cassidy took stock of her appearance: raggedy shorts, an ancient tee shirt emblazoned with "A woman needs a man like a fish needs a bicycle," dust from litter sticking to her sweaty face. Dropping the broom, she rubbed an arm across her forehead, brushed off her shirt and ran fingers through her hair, then dashed off to answer the door.

As she rounded the divider into the waiting room, she could see a face through the window in the door. Her mother's face, sharp creases like parentheses on either side of her mouth, connoting disapproval.

15

VILLAGE DAY

She unlocked and opened the door. "Mom, what's wrong?" Cassidy had trained her mother never to show up without calling first so she wouldn't interupt sessions.

"Why's the door locked?"

Cassidy glanced over her mother's shoulder into the glare of remorseless light that pinpointed every bright yellow dandelion rearing its head above her overgrown grass. "Is something wrong? I thought I'd been caught looking like a ragpicker by one of my clients."

"Yes, something's wrong." She pursed her lips. "But I'd rather come in first, if you don't mind."

"Sure. C'mon in." She grabbed the cat, who was sticking her nose out the door, sniffing air.

"I told you no one would take it and you'd be stuck."

Her mother sniffed, mirroring the cat. "And the *smell*. It's worse than ever."

Cassidy glanced at her watch, then led her mother into her office. "I assume you did not come over just to say I told you so."

After settling side by side on one of the sofas, her mother said, "Yesterday I tried phoning you three times and you never returned my calls. But I still assumed you were coming for dinner . . . "

"Oh shit." Cassidy thumped her forehead. Her mother sighed.

"I'm sorry, I forgot. I said I'd get back to you about Wednesday and it slipped my mind."

"You told me you'd be there, so naturally I was expecting you. Even though you didn't return my calls. So despite the heat I went ahead and made tuna casserole. And then I waited." With an accusing look, her mother pulled a used tissue out of her purse and blew her nose, ignoring the Kleenex box on the wicker table. Cassidy remembered Carla describing how it felt to wait for someone who never arrived.

"I didn't say I was coming. I distinctly remember—I said I *may* be able to make it on Wednesday."

"When you weren't there by eight, I started worrying you were in an accident or the hospital or something. Working with these crazy people, anything could happen."

You don't know the half of it.

"The least you could do," her mother continued, "is return my calls."

"When did you call?"

"Can't you keep track of anything?" Her mother studied

her from under lowered brows. "Is there something you're not telling me?"

"I never got the messages. You sure you didn't just hang up? I know you hate talking to the machine."

"It's not a man again, is it? I hope it's not Kevin, after all the trouble he's caused. I always thought Kevin was a lot like your father, you know."

"Now, Mom, listen. Are you sure you really did leave a message? This is important. If my machine isn't working, I need to know."

"Of course I'm sure. I called three times yesterday afternoon and you never bothered to call me back."

"Mom, I told you. I didn't get the messages."

"But you said you'd call back about dinner."

"I know. It's my fault. I forgot." She glanced at her watch. "Bad news about the machine. I can't afford to lose messages—ever—so I guess that means I'll have to replace it. If there's any room left on my credit card."

"You could talk to your grandmother."

"Mom, I've got a client coming at one and I have to get ready."

"That's more than an hour from now." Her mother got up, went into the kitchen and returned with a glass of water, which she dumped on the wilting coleus. "The other thing I wanted to mention, your grandmother'd really like to see you. I thought maybe we could go together on Sunday."

Cassidy brushed foam crumbs into a neat pile and poked them through an untapped crack, back inside the seat. "I'd like to . . . but Sunday's out."

The room was silent. Her mother's eyes narrowed.

Cassidy's foot jiggled.

"There *is* a man."

Cassidy uncrossed her legs, planted her feet firmly on the mustard carpet. "We are not going to have this conversation."

"I don't understand why you never tell me what's going on."

"There's nothing going on. Now . . . " She rose from her chair and stood waiting. Her mother resisted for a moment, then sighed and got up.

Cassidy took her mother's arm and walked her to the door. "Next time, call ahead. It's too hard on me when you show up unannounced."

"No point in calling when you won't return my messages."

≈ ≈ ≈

Friday afternoon Cassidy returned from Dominick's, a supermarket near her house, and pulled her car into the garage. She slid the giant brass keyring around her wrist, picked up her handbag and the plastic sack filled with kitty litter and cat food, and trudged through the heat toward her back door.

Moving along the chain link fence toward her gate, she looked despairingly at the crop of bright yellow dandelions that threatened to vanquish her grass. A car passed, but she was too distracted with the heat and the dandelions to notice.

Every client walking in the back door can see by the dandelion count my life is totally out of control.

As she passed through the gate, she heard the sound of

a car door and turned to look behind her. A black sedan had parked in her driveway. *Ohmygod!* Her jaw went slack. Her fingers loosened, plastic sack slipping to the ground. She managed, just barely, to tighten her grip on her handbag before that got away from her too. Sweat broke out on her forehead. After a moment of frozen gaping, she bolted for the door. Thank God her keys were out. She opened the screendoor and pushed the key at the keyhole, fumbled, tried again. *Don't look,* a voice screamed in her head, but she couldn't stop herself. A man in a suit was power walking toward her gate. This time the key went in. She thrust the door open, kicked the cat out of the way, slammed it shut, then dropped the bolt into place.

Through the window in the door she saw the man come flying up the steps. He moved with catlike, sinewy grace, stopping in front of her door no more than two feet away to look at her through the glass. The same face she had glimpsed through the rear window driving away from Walgreens. Not a drop of sweat on him. What was he, some kind of android that didn't feel the heat? He rattled the doorknob, but without urgency, simply letting her know that if he chose to come in her paltry lock wouldn't stop him.

Letting go of the knob, he made eye contact. She couldn't move. He had a craggy tan face, razor cut dark hair that was perfectly in place, dark fathomless eyes. His full lips parted in a sensuous smile that said killing and love making were all the same to him. He winked, then turned and disappeared.

Her legs got suddenly weak. She sucked in air through her mouth and went to stand at the kitchen sink where she grabbed hold of the counter to keep herself upright. Gradually, her heart stopped racing and she was able to gulp down a half glass of water. She set the glass on the counter and the cat jumped down from the refrigerator to sample it.

"Just wanted to spook me," she told the cat, "same as when he tailgated me on the drive out to Honor's."

She pulled a kitchen towel off the rack below the sink and wiped the sweat off her face. "I suppose, if you look at it from his point of view, it must get boring sitting in the car all the time. I can see why he might want to liven things up." She shuddered, thinking of herself as the pathetic little mouse providing entertainment for the sleek black cat that was stalking her.

An hour later she mustered the courage to venture out and pick up the litter and cat food cans laying on the walkway up to the door.

„ „ „

Almost one o'clock Sunday, Cassidy was regarding herself in the full length mirror. Her pursed mouth, enclosed by parentheses creases, reminded her disturbingly of her mother. She had on dusty rose shorts and oversized cranberry tee. White pants with a hot pink shirt, a black-flowered sundress, and an electric blue playsuit lay in heaps on the bed, the cat burrowing through them.

She ought to wear the shorts. The shorts were perfectly adequate. There was nothing wrong with them. Nothing right either. The shorts were ordinary. Boring. She glanced longingly at the sundress, which fit sleekly, emphasizing her slender figure. She had discarded the sundress because of its revealing neckline. She was sure to run into a client if she wore the sundress. She reconsidered the pants, which she had discarded because they were polyester. Everybody disdained polyester, although she secretly liked it because it didn't look continuously wrinkled, as did her unironed natural fibers. *Why are you doing this?* She bounced back to the playsuit. The playsuit was not boring. It also showed off her figure, although she'd initially discarded it because she'd have to go braless and she didn't want to send the wrong signals.

If braless wasn't the signal you wanted to send, you wouldn't be dying to wear it.

No you don't. This is not what you want. What you're looking for is someone who wears three-piece suits and grows tomatoes in his back yard.

"What the hell," she muttered. Ripping off her shorts, shirt and bra, she tossed them on the bed, where the cat wrestled them into submission. As she grabbed up the playsuit, the back doorbell rang. Odd. Zack usually came in the front. She grabbed a pair of earrings. Garnet and gold dangles, a gift from Gran, her only piece of good jewelry. No, too pretentious.

He called from the foot of the steps. At the sound of his voice, the cat went zipping down. Cassidy yelled back, asking him to wait on the porch.

A few minutes later she joined him, leaning against the oak door next to the wicker couch where Zach lounged. He had a glass of wine in his hand and an enraptured cat on his chest, her nose just inches from his chin. Wind chimes jangled in a snappy breeze. Two helmets clumped on the seat beside him.

He looked up. "I came in the back door."

Noticing the pile of magazines on the plastic chair, she wished she had thought to put them somewhere else.

"I shouldn't have been able to. It should've been locked."

Her shoulders stiffened. She could feel tightness in her arms and had to stop herself from crossing them.

He sighed. "Why won't you do what I asked? Even if you don't think it matters, why not do it just to humor me?"

"I don't know." She flexed her shoulders and breathed in. "It's just that it's hard to remember." Removing the magazines, she dropped into the chair.

"Well, try to do better." He held up his wine. "Couldn't find any beer. You want a glass?"

"Too early for me."

He cocked his head, giving her a sharp look. "You know, therapists like to create the impression they're non-judgmental. But as a group, I've found them second only to cops."

She grinned sheepishly. "Occupational hazard. Do the helmets mean we're riding a motorcycle?"

"That okay with you?"

She smiled broadly. "When I see motorcycles go by, I always think they look so cool."

He patted the couch. "Come over here so we can look at the schedule together." She sat beside him and they studied the listing in the local paper.

"Free massage at Scoville Park. What kind of massage, I wonder?"

"Not the kind you think. Oh, look. The Montessori school's having an open house. Mrs. Kowalski hosting. That's Luke's teacher."

"Mrs. Kowalski," Zach mused. "Last time I saw her I was in high school. Stopped by to tell her how I was doing."

"Want to see if she still remembers you?"

"Why? You have an interest in Montessori?"

"Well, I was just thinking, I wouldn't mind hearing what she has to say about Luke."

"Let's go then."

ès ès ès

Zach walked ahead of her across a room filled with child-sized tables toward a white-haired woman with her back to them, tacking children's drawings up on a bulletin board.

"Mrs. Kowalski," Zach called out to her.

She turned around. Her face was blank at first, then broke into a cheerful smile. "Well, if it isn't little Zachary Moran." She was small and round, with a happy-face head mounted on a nearly neckless body, an animated snow woman. She moved around in front of her desk and boosted herself up on it, her stubby oxfords dangling several inches off the floor.

"Didn't think you'd remember me after all this time." Zach stopped a few feet in front of her, hooking his thumbs into the back pockets of his jeans. Cassidy came around to stand beside him.

"Took me a minute. But you know, the older I get, the clearer the early memories are—back when I was a spring chicken." Her voice had a pleasant, burry sound. "It's always a treat when one of my kids returns for a visit. Almost all of them come around sooner or later."

Zach grinned. "None of us ever gets away, do we?"

"Hardly ever." Her face melted, crumpling inward. "Except for your brother." She shook her head. "Couldn't believe it. You know, you boys don't fool me very often. But he sure did."

"I couldn't believe it either," Zach said. "Still can't."

"You know, I've got Luke in my class this year. I always like it when I have my grown-up children's children. Only . . . this is too much of a repeat." She shuddered. "It's just awful to see Luke going through the same thing that happened to his father. I remember so clearly." Her eyes moved away from them, looking back in time. "The amazing thing is, it happened to both boys right when they turned five."

Cassidy cocked her head, listening more closely. *What's this about Ryan turning five.*

"Before his birthday," Mrs. Kowalski continued, picking up a ceramic apple from her desk and folding both hands around it, "Ryan was such a good little kid. Too good, maybe, too grown up for his years. But basically he seemed okay. And then everything changed, almost overnight. Seeing Luke go through this thing now, it's as though somebody blew out the pilot light inside of him. It's been bringing back memories of how the same thing happened to his daddy. It's just so amazing, the way history repeats itself." She dropped the apple onto her desk.

"What a memory. How do you keep all your kids

straight? You must've had hundreds over the years." Zach shifted his weight into a looser, younger-looking stance.

"I have to admit, as I get older, some of the memories from last week are kind of fuzzy. But all my kids are different. All special in their own way. I can still see Ryan. Luke looks so much like him. I can see him wearing that cute little sailor suit he liked so much. I remember him telling me his mommy didn't want him to wear it all the time, but he did anyway. And then, after his birthday, his fifth it was, I don't think I ever saw him wear it again."

Cassidy's brows pulled together. *I don't get this stuff about Ryan's fifth birthday.*

Mrs. Kowalski pushed herself off the desk and stepped closer, her voice taking on a confidential tone. "He got so quiet. Stopped laughing and playing with the other kids. And so angry. He used to get into terrible fights. It really got to be a problem. I remember talking to your mother and father about it. No wait," she looked confused.

"I had a different father," Zach said.

"Anyway, I know I was surprised they looked so much alike, and Ryan looked just like they did, all three of them—Ryan, his mom and dad—like clones, not like you at all. And now I see the changes in Luke. He sits in the back by himself, refusing to play, sucking his thumb when he thinks nobody's looking."

Zach said, "I can see the difference too."

Mrs. Kowalski's round blue eyes, bright and lively as a squirrel's, bounced over to Cassidy. "I'm sorry, I didn't even get your name. I've just been so beside myself about Luke. And then when I saw little Zachary here, I forgot my manners."

Zach introduced them.

"This is a fine young man you've got here," she said to Cassidy. Then, to Zach, "Your family never properly appreciated you. But maybe that's just as well. When I had Ryan in class, his mother and father kept coming in all the time, checking up on everything. But you know, I don't think all that attention did him any good. There were things that happened. Things his parents covered up. I knew that boy was going to have problems."

16

BUMPING INTO A BLONDE

Zach abruptly straightened. "What kind of things?"

Tightening her lips, Mrs. Kowalski shook her head. "I may be a garrulous old lady, but I don't tell tales out of school. There are some things best forgotten. Anyway," she turned to Cassidy, "as I was saying, this's a good man you've got here. I'd recommend you hang onto him."

Cassidy took an imperceptible step backward. *You may be a sweet old lady, but you overdo it where 'your boys' are concerned. This is not necessarily the little Zachary you remember.*

After chatting a few minutes more, Mrs. Kowalski insisted on hugging Zach, who looked uncomfortable, and they parted.

"What a sly old matchmaker," Cassidy said. "I thought she was going to try for a wedding date, right on the spot."

"Yeah, but she really is a sweetheart."

"Only in Oak Park. Even with all the change and controversy going on, this place is still so stable or entrenched or something you actually can find people who've been teaching at the same school for more than forty years. And remember everything about everyone."

"Her memory's incredible. But she's slipping a little. Some of the details weren't right."

"You mean about the parents who looked so much alike? Ryan's father died before he was old enough to be in her class, didn't he?"

"Killed in a car crash about a month after Ryan's third birthday, which was before he went to Montessori. It must've been Mildred and Martin she was talking about. They were more of a couple than Mildred and my dad."

"Really interesting, what she had to say about Ryan. Any idea what the mysterious problems were?"

He shook his head. "Nope. Although, now that I think about it, I always felt there were secrets everybody knew but me."

&a &a &a

Waiting for the light to turn, Cassidy watched the crowd on the opposite side of Lake Street drift past. A brown-skinned, turbanned man moved through the throng in a straight line, eyes gazing off into space as if he were the sidewalk's only occupant, a sari-wrapped woman following sedately three steps behind. A helmeted cyclist hauled two small kids, one black, one white, in a kiddie trailer behind his bike.

A few minutes earlier, she'd left Zach in the bank parking lot, in line at the Kiwanis' food stand, while she crossed Lake Street to use the library rest room. Through a gap in the crowd, she spotted him standing toward the far end of the parking lot, tipping up a paper cup to empty it. He tossed the cup in a trash can and started to take another bite of his brat, then stopped, hand halfway to his mouth. His gaze fastened on someone approaching in the stream of people on the sidewalk. Cassidy looked also, trying to figure out who had caught his eye.

A blonde woman tugging a young boy along beside her stopped suddenly and waved at Zach. Starting towards him, she tried to drag the child along with her, triggering an angry scream from the boy and a lurch in the opposite direction. The woman knelt and talked to him, but he continued to cry. She finally picked the boy up, even though he struggled against her, and carried him off in Zach's direction.

Cassidy darted across the street, forcing a car to slam on its brakes. She ran up to take her place beside Zach, arriving just seconds after the blonde.

"Hi," Zach greeted her. "This is Yvonne. Yvonne, this is Cassidy."

Yvonne had masses of loose curls that tumbled around her tiny perfect features and brushed against the top of her strapless dress. Her trim body was tucked into a shiny pink and white sheath, the fabric so thin her nipples showed through. She glinted in the sunlight, bedecked with gold chains, rings, and dangling cluster earrings that had to be diamonds, not rhinestones. Yvonne looked as delectable as a mound of vanilla ice cream covered with pink raspberry sauce, gold sparkles, and whipped cream.

The picture was flawless except for the child hiding behind her, a death grip on her legs.

Cassidy made her face carefully blank, the way she did in sessions when a client said something she hated.

Zach stuffed the last bite of brat into his mouth, hooked his thumbs into his back pockets and looked at Yvonne with evident pleasure. Yvonne touched her bright pink fingernail to her matching bottom lip and returned the look. Cassidy folded her arms across her chest. When she couldn't stand the silence any longer, she blurted, "So . . . you must be a friend of Zach's."

Yvonne allowed her mouth to turn up slyly at the corners. "Friends, yes. You could say that." Cassidy's jaw tightened.

"Sorry Chucky's making such a scene." Stooping, Yvonne tried to soothe the child, who stopped whimpering but continued to hide behind her legs. She straightened and spoke directly to Zach. "So, babe, what've you been up to?"

"What I've been doing mostly is helping Ryan's wife pick up the pieces. You heard about Ryan?"

Yvonne tried unsuccessfully to look downcast. "What a shock. I know you two weren't that close. But still, it must have been . . . a real shock. So, how's the family doing?"

Zach shrugged. "Well as can be expected. It's not something you bounce back from right away."

Cassidy watched Zach closely, monitoring his responses. He appeared relaxed. Pleased to be having this conversation. Not in any hurry to end it.

"Know what you mean." Yvonne showed the tips of tiny, perfect teeth in a half-smile that seemed out of keeping with her words. "One of my friends, her father killed himself. That girl was a basket case for months. I thought she'd never snap out of it."

Snap out of it. The words grated on Cassidy like ground glass rubbed over her skin. She peered down at the boy, noticing for the first time that he was about Luke's age and had the same light, Nordic coloring. The resemblance had initially escaped her because his behavior was so dissimilar.

"So, how's Mildred doing? I know this isn't your favorite topic but your mother doted on that man like he was the second coming." Cassidy's head jerked up. She studied Yvonne, wondering just how much she knew about the Lawrence family.

"You'll have to ask her."

"Doesn't give much away, does she? Always comes across like she's so strong. But that woman's had a lot of tragedy. All those deaths. And suicides too. Suicides are the worst. I couldn't believe how hard my friend took it when her father hung himself."

Cassidy moved her eyes back to the little boy. He had poked his head out from behind his mother's legs and was anxiously regarding Zach. His skin was pasty, his eyes darkly circled. Snot was smeared across the lower half of his face.

Something's wrong with this child.

"Enough about Ryan," Zach said. "Everywhere I go,

that's all anybody talks about. What about you?"

"Oh, everything's pretty much the same. My personal life's pretty boring." She sent him a significant look. "Chucky's giving me a hard time. He's been weird lately. Don't know what's got into him."

"Well," Zach said. He took a moment to consider. "Guess we better be moseying along. It's good to see you."

"Same here." She lowered her eyelids slightly. "Maybe we could get together sometime. Have lunch."

What a nervy bitch.

"Who knows?" Zach responded. "Well, keep in touch." He turned away. "C'mon Cass, let's see what's next on the agenda."

"I'm getting a sundae," she announced. She stalked off in the direction of Unity Temple, Zach hurrying to catch up. He reached for her hand but she yanked it away. Keeping half a step ahead, she approached a large cement building distinguished by the flat surfaces and horizontal planes of a Frank Lloyd Wright design. A thin, elderly man in the red and white stripes of an old fashioned soda jerk stood on the porch steps hawking sundaes. "Hey, you," he said, pointing at Zach. "Buy your best girl a sundae?"

Cassidy marched up to the booth, ordered a chocolate sundae, and laid down a couple of bills before Zach could get his wallet out. She picked up her dish, strode across to one of the picnic tables, and plopped down. A moment later, Zach settled beside her and dipped into his ice cream.

Halfway through her sundae, she said, "All right, who is she?"

His eyes sparkled. "I wondered how long you'd be able

to hold out."

"You could've just told me."

He lowered his spoon, his face more serious. "The reason I did it is, you always act so above-it-all. I wanted to see if you really are human under that therapist facade. So, what do you want to know about Yvonne?"

Above it all? Just because I don't kowtow and agree with him all the time? "Everything."

He cocked an eyebrow. "Okay, I went out with Yvonne for about three months. Seemed like we weren't getting anywhere, so I confronted her. She admitted she was involved with somebody else—an older guy. He refused to commit, so she'd started dating me in an attempt to get him out of her system. Actually, I suspect the real game was to make her boyfriend jealous. Anyway, when I found that out, I stopped seeing her. End of story."

"Well . . . " She wanted to yell at him some more but couldn't think of anything else to say. "Okay." She patted her napkin at the ice cream that had dripped down the front of her playsuit. "If that's all, how come she knows your whole family history?"

He shrugged. "I doubt she got it from me. I certainly didn't go around talking about my family. Which is hardly surprising, since up until Ryan got his brains blown out, I didn't go around thinking about them either. Who knows? Everybody's connected. Maybe her sister does Mildred's nails."

She tried imagining Mildred gossiping with her manicurist but the picture didn't work. Everybody was *not* connected. There were, in fact, a number of circles that did not overlap. Her friends, for instance, did not consort with the Lawrences. As she thought about it further, Yvonne impressed her as something of an anomaly, not quite belonging to either of the main Oak Parkish groups: neither the old-money, heirs-to-estate crowd nor the young-professional, liberal-newcomer crowd. Something about the way she talked and the diamonds dripping from her earlobes seemed dissonant.

"What kind of work does she do?"

"Secretary."

Diamonds on a secretary, huh? She bit back a comment that, if it had come from Zach, would have outraged her feminist sensibilities.

17

FIFTH BIRTHDAYS

"I'm done." Cassidy tossed her crumpled napkin on the picnic table and stood up, noticing that Zach's napkin was still neatly folded. *How is it that other people manage to eat so tidily?*

He extended his hand and she put hers into it. They meandered down Lake Street, which was raggedly festooned with clumps of people, spurts of jazz, folk, and carousel music, smells of charcoal, popcorn, and beer. In front of the Baptist Church, families were being enticed with pony rides, games, and a clown. On the lawn next to the Congregational Church, a string quartet played Bach. They stopped to listen.

Cassidy said, "You said the relationship wasn't going anywhere because *she* wasn't interested. How about you?

Were you interested?"

"I was frustrated, so I guess that means I wanted more."

Cassidy stared at the violinist, who had a dreamy look on her face as she moved the bow ever so lightly. "Were you in love with her?" she asked in her small voice.

Sighing, Zach drew her off to a quiet spot next to a large elm. He rested one hand loosely on each of her shoulders. "Generally, I don't fall in love. I try not to, and I try not to do anything that would lead a woman to fall in love with me. I enjoy having someone in my life. I like having someone to do things with, someone to talk to. I like having a regular person to sleep with. But basically, I'm happy with my life the way it is. I don't want complications."

"I see." She broke away, showing him her back. *What do you want? You want him not to tell you?* She turned toward him and stretched out her hand.

ล ล ล

It was early evening when they got back to Cassidy's. He accepted her invitation to stay for a glass of wine, so they settled on the porch with the half empty jug of Carlo Rossi's and watched a rosy glow spread above the Oak Park roofline.

The cat was insane with delight at having both of them for an audience. She lay on her back and showed her tummy, squirmed around, leapt straight up and jackknifed in an attempt to capture her tail. Zach pulled out a handful of pistachios and threw one to the cat, who instantly scooted it to the far end of the porch like a Bulls player dribbling a basketball. He piled the rest on the bench in front of them and proceeded to crack one at a time, sticking some in his mouth, some in Cassidy's.

"What shall we name her?" he asked. "How about Milli Vanilli? That's got a ring to it. Or something more literary. Colette, maybe."

"You're so worried about the emotional trauma of namelessness, you take her."

They watched the cat, sipped wine, munched pistachios.

"You know," Cassidy said, "I've been thinking about what Mrs. Kowalski said, and the ages are wrong. She said Ryan changed right at the time of his fifth birthday. But nothing happened then—at least nothing I ever heard about."

"I figured she mixed it up with his third birthday. That's when his father died." Zach poured more wine, then plunked the jug on the floor and set the lid on the bench next to the pistachio pile.

"But would he've been in Montessori before he turned three?"

Zach sat up straighter. "I don't think so."

"She seemed so specific, so certain about the changes." Cassidy mulled it over. "And equally certain about the age."

The cat jumped on Zach's lap, then snuggled into a space between them.

"Hardly surprising she got the details wrong. It's been—what?—around forty years."

Cassidy wiggled her fingers to get the cat's attention. "Even so, I can see how she'd remember. Early memories do get clearer as people age. Plus, it'd make a real impression, seeing a child go through major behavioral changes. Especially if there were mysterious 'problems' and parents giving her a hard time."

"Funny she mentioned that sailor suit. I've got a clear image, photo of Ryan in a sailor suit Mildred used to keep beside her bed. Seems like somebody told me it was taken on his fifth birthday."

Cassidy remembered Ryan's dream about someone threatening Luke on his birthday. *Should I tell Zach about the dream?* "That photo gives me an idea. Maybe we could find out more about Ryan's fifth birthday if we looked through some old pictures. Your mother have any albums going back that far?"

"Does she ever." Zach stretched one arm along the rim of the couch behind her shoulders. "She's a card-carrying pack rat. Everything is packed away somewhere, either in albums or boxes in the attic."

"Could you get hold of the albums?"

"I could probably find a way."

Zach finished the last of his wine, then said, "Much as I hate to disturb the cat, I better be going."

He started to get up but she put her hand on his arm. "One more thing." The cat threw him a disgusted look, stepped daintily over to the unoccupied portion of the couch, and stretched.

He gave her a *Now-what?* look.

"This really is none of my business . . . " Cassidy hunched her shoulders, pulling inward. "Ryan mentioned you'd lived with somebody for several years, then left. And I was wondering . . . "

Zach regarded her from under his brows. "You're right, it's none of your business." His voice clipped. "But go ahead. What were you wondering?"

"Well, what I wanted to know is . . . I wanted to know why you left."

"You're familiar with the phenomenon of men avoiding commitment?" He started to get up and she pulled him back down. The cat pounced into the middle of the pistachio pile, grabbed the Carlo Rossi lid, and shot out of sight.

Cassidy glanced down at the jug, which contained several inches of wine. "Just because the lid's gone does not mean we have to finish it." She took a deep breath and plunged on. "So, what is it you want to avoid?"

"Never date a shrink. They won't let you off the hook." He sat forward, hands on knees. "I don't know that I can explain." She waited, hand still on his arm. He sighed. "I really did care for Lisa. She was very nice, we were pretty compatible. I didn't want to hurt her. But when we hung out together too much, I felt like I couldn't breathe." Cassidy removed her hand.

"And of course, the more I pulled away, the clingier she got. Finally she was talking marriage all the time, and I knew I couldn't go through with it. I figured the longer I stayed, the worse it would get. So I left."

"You were doing her a favor, right?"

"You've got lousy timing, you know that, McCabe? I was expecting a long, juicy tongue kiss. And now, I'm out of the mood."

You just did yourself a favor. Zach's obviously another noncommittal jerk. Scaring him off's the best thing you could do.

ɞ ɞ ɞ

Cassidy did not sleep well that night. She dreamed Kevin was pursuing her through dark alleys on a motorcycle with a blonde clinging tightly behind him. Just as he started to run her down, her eyes flew open.

She awoke Monday morning to face an empty day, no clients until evening. *Too much time to think. Better when I'm working—don't have to worry about my own problems. So who needs who? My clients need me or I need them?*

At midmorning she got out her bike and rode off to the forest preserve. It was another mild, clear day, and a couple of hours pedaling through the woods got her mind off Ryan and Public Radio Voice. On the way home she stopped at Erik's, a popular lunch spot in the middle of town.

She was headed toward the salad bar when someone called her name. *Oh shit. Never go to Erik's when you look and smell like a mud wrestler.* Scanning the dining room, she saw two arms flapping like wings. Maggie. *Worse than oh shit. Maggie's been leaving messages for over a week and I haven't answered. What's the matter with me? Why am I avoiding my best friend?* Cassidy wove her way through the crowded tables.

Maggie put her hands on her hips and gave her a mock glare. "Surprised you've got the nerve to show your face." A lesbian therapist specializing in women's issues, Maggie was softly feminine with short, light brown hair curling around a scrubbed, pretty face devoid of makeup. "I must've left five messages on your machine. You mad at me or what?"

Can't tell her I just didn't feel like it. "What," Cassidy said, feeling stupid.

"Don't try any of that funny business with me," Maggie snapped. "I caught you fair and square, so now you've got to confess. What's going on?"

"It's just that, I've been busy. I meant to call but . . . " Cassidy shifted her weight from one foot to the other.

"But what?"

Cassidy shrugged. "Oh, you know how I am."

"That's what worries me. Usually when you hole up like this it means something's wrong. Now, 'fess up."

"No, really, I'm fine." She smiled weakly. "Look, now that you've caught up with me, why don't we set a date for lunch?"

They made plans to meet the following week.

Cassidy got in line at the salad bar and picked up a plate. She piled on spinach, lettuce, raw veggies, cheese, bacon, water chestnuts, chopped nuts, and dressing, then took a table by the window. As she poked at the food in front of her, she admired the arrangement of colors—red, orange, white against a background of deep green—but felt little interest in chewing and swallowing. Across the aisle sat two men in business suits, a young black with a toddler squeezed in beside him engaged in rapid-fire conversation with a balding white guy, daily planner next to his plate. Daddy taking his son to work? The black guy was saying, "We've gotta do something about gangs in the schools . . . " A thin, elderly man, sparse strands of white hair combed across shiny pate, wearing a dark suit and tie, pedaled up and parked his bike outside the restaurant. A woman's voice, measured and confident, came from behind her, "I talked to the village president for over an hour about the new recycling plan."

Sensing movement, she looked up to see a tall, slender man, white hair thick and gleaming, faded eyes framed by owlish, wire-rimmed glasses, bearing down on her.

He stopped behind the empty chair on the other side of her table. "Mind if I join you, Miss McCabe?"

18

CHANCE ENCOUNTERS

She remembered where she'd seen him. "Mr. Lawrence?" Martin Lawrence, Ryan's uncle. "Uh . . . Make yourself comfortable."

He lowered himself into the chair, took off his wire-rimmed glasses and rubbed the bridge of his nose. Tired blue eyes looked up at her from under craggy brows. Involuntarily, her eyes widened. She had a sudden, uncanny sense of seeing Ryan in his face. Her breath caught and she blinked back moistness. He raised his head and the likeness was gone.

He hooked his glasses back, one slender earpiece at a time. "I hope you don't consider this presumptuous, my offering advice. But I fear you may find the legal system a bit intimidating."

She nodded, not trusting her voice.

"I know the papers were served a week ago Thursday, and the fact that they haven't been answered makes me wonder if perhaps you have not as yet turned them over to your attorney. If you have not procured legal counsel, it's essential to do so."

"I didn't know there was such a rush." Voice sounded mumbly. Her back stiffened in anger—at herself more than anything.

"Once you've put it in the hands of a competent attorney, it will ease your mind. He'll take care of everything. Most cases of this nature are settled out of court, you know."

She nodded again, feeling like a tongue-tied child in the presence of a kind but formal teacher. What could she say? *Loan me money for the retainer—then you two legal ghouls can split whatever's left?*

"You must understand, it's required that you answer the petition. You cannot simply ignore it."

You're playing my song. But you're up against some stiff competition. If Public Radio Voice gets there first, I won't need an attorney.

"I'll take care of it." Her voice firm. She placed her hands on the table, fingers laced together.

"The thing I like least about the law is its adversarial nature. Although I understand why my sister needs to do what she's doing, and I certainly intend to put forth every effort on her behalf, I'm not altogether pleased. Ryan's death has been a tragedy for all of us, and I would prefer to see the suffering end as soon as possible."

"Then why not drop the suit?"

"Mildred sees things differently. And she's very head-strong, as I'm sure you've heard." Giving her a kindly look, he stood up, expressed appreciation for her willingness to talk, and left.

She regarded her barely touched plate, the colors now garish and unappetizing. The thought of putting one more forkful in her mouth made her want to gag. *Treating yourself to lunch so you could feel better was not a great idea.*

She stood up abruptly, knocking her chair into the chair behind her. *Slow down. Don't go running out of here like a scared rabbit.* She took a deep breath. Her eyes wandered around the crowded dining room, then zoomed in on a face, a man in a charcoal suit seated in the far corner of the room. He made eye contact, smiling slowly. Her chest thudded. Was this the same man who'd followed her out of Wal-greens? She couldn't be sure. Was the smile because he thought she was flirting? Or because he wanted her to know he was after her? Her imagination was playing tricks. She was being paranoid again.

ra ra ra

At six o'clock Cassidy sat in her office waiting for Connie, a woman who'd shown up regularly every week for three years. This week she did not appear.

After seeing her other two clients, Cassidy sat down at her desk and tossed a handful of coins into the wine bottle, money she was squirreling away for Maggie's birthday dinner. They'd taken each other out for several years now, but considering her nonreturn of phone calls, Maggie might not be speaking to her by the time her birthday came around.

She should've called back and admitted her life was a mess. She also should've been putting more coins in the bottle, because at this point she damn well owed Maggie more than a burger at McDonalds.

She reached for the phone to call her missing client, but before she could pick it up, it rang.

Zach said, "I picked up those albums today, and it'd probably be better to go through them as soon as possible."

"You'd prefer to get them returned before Mildred finds out?"

"How about we get together tomorrow around nine?"

She shuffled through the clutter on her desk looking for her calendar, knowing already she had only one early evening client. "That'll work."

"Thought maybe you'd like to come to Marina City, see my place. The view here is terrific."

She paused. Actually, she would like to see his condo. But after mentally replaying the I-don't-want-commitment conversation, she decided against it.

She finished with Zach, then dialed Connie's number. After ringing a long time, the phone was answered, a groggy "Hello." Cassidy asked about the missed session.

"Didn't you get my message?"

"Machine must be acting up. When did you leave it?"

"Round noon. Said I was going home sick, I'd see you next week."

Cassidy wished her a fast recovery.

Another missing message. After losing those first calls, she'd tested the machine by having her mother leave messages, and it had worked perfectly. She'd convinced herself the initial malfunction was a fluke. Now this. She pictured the man who'd smiled from across the room at Erik's. An icy feeling crawled up her spine.

ò€   ò€   ò€

"I brought these over because I said I would, but I really can't see the point to it. What do you hope to get out of digging around in all this ancient history, anyway?" Zach thunked down a cardboard box on one of the black vinyl sofas. The cat leapt up and snuffled his hand.

Standing just inside the doorway, Cassidy rocked from one foot to the other. "You want something to drink?" His movements were reflected in two wide black windows, the overhead spreading soft light that scarcely reached into the corners.

"If I'm going to have to look at all these images of an idyllic past that never was, I definitely want a drink."

She disappeared into the kitchen, returning a minute later with two glasses of wine. Even with door and windows open, at night the small room enveloped them like a cocoon.

"Okay, McCabe. Enough tap dancing. Before I subject myself to this, I want an explanation."

She cocked her head, grimacing. "I can't say exactly. We keep picking up odd bits of information about Ryan's childhood. So I thought looking at old photos might help figure out what happened."

He sat down, patting the patched vinyl for her to sit beside him, and pushed back the wicker table so he could stretch out his legs. "So what? What does anything that happened almost forty years ago have to do with our current situation?"

"I know it's a long shot." She sat, her legs not quite touching his jeans. The cat stood on hind legs to sniff at the coleus, chew the leaves.

"You therapists always have to go back to childhood to explain everything. If somebody can't get it up today, it's because he got whacked for masturbating at the age of six."

"What's all this sarcasm about, anyway?"

"I don't happen to buy your Freudian theology, that's all." His voice challenging. "This whole idea that people are helpless and everything's determined by childhood offends me. I think people are better off putting their pasts behind them instead of endlessly whining about their dysfunctional childhoods."

Her back stiffening, she pulled away. "I thought you possessed at least a modicum of enlightenment. Way you're talking now, you sound like a Neanderthal."

"Look, I don't mean to insult you. I know therapy is like religion, and generally I stopped badgering fundamentalists after my sophomore year."

"Are you saying you don't believe there's *any* connection between what happened in childhood and people's problems as adults?"

"People see what they want to. You know as well as I do it's all hypothesis, an article of faith. Right now psychotherapy's trendy, but there's no research to back it up."

"That was quite a speech. Can I take it to mean you'd prefer not to look at pictures from your childhood?" Coleus apparently not to her taste, the cat stalked over to curl up on the directors chair.

"You can take it to mean I felt like spouting off." He reached over, put an arm around her shoulder and pulled her closer. "Now that I've got it out of my system, I'm ready to look at pictures." Taking a musty album out of the box, he spread it open across both their laps.

They flipped rapidly through the first one, which spanned Mildred's high school years and ended just before her first marriage at the age of twenty. The faded black and white snapshots showed Mildred as a perky young girl paired up with lots of different boys.

The next album contained wedding pictures in color, new home pictures, and pages of baby pictures. The last photo showed Mildred holding Ryan on his third birthday, her husband on one side, Martin on the other.

The third album started with wedding party shots of Mildred and her new husband, none of which were quite in focus. Cassidy squinted at the blurry images of Zach's father, trying to see a likeness. Although none showed a clear view of his face, she experienced a faint sense of recognition.

"Queen Mildred and her peasant husband," Zach muttered. "A marriage straight out of the Addams family. They met a few months after Ryan's father died. I think she was feeling itchy. He was a creative type—called them beatniks back then. I don't think she ever intended to marry him. Just wanted a fling. But pro-choice wasn't much of an option back then."

The next few pages were entirely taken up with Ryan's third and fourth years, chronicled by dozens of photos showing a cheerful, active, outgoing child. Zach was born shortly after Ryan turned four, but aside from a handful of photos in which Ryan was holding his brother, the new arrival was conspicuously absent. Even more absent were parents and other adults, who appeared not at all between wedding pictures, taken when Ryan was three and a half, and fifth birthday pictures.

Several pages were filled with a blonde, sailor-suited cherub who shared center stage with Mildred and Martin on the occasion of Ryan's fifth birthday. The one-year-old Zach was occasionally visible in the background. Mildred's second husband was nowhere to be seen.

Cassidy stopped at a close-up showing a radiantly excited little boy in front of a birthday cake with five candles. "If I had pictures of Ryan and Luke side by side, I wouldn't be able to tell them apart." She turned the page and came upon a group shot. "When I look at these, I have to remind myself that Martin's not the father."

"Ryan's dad was Martin's best friend. I always had the impression Martin felt some sort of obligation to step in when he died."

"I wonder why Martin never married."

"He did, but it only lasted a few years. Nobody much talked about it. Seems like he married some woman with a kid, then she died and the kid went to live with his father. Now that I think about it, she may've committed suicide, probably the reason it was all kept so hush-hush."

"Not good. We lose another point on that one."

"What do you mean?"

"Suicides tend to run in families. A suicide in a previous generation increases the odds Ryan'd do it."

Zach looked skeptical. "That doesn't make sense. Now if you were talking about her son, I can see how it might apply. But Ryan?" He shook his head. "This is pretty irrelevant, but I seem to remember hearing that the stepson— Frank, I think his name is—"

The phone rang and Cassidy jumped up. *If it's Public Radio Voice, Zach'll make you explain.* She slowly eased back down. After four rings, the machine took it.

"What was that about?"

Her eyes returning to the family group, she realized something was nagging at her. "Do Martin and Mildred both have a lot of money?"

"They've never had a heart-to-heart with me about their investment portfolios, but I'd guess neither of 'em has to worry about being homeless in their old age."

She traced a box around the photo with one fingernail.

He barked out a short laugh. "What? You think I whacked Ryan so I could be sole heir? The odds are, Mildred'll leave her money to her women's club and Martin'll leave it to village projects before anything trickles down to me."

"Stop trying to read my mind," she said irritably. Turning the page, she came upon a series of post-birthday pictures. She examined the little boy in button-down shirt and cotton pants. "Something's different."

19

OLD PHOTOS

"What is it?" Zach asked.

"On the other side of his birthday, when you study the face and body language, he seems changed. More withdrawn, closed up. That wide open, on-top-of-the-world smile doesn't show up anywhere. In these later pictures he's a sad, beaten down kid." She gently rubbed a finger over an image of Ryan huddled on his back steps.

"If you hadn't heard Mrs. K on the subject, do you think you'd have noticed?"

"Maybe not. But now that I'm looking, I can see it. What do you think? Am I imagining it?"

"No, I see it too. Maybe he was just going through a stage. That's what kids do, isn't it?"

"Mrs. Kowalski knows more about five-year-olds than

just about anybody in the world and she didn't think it was a stage."

"I admit, you've got my curiosity going, even though I was determined not to get sucked into any shrink-type, childhood history theories."

"What do you suppose happened?" Her eyes narrowed. "Could he have been abused?"

"I doubt it. Ryan got so much attention, he was so overprotected, it's hard to imagine. I was a more likely candidate." A muscle rippled in his cheek. "But . . . I wonder if it could've been the fighting. Mildred and my dad used to have some real knuckle-busting brawls. I think Ryan slept in the same bed with Mildred until he was six or seven, which means he would've been right in the middle of it."

"That could be it. It also fits with his having such a reaction to Luke's fifth birthday."

Zach looked puzzled.

"Luke's birthday could've brought back the feelings he experienced when he turned five. Children can get really terrorized when their parents fight. That also would explain the close tie to his mother, the antagonism toward his stepfather."

"I suppose that all makes sense but it doesn't take us anywhere." A breeze carrying the scent of budding plants whipped through the window.

In the next album, Cassidy mused over ten-year-old Ryan with a headlock on Zach, whose mouth was spread in an idiotic grin. Ryan stood out as slender, angular, golden. In comparison, Zach appeared uncombed and unkempt— darker, stockier, more ordinary.

"You certainly are enjoying yourself for a kid who's taking lumps from his brother."

"That was before I got smart." Head straightened, voice got more clipped.

"Oh?" Cassidy said, biting back the *Tell me about it* therapist-speak.

"When I was a kid, I thought Ryan walked on water. Didn't matter that he treated me like a punching bag and made me into his personal slave. I was fucking grateful he'd bother to beat on me."

"I guess little brothers feel that way a lot." The clock chimed ten times. The cat oozed out of the director's chair, stretched, then hopped onto the stack of albums, where she struck a pose waiting to be admired.

"I probably had a worse case of hero worship than most, given that Ryan was the only person in the world who knew I existed. I used to think he paid attention 'cause he cared, 'cause he was a such a good guy. But I finally figured out there was a big payoff for him in having somebody to boss around. It took some rough lessons before I caught onto it."

Her foot started jiggling. "What happened?"

"The time he really zapped me was my sophomore year. Until then, I usually did whatever he said but I was getting pretty sick of it. Anyway, he told me I had to go out for football. He'd been a big star, of course, and he considered football the only real sport, so I had to play and follow in his footsteps. But what I wanted was to mess around with the guitar and smoke dope and hang out with a whole different crowd."

She rubbed a loose edge of tape, trying to get it to stick.

"I can see why he might not have totally approved."

"When he finally got it through his head that this time I wasn't going to give in, he got back at me in a big way. Mildred had a diamond necklace she'd inherited from her grandmother, which he made off with. He waited until everybody was all worked up about the disappearance, then showed up with necklace in hand, announcing he'd found it in my desk. Everybody believed him, of course. And if that wasn't enough, he convinced Mildred—never very difficult for him—I was so screwed up I needed head shrinking. So she forced me to see a counselor that whole year." A disgusted look crossed his face.

Ryan was just a kid. Brothers do things like that. She bit her bottom lip. "So that's why you were so . . . well, so distant, so cut off. It makes more sense now."

He leaned back. "There's always a reason. One of the things I like about digging into a story is that once you've got enough information, everything makes sense."

The cat jumped onto the album that was spread across their laps. She tried to sprawl out on top of the pages but they pushed her away. She left in disgust, wandering over to the other sofa where she began chewing and tearing at one of the remaining buttons.

They were in the middle of the next album when Cassidy noticed a photo showing an uncomfortable-looking teenaged Zach standing next to an older man who had his arm around Zach's shoulder. It was the first clear view she'd seen of the man's face.

"Jerry!" She blinked, looked again. "That man in the picture is the guy who talked to me at the wake. The one who was celebrating." She stared at Zach, who had an odd look on his face. "Jerry's your father. He said Ryan had a personal grudge—that's because he was the stepfather. You knew that guy was your father all along, didn't you?"

"Well, uh, I kind of guessed." He shifted away from her on the sofa.

"You knew Jerry was your father and you didn't tell me."

"I guess that's right."

"You guess?" Anger rose in her chest. "What do you mean, you guess? Why the hell didn't you tell me?"

He shrugged, looking toward the opaque, black window. "Don't know. I suppose I should have mentioned it, but . . . I just don't know."

"You're not getting off that easy. There's always a reason, remember?"

He gave her a straight look. "Yeah, there's a reason. I just don't know what it is."

"What were you thinking when I told you that story about his getting blackballed by Ryan?"

"I was thinking, what a mess . . . his whole life's a mess."

"Do you care what happens to him?"

He lifted one shoulder, that odd look on his face again. "Not really."

She took a deep breath. "Remember how you yelled at me because I didn't tell you all about Public Radio Voice? You want me to tell you everything and you don't even mention that this guy who hates Ryan's guts is your father."

Always snooping into everyone else's business. Doesn't give anything in return. Another goddamned withholder.

"Yeah, I should have told you."

"Not good enough. You can just pack up all these moldy old albums you didn't want to show me in the first place and get out of here."

≥≈ ≥≈ ≥≈

It won't kill you. Just a couple of hours. Besides, she's fixing strawberry shortcake.

The salmon sky showing through her bedroom window reminded Cassidy that her mother was expecting her at seven-thirty, a mere five minutes from now. She pulled her burgundy and rose silk dress over her head and tossed it on the satin comforter. The cat pounced. Cassidy yelled and the cat buried her head under the skirt, leaving her tail and haunches exposed. Cassidy pulled the dress off the cat's head, grabbed her by the scruff, and extricated her claws.

"You're ruining everything. All my clothes have snagged threads and cat hair. My furniture's in a state of rapid deterioration."

She picked up the cat, who chewed the ends of her shoulder-length hair and purred. "I should have a Doberman instead. What good is a cat?"

The cat crawled onto her shoulder, then looked around for some place higher. Cassidy dutifully lifted her onto the top of the six-foot wardrobe in the hall. Eyes glinting maniacally, the cat lashed, claws-out, at the top of her head.

Cassidy jumped out of range. "If I had a dog, he'd be grateful. Dogs are good at gratitude. Unlike cats and men." She heard her mother's voice, at the end of her rope, *I hope you have a kid who turns out just like you.*

She should be nicer to her mother, who went out of her way to cook special dinners. Maybe she ought to wear something decent, just this once, instead of ratty shorts and tee. She pulled the burgundy silk back over her head, then took out Gran's earrings, garnet and gold, her favorites. Her mother would like to see her wear the earrings.

She was poking one into the hole in her earlobe when the phone rang. She lay the earrings on the television and picked up. Zach's voice, low pitched and tense. "Scott's resurfaced. The police brought him in yesterday for questioning, then let him go. This morning he landed in an emergency room with an overdose."

"How's he doing?" Dropping into her desk chair, she scribbled dark zigzag lines across an unopened telephone bill.

"Don't know. I just hung up from talking to Kristi. She's at the hospital now, pretty hysterical."

"I can imagine."

"Anyway, the reason I'm calling is, she wants me to hold her hand while she waits for him to get conscious. I thought maybe you'd like to go along."

This does not sound like fun. Remember, your mother's waiting. She made strawberry shortcake especially for you.

"I've got plans. Besides, you're the one she called."

"Men are no good at this kind of thing."

I grant you that. She touched the chipped corner of the desk.

"You're a shrink, this is what you do."

"Thought you didn't have any use for shrinks."

"So, will you do it?"

"I don't think . . . "

"Pick you up in ten minutes."

Oh shit. Now I've got to deal with my mother. She dialed the number and let it ring. Her mother refused to get an answering machine, insisting that she was always home. The problem was, she spent inordinate amounts of time in the bathroom, during which the phone went unanswered. Cassidy counted twenty rings and hung up.

Zach picked her up and headed across the city toward Ravenswood Hospital on the far north side. After driving in silence for some time, Zach said, his voice more tentative than usual. "I fucked up not telling you about Jerry. It's just that, the way I usually operate is, I ask people questions and they do the talking. It's a long-standing habit."

"That doesn't make it okay."

"You do the same thing, which is the reason we've been butting heads."

"Not me. I don't do that."

"I'm not used to being pinned down, and my tendency is to retreat into my old bad habits. But you don't let me get away with it."

"That must be frustrating for you," she said in a snide parody of her therapist voice.

"Yeah, it is. But you're right, I should've told you."

He's a sneak. A manipulator. Don't let him off.

"Well . . . " she started, trying to think of a sharp comeback, "I still don't understand why you didn't tell me."

"Just an automatic response. I grew up watching Mildred and Ryan ridicule him. And I started making fun of him too. Then I got to pretending Ryan's father was my real father. So I guess I just reached the point where I never acknowledged him." He glanced over at her.

She could see he didn't enjoy talking about this. "What's it like now? You ever see him?"

"He calls from time to time. Usually when he's in some kind of jam. Sometimes he hits me up for money, sometimes he just wants to bitch."

"Do you give him money?"

"Sometimes."

№ № №

Kristi was alone in the blonde-wood-and-glass, apricot-and-aqua visitor's lounge of the hospital detox center. She was seated on a spartan couch in a folded-up position, her legs pulled close to her chest, her head buried in her arms, snarly hair tumbling over her forehead.

She looked up, revealing a red, puffy face. "Thank God you're here," she said thickly. "I was so afraid . . . I mean, what if he never . . . I couldn't stand to be here all alone."

"Of course not." Cassidy perched on the edge of the apricot cushion and wrapped her arms around Kristi, breathing in her body's acrid scent, a mix of expensive perfume and sweat.

Zach sank into a low-slung aqua chair across from them. "He's going to be all right." He got up and walked over to Kristi, raised one hand as if to pat her on the head, then let it drop. He returned to his seat.

Kristi sat up straighter and raked her fingers through her crinkly hair. "I've been thinking about so many . . . I want you to understand what ... Ryan did terrible ... but it was my job to take care of him. And I didn't do it." Her face went from guilt to despair.

Murmuring encouragement, Cassidy shifted away from her into the corner of the Scandinavian couch.

"Right in the beginning, when I first started seeing Ryan, there were things ... Ryan did things. When Scott was little, I never had much ... I was always so busy trying to straighten out my own ... So when Ryan came along, the poor kid was starved for ... I think he really wanted Ryan to be his dad."

"What went wrong?"

Kristi's eyes glistened. "Ryan was so ... he was really, you know, moody. Sometimes he was just wonderful. He made us both feel special and important. Sometimes Ryan acted like he loved Scott the way a father ... "

"So what went wrong?" Cassidy repeated softly.

"It was like he turned into somebody else. Like there were two people in the same body. A good Ryan. And a bad Ryan."

A borderline. My God, Ryan was a borderline. Two years in therapy and I never suspected.

20

A PUNK'S PERSPECTIVE

"I know what you mean." Zach stretched out his legs, crossing them at the ankle. "I've seen it too."

Cassidy's chest tightened. She wished Kristi would shut up.

"The first time I really saw it . . . it was only a few months after we started dating. Scott would've done anything to get Ryan's approval, and what he did was, he saved up his money and bought him a wallet. For Father's Day. And Ryan said . . . he said he wasn't Scott's father and Scott had no business giving him . . . he said it was just a cheap piece of shit. I thought it must be my fault, I must have done . . . Anyway, Scott went running out of the house and then

Ryan cut the wallet into little pieces and stuffed them into the knapsack Scott took to . . . " Rage flashed across her face.

"What a terrible thing." Cassidy swallowed, trying to keep down the taste of bile in her throat. All this time she'd been blaming Kristi for Ryan's problems, thinking he would've been happier with her than with Kristi. The truth was, Ryan would've chewed up anybody.

"What's really terrible is, I didn't do anything about . . . I thought if I was better at making Ryan happy, if I kept Scott from getting in his way . . . Oh, Cass, I knew what Ryan was doing to him. I knew it and I went ahead and married him."

Taking Kristi's hands, Cassidy forced herself to look into the tear-filled eyes. "I don't know that I could've done any different."

"The worst thing about . . . there was the good Ryan, and that's what made it so . . . If there'd only been the bad part, then I could've . . . but the good part was so good. When he was the good Ryan, he could make all my fantasies come true."

Cassidy whispered. "I know how that feels."

"It was tearing me apart. Scott and I both tried . . . we tried so hard . . . I don't think he ever really believed we loved him. I watched Scott go from this sweet little kid who . . . I saw him get desperate and angry and . . . it almost seemed like he wanted to kill somebody, or kill himself, and now . . . "

Covering her face with her hands, she drew long moaning breaths. Only a few tears dripped through her fingers.

She seemed to have used up all the tears and now was experiencing an emotional collapse that was all dry heaves and convulsive sobbing.

 је је је

The clock on the aqua wall said eleven-thirty. Zach put down his copy of Newsweek. "I've been thinking some more about Ryan. You told us what happened the night he died, but what about during the day? Anything out of the ordinary?"

Kristi glanced up, her eyes startled. "During the . . . well, I don't know, it's hard to . . . Time's all jumbled . . . I wonder what's taking so long? What do you think it means, that it's taking so long?"

"It doesn't mean anything," Cassidy massaged the back of her own neck. "It just takes a long time to come out of, that's all. Try to remember. It'll help get your mind off what's going on now."

She stared straight ahead, her eyes defocusing. "Oh yeah, there was something . . . Luke and I drove Martin to the airport. He called around noon to say he had to go out of . . . Something he couldn't get out of. He'd have to miss Luke's party and wanted us to see him off. So Luke and I put him on a . . . Luke thought that big plane was so cool—started buzzing around with his arms spread out saying 'New York, New York.' "

Zach said, "Martin was in New York that night?"

"That reminds me, did you know Martin's stepson got back in touch? I guess he's been in Chicago awhile now. Martin told me he's planning to get some of the family together for dinner. But what I started to say is, when I put the car away, Ryan was just coming down from his study over the garage. I was really surprised. He's never home in the middle of the . . . "

A nurse appeared in the doorway. Kristi jumped up. "Is he . . . he's not going to . . . is he all right?"

"He's going to make it. This time. You his mother? C'mon, you can see him for a few minutes."

After about ten minutes, Kristi walked back into the lounge, a desperate look on her face. She slumped down next to Cassidy and grabbed her hand. "You've got to talk to—He looks terrible and he's not . . . Please, Cassy, talk to him."

Oh shit. I can't stand punks. Haven't the slightest idea how to work with them.

"I'd like to help, but . . . I don't have any experience with adolescents. You're his mother, you'd know better how to . . ."

"I don't know what to say," Kristi interrupted. "He's so angry. You're good with words, Cass. You know how to—"

"Why don't you?" Zach chimed in. "I know this won't be easy, but what've we got to lose?"

Nothing for *you* to lose. *I do not want to do this.* "All right, I'll give it a try. But don't get your hopes up."

Scott was lying with his head turned away from the door, so still she thought he was dead. Her leg muscles twitched; hairs rose along the backs of her arms. She spoke his name and he slowly turned to face her. Yellow skin rubber-coated his skull. Slitted eyes peered out of rubbery folds.

"Who're you?" he rasped.

"I'm Cassidy. Friend of your mother's."

"Cassidy. The McCabe bitch. That shrink the dick was seeing. I heard her, like, talk about you but it didn't sound like you were a friend. Shit, Ma's such a flake, she thinks everybody's her friend."

"She asked me to talk to you."

He laughed hoarsely. "You gonna give me religion, or what?"

"I'm only here 'cause your mother's beside herself. Me, I haven't got a clue what to do. You want to kill yourself, there's no way I can stop you."

The room was silent except for the whirr of machinery and his ragged breathing. She eased into the chair beside his bed. His eyelids drooped. She tried to imagine what it would be like for a twelve-year-old to find the wallet he'd given as a gift chopped-up in his knapsack.

"Sometimes I wonder," she said, her voice gradually sliding into a slow, rhythmic cadence, "what it might be like . . . to want to die . . . to want to die so bad . . . that nothing else matters . . . nothing at all . . . not your mother . . . or your friends . . . or your dreams of the future . . . nothing at all." As she watched, his face started to relax. "And when I think . . . about what it would be like . . . to want to die . . . I imagine you would have to have . . . a part of you . . . that has a lot of pain." A muscle twitched in his cheek. "There must be . . . so much pain . . . it must hurt . . . so much to live . . . and the part of you . . . that feels the pain . . . must be getting . . . closer and closer . . . to the surface . . . it must be getting . . . harder and harder . . . to find ways . . . to keep the pain away."

His head jerked. He turned to face her. "What the shit you think you're doin?"

"Would you let me talk . . . to the part of you . . . that feels the pain?"

"No! Shut up. Go away."

"I promise . . . I won't do anything to hurt you . . . I won't make it worse . . . I just want to say . . . to that part that's been hurt . . . so badly . . . that it wasn't your fault. You shouldn't have been . . . hurt like that . . . you deserved to have . . . a mother who could protect you . . . and a father who could love you." Her voice dropped even lower. "You deserved to be loved."

One tear leaked out of the corner of his eye. He turned his face away and pulled the covers over his head. She wiped a hand across her sweaty forehead and waited for what seemed like a very long time.

Finally he pulled the covers away and looked at her. "You shouldn't of done that. Nobody ever makes me cry. I don't let anybody make me cry." His voice was thin, exhausted.

"Takes courage to cry."

"You're full of shit."

"Will you get some help?"

"I don't know."

"Your mother wants you to get help more than anything."

"Not more than she wanted to keep the dickhead around."

"He's dead. And she's sorry she let him do what he did to you. Will you get some help?"

"I don't know."

Feeling the heaviness in her stomach she had carried around for days after Ryan died, she stood up. "Well, I guess there's nothing more for me to do."

"Wait! I got to tell somebody. Might as well be you."

She sat back down. "What is it you've got to tell?"

"About Ryan. What happened that night. I was so pissed. I said I was gonna, like, kill him, and I really wanted to do it, you know? So I ran outta there and I hung out for awhile and smoked some joints and cooled off. And then I got to thinking that this time maybe I'd gone too far. Maybe I'd got him so mad he'd call the cops on me. I was scared he'd put me away. So I thought maybe I could get around him. Usually, I wouldn't do it. But when I really wanted to, I could get around him. All I had to do was tell him he was right about everything. Like he was a prince of a guy and I was a worthless shit, and then he'd usually be okay for awhile. So I went back to the house. He was in his study and I went up to talk to him. But he was, like, he was kinda weird, he didn't seem to remember the fight or nothin'."

"What exactly was he doing? Tell me everything you remember."

"He wasn't doing nothin'. He was just sittin' at his desk and he seemed kinda excited or something, and he goes, *'I don't have time now. I've got something important to take care of.'* And then he goes, this is the really weird part, he's got a picture of Luke in his hand and he goes, *'Something I've got to do for him.'* Like it was for his birthday or something. But the way he said it, and the way he was so sorta excited, it didn't seem like just a birthday. Oh yeah, and then there was something else, only I'm not sure about this part. I think he muttered something like, '*Always known there was something wrong with me.*' "

"Was there anything else? Try to remember."

"I don't know. Yeah, maybe. Seems like he had a newspaper, a *Post*, on his desk and he'd circled one of the stories in red. But that's all there was. Nothin' else."

"Then what? After you left?"

"I figured he wasn't gonna turn me in so I just went out and partied and it was, like, real late when I came in. And the light was still on and I was curious. I guess I was so high I didn't exactly know what I was doing. So I climbed the stairs and opened the door and . . . shit, I couldn't believe it. It was like . . . it was sorta what I always thought about doing . . . For a minute, I wasn't sure, I thought maybe I'd done it and forgot. And then I got ahold of myself and remembered he always had a big wad of money on him. And I just decided I'd take it. I figured the fucker, like, owed me, you know?" His eyes met hers, looking for something. Found it and looked away.

"Why'd you disappear afterwards?"

"I just had to get outta there."

"What happened after that?" She wished it would be okay to touch him, maybe stroke his forehead. But she knew it wouldn't.

"Nothin'."

"What made you O.D.?"

"I just wanted to . . . I wanted to, like, make the pictures stop."

"I think I get it. Well . . . what do you suppose? You

suppose you might be ready to start getting straight?"

"How should I know what I'm gonna feel like when I get outta here?"

⁖ ⁖ ⁖

She returned to the waiting room and told Kristi that Scott seemed to be better. "Don't count on it—but he might be willing to go into treatment."

Long after midnight her exhausted body collapsed into the passenger seat of the Datsun. She closed her eyes, wishing she could doze on the way home, but they popped open. Although her mind had fuzzed out hours ago, her head was still buzzing the way it did when she drank too much coffee. She opened her mouth and tried to deliver a coherent account of Scott's story.

Zach, who looked as fresh as if he'd just stepped out of his morning shower, gave her a quizzical look. "Why was he so hot to tell you, anyway?"

"Hard to say. I was an outsider—somebody safe to talk to. That's one of the reasons people go into therapy."

"If what he said is true, this is the first tangible piece of evidence indicating it was murder, not suicide."

"Huh? You'll have to spell it out. I'm too tired to make sense out of anything on my own."

"He saw a photograph and a newspaper with a story circled in red. Neither of those items was found when the body was discovered. Therefore, somebody else came into the room after Scott left. Not quite evidence of murder, maybe, but at least evidence somebody else was there."

Cassidy leaned back against the seat and tried again to

close her eyes. This time her lids stayed down. "There's something else I've got to tell you before I chicken out. When Kristi was talking about Ryan's craziness, a light bulb went off in my head, and I recognized what was wrong with him. He was a borderline. I should've seen it sooner but I didn't."

"What's a borderline?"

"A borderline is somebody who's very sick. Much sicker than I realized. I'll explain it all later, when I get my brain cells started up again. But anyway, borderlines get to be borderlines because of their childhood experiences. I think we need to find out more about his fifth birthday."

"I still don't see how something that happened back then could have anything to do with somebody killing him now."

"I'm not saying it did. But I still think we should find out as much as we can."

"All right, I'll humor you. We can put our heads together and analyze his childhood. But only if we do it over dinner tomorrow night."

21

BORDERLINES

Cassidy felt a pain in her toe. A sharp, needlelike object was stabbing the big toe of her right foot. As she struggled to sit up, the cat dashed away. Wobbling to her feet, she got down on her hands and knees and pursued the cat into the farthest corner under the desk. After disposing of the cat, she discovered she'd forgotten to set the alarm. If she didn't hurry, she'd be greeting her first client in Kevin's *Springsteen* tee shirt.

She made it through her morning sessions, then went upstairs to face an unmade bed, last night's clothes strewn around the bedroom, the steady, unblinking eye of the answering machine. The fact that her mother hadn't called to complain was a bad sign.

She decided to straighten first, apologize later. She

hung up clothes and made the bed, then noticed a lone gold and garnet earring on the television. She crawled around the floor, peering under furniture, but did not expect to find it. When napkins and lids disappeared, not to be seen again, it was no big deal. But an earring her grandmother had given her was another matter altogether. She'd known from the minute she reached for that can of tuna she'd end up feeling dumb for having once again failed to follow her mother's advice. Why didn't she ever learn?

She stood up, brushed dust off her hands, tossed the auburn tangle out of her eyes. She glanced around, hoping the cat would be available to yell at, but the creature had a sixth sense about the timing of disappearances.

Since the cat was in hiding, she had no one to blame but herself. She plunked down in front of her desk, ready to do penance. *If you want to behave like a brat, you have to be prepared to eat worms and grovel. After all, it's the only pleasure she's got.*

Cassidy saw her mother sitting by the phone, that familiar, disapproving look on her face. She grimaced and picked up the receiver.

"So," her mother said, "what is it this time?"

"I can't tell you how sorry I am about missing dinner. I got a last minute phone call from a friend with a kid in the hospital who needed hand holding. I tried to get hold of you but you didn't answer."

"Do you know what it's like to sit for hours, wondering what's happened?"

Cassidy pictured herself waiting for Kevin with no idea when he might show his face. "You must've had a really bad night."

"This friend—man or woman?" Her mother's voice turned sharper. "All of a sudden, things keep coming up. You forget to call, you don't have any time."

"What would you do if you got a crisis call from a friend and couldn't reach me?" Cassidy rose and stepped over to the window, where she watched three small children chase each other in the yard across the street. The cat, suddenly appearing out of nowhere, jumped onto the windowsill and nuzzled her hand for petting. Down toward the end of the block a green car was parked at the curb. From this distance she couldn't tell if the windows were tinted, but the tightness in her chest told her they were.

"Something's going on, Cass, I can smell it. And it smells like you're involved with another one of those unreliable, playboy types, and you don't want me to know."

God, I must be leaking pheromones like crazy. "I'm sorry and I want to make it up to you. Just tell me, what can I do? Anything at all." *You shouldn't have said that.*

"Well, I've still got the strawberries and whipped cream. Why not come over tonight?"

The cat stood, hind legs on the windowsill, and swatted at the phone, claws digging a bloody furrow across the back of her hand.

"I wish I could, I really wish I had tonight free." A sick, guilty feeling settled in her chest. "But I've already made other plans."

Cassidy slapped at the cat, who jumped across to go treasure hunting on her desk. She endured a pained silence on the other end, then wrapped it up with her mother. Hands on hips, she glared at the cat, whose entire attention was focused on digging through papers and pretending she didn't exist.

"This time you've gone too far."

Large cat-eyes dominated by wide black pupils—her wild look—stared into Cassidy's.

"Everything you've run off with has disappeared into some black hole. Now it's an earring passed down by Gran."

The cat stood alert on all fours, tail switching, stare black and unwavering.

"How could you do this to me? All these other problems, now you're picking on me too." Hearing the whine, hearing her mother's voice come out of her mouth, she felt a stab of embarrassment but couldn't stop the words.

"Why am I yelling at you? The real question is, what's the matter with me? I should've taken you to the pound that first day after you ruined my sleep and made me screw up Ryan's session."

The cat deliberately pushed her ceramic mug full of pens off the desk, then raced out of the room.

"Shit!" She pounded her fist on the desk, then got down on the floor and picked up the pens. Satisfying though it might be, screaming got her nowhere. The earring was gone, the cat in hiding. *Time to stop obsessing and get something done.*

One tough call—apology to her mother—out of the way. Might as well keep going and make the other. She'd ransacked every corner of her mind to come up with a lawyer who might be willing to represent her without a retainer. Then she remembered her grandmother's attorney, whom she'd met a few years back. He might do it, but she'd procrastinated about making the call. The thought of having to beg made her cringe.

She got through to him right away. He told her to put the papers in the mail and forget about it until further notice.

ta ta ta

It was after dark when Zach picked her up that night and drove to Kinzie's, a restaurant she remembered fondly from the less-impoverished days before her divorce. The hostess, who seemed to know him, seated them side by side at an intimate corner booth with a round table. He ordered a Beaujolais while she studied the three-page menu, debating between the spinach salad, which was cheap, and the lobster dinner, which called to her in siren tones.

The mini-skirted waitress approached. She had the face of a fiftyish sun worshiper above a Nautilus body that looked twenty years younger. She poured wine, then smiled at Cassidy, pencil poised.

"I'm not sure. Take his order first."

Zach ordered ribs.

The waitress smiled in her direction again. "Need more time?"

"No, that's all right." *Make up your mind.* "I'll take the, uh . . . spinach salad."

When the waitress was gone, Zach looked at her quizzically. "Why do I get the idea that wasn't your first choice?"

She took her time unfolding the napkin and spreading it across her lap.

"Look, I'm not running a tab." Zach put his elbows on

the table. "I don't expect you to pay up later. Even we Neanderthals have gotten beyond that."

"I never thought you were. But maybe I am."

"Don't you think it's just as bad to keep score on the receiving end as on the giving end?"

"When you're on the receiving end, you have to." She tapped a wine colored fingernail on the white tablecloth. "Now leave me alone. This is not what we came here to talk about."

Zach sipped some wine. "Right. You were going to tell me about borderlines."

She took a deep breath. "It's hard to know where to start. First of all, borderlines are different from people who have some kind of mental illness. Something goes wrong early in life that prevents the borderline from developing a normal self or ego. So it's not a problem you can fix."

"Are you saying it's incurable? Like AIDS or something?"

"Some therapists claim to have success with borderlines but it's doubtful. Usually treating a borderline is more of a holding action."

Zach looked unconvinced. "This all sounds a little voodoo-ish to me. If Ryan was so sick, how come nobody knew it, not even you? And how was he able to manage so well? He did a better job of maneuvering than anybody I know."

"Borderlines can be quite successful in their careers. But their relationships are always a disaster. They have two distinct sides, and they swing back and forth—just like Kristi said. The good side is intensely warm, exquisitely attuned to their partner's needs, more so than any normal person. And the bad side is incredibly rageful and cruel. Which means a relationship with a borderline is always a nightmare."

"This is hard to believe. You're telling me that Ryan's basic personality, the behavior I always chalked up to personal idiosyncrasy, is actually a pattern or some kind of syndrome."

"If you'd seen as many of these people as I have, you'd believe it. Another feature of borderlines is that they tend to be self-destructive and sometimes end up killing themselves. Which brings us full circle."

The waitress brought a loaf of warm homemade bread and a salad for Zach. Cassidy sliced the bread, offered it to Zach, then took two pieces for herself. Consuming the first piece and washing it down with wine, she realized how completely empty she felt.

Zach finished his salad and pushed his plate back. "Look, I know this sounds critical and I don't mean it to come across that way. But if you've seen a lot of borderlines, I'm still wondering why you didn't pick up on Ryan sooner."

She brushed the breadcrumbs into a pile, pushed them off the edge of the table into her hand and dropped them on her bread plate. "Is it really necessary to go into this?"

"You can always tell me to butt out."

"Confession is supposed to be good for your mental health. At least, that's what I always tell clients. So here goes. One reason I screwed up on Ryan's diagnosis is that he only showed me his good side. He was splitting between

Kristi and me. He saw Kristi as the bad mother, so he was showing her his bad side. He saw me as the good mother, so I got the good side." That rush of sadness in her throat again. She raised her glass and took a large swallow. "But that isn't the main reason. The main reason is something I've only just now admitted to myself. I was idealizing . . . No, that's minimizing. It was more than that. I was attracted. And that kept me from seeing him the way he really was."

Zach sat up straighter. "*Attracted?* Aren't you understating a little? How about *a crush, infatuated,* maybe even *fell in love.*"

She watched her hands crumple the napkin in her lap.

"Well, why not?" A muscle tensed in Zach's jaw. "Why shouldn't his shrink add her name to the list? God knows everybody else did." He picked up the wine bottle and refilled both their glasses.

"Look, I'm not proud of it."

"No reason to feel bad. After all, shrinks are human too."

"Well, I do feel bad." She lowered her chin. "It prevented me from giving him the best possible treatment."

"So what? Doesn't matter. Borderlines can't be cured anyway." He turned his head and scanned the room. "Service is slow tonight."

"Well . . ." She mashed crumbs into the breadplate. "Shall we move on to the next item?"

"After dinner. I don't feel like talking about Ryan's childhood just yet."

"Are you upset? I mean, does it bother you that I was . . . well, infatuated?"

"I'm just hungry, that's all. Can't think on an empty stomach." He jabbed the tines of his fork into the table, making indentations in the thickly padded cloth.

After they had finished their meal, Zach placed his still folded napkin on the table and turned in her direction.

How does anybody manage to eat ribs and end up with a napkin looking like it just came out of the laundry?

"Okay," he said. "My stomach's happy. Let's talk about childhood secrets."

Cassidy needed to use the restroom before they started, so she excused herself and walked to the other end of the restaurant. When she emerged a few minutes later, she noticed a tall, attractive man standing next to the table talking to Zach. He straightened and headed toward the door, affording her a glimpse of boyish face topped by thick sandy hair. *Tony Chiparo? Couldn't be. Why would he be talking to Zach?*

She returned to the table and seated herself. "Who was that man?"

"Some guy who stopped to say he liked my article on judges."

"How'd he know who you were?"

Zach shrugged. "Every so often somebody recognizes me. Well, you ready to strategize?"

"Have you thought of anything?"

"Regrettably, there is something that keeps forcing itself on my attention. Much as I've been trying to avoid it, the reality is, if we want to learn more about young Ryan, we've got to tackle our mutual mother. Since you're so hot on pursuing this childhood angle, we might as well get it over with."

"There's no reason for both of us to do it."

"Right. You can do it."

"I'd never get my foot inside the door. But you're her son. She has to talk to you."

"How little you know the Dragon Lady."

"Seriously, I could give you a list of questions."

He shot her an indignant look. "You're the one wants to know about his childhood. Personally, I lived through it. That's enough for me."

"Okay, let's make it a team effort. But considering that she and I are legal adversaries, seems like it'd be impossible to get her to open her mouth with me in the room."

"I'll come up with something." He laid his arm around her shoulders. "Well, chief, is that it? We done with the briefing?"

"One more thing. We might be able to learn something by going through old memorabilia. You know, scrapbooks, art projects, that kind of thing. Mothers always seem to have stuff like that stashed somewhere."

"Everything that ever came into the house is packed away in boxes in the attic. Only question is, which box?"

"I'd like to have a look."

He lowered his head and glowered. "You don't know what you're asking for. She's been stuffing boxes away for at least fifty years."

"Don't you want to go treasure hunting?"

"Haven't I given in to all your demented ideas so far? Okay, I'll take you into the attic. After we get done mucking around in the cobwebs and dust, do I also get to take you into the shower?"

"We'll see."

When he parked in front of her house, she sat still for a moment, then moved fractionally closer instead of diving for the door. He took her face in his hands and gave her a kiss that was a little shorter, a little harder than the one she received the night they had pizza.

"Do I get to come in?"

"Not yet."

22

THE ATTIC

Cassidy held a drawing torn out of a child's wide-lined tablet up to a dormer window thick with grime. She and Zach, working at opposite ends of Mildred's cavernous, L-shaped attic, had been digging through boxes for more than an hour, and this one drawing, taken from an envelope labeled "kindergarten," was the first item that flagged her interest.

The envelope had been stuffed with crayoned pictures, the majority of which were dense shapes made by a black crayon pressed heavily against the paper. Many contained repetitive circles forming a dark vortex, an image reminding her vaguely of Van Gogh's darker works.

The drawing in her hand was the only one containing any shape that could be considered remotely human, and even here it was no more than a stick figure pushed off to the corner. She'd carried it over to the window hoping to find enough daylight to get a good look at it. The window was at the far end of a cozy, boxed-in space, the kind of hideout children loved. She could envision Ryan as a small boy curled up on the window seat playing with the toy cars she'd found in one of the boxes she'd opened earlier.

Examining the picture under the failing light, she detected a red squiggle protruding from the midsection. Black lines had been scribbled across the figure, making it difficult to interpret. But assuming the stick-figure shape under the heavy lines represented a child, what was the red mark? A penis? Blood? Or was she simply imagining that the black lines in the corner were somehow different from the black lines in the middle because she so desperately wanted to justify having dragged her detection partner into her current lunacy.

She considered having Zach, whom she had not seen since the beginning of their dig, take a look at it. She started to move in his direction. *Not a good idea. Zach's not exactly what you'd call sympathetic to Freudian interpretation.* Having to defend herself against ridicule would only make her more insecure.

Yeah, but what about the way you jumped all over him for not having been completely and instantly forthright?

Folding the picture carefully, she carried it to the far end of the attic and tucked it into the handbag she'd dropped in the corner. She returned to the box in which she'd found the drawings, put the envelope back, and closed it. She grabbed the box directly beneath it, hoping for a vein of gold, but the next box, and the surrounding boxes after that, yielded nothing.

A few minutes later Zach came hurrying around the corner. "I lost track of the time. We'd better get out of here."

"Already? Why, it only seems like a week's gone by since we first got here." She wiped her gritty hand on her shorts and pushed her tangled hair out of her eyes.

"Scrounging around in someone else's trash in a stifling attic's not as much fun as you expected?"

"Shouldn't I put the boxes back?"

"Remember, I told you—whenever Mildred goes to the Lake House, she always gets back before dark." He started for the stairs.

"Wait." She raced to the far end of the attic, grabbed her bag and dashed to where Zach was standing at the head of the stairs. With Cassidy at his heels, he sprinted down to the second floor and hurried along to the end of the hallway. The next flight of stairs led down to the front door. Just as he reached the top, he came to an abrupt halt. Cassidy skidded up against his back, her hands grabbing his sides and her teeth biting the tip of her tongue.

Peeking under his arm, she saw Mildred at the foot of the stairs. *Oh shit. Why'd I have to get caught looking like such a mess? Maybe I ought to use hair spray—naw, that's going too far.*

Mildred and Zach regarded each other. Finally, Zach broke the silence. "Well. I really didn't expect I'd run into you."

"Evidently not. Although it seems like that little person whose head is sticking out behind you is the one who did the running into." Mildred's voice had the same staccato quality as Zach's when he wanted to put Cassidy in her place.

"So, since you had the bad timing to surprise us like this, why not join us in a drink?" Zach started down, taking the steps with a slightly pronounced jauntiness. He brushed past Mildred, standing straight-backed in the entryway, and headed for the liquor cabinet in the sunken living room. Cassidy, her heart racing, stayed one step behind.

Mildred took up a position in front of the window where she stood with her hands at her sides, watching Zach pull down the door on the gracefully carved gold and white cabinet. The room was done in French Provincial, with champagne walls, sheer white fabric draped around the windows, and taupe carpeting.

Anybody who lives in a house like this should never've had kids.

"I presume you'll have your usual DuBonnet, Mother."

"Yes, thank you." She was a tall woman, as tall as Zach, with large shoulders and narrow hips. Her short white hair was beautifully sculpted; her skin, though covered with a fine skein of wrinkles, reminded Cassidy of an elegant suede jacket she'd once owned. The eyes were Ryan's eyes before his depression: clear, intelligent, full of life. Right now, they showed pinpricks of angry light.

Zach served Mildred, then turned to Cassidy. "What'll you have? Sherry? Scotch?"

"Sherry," she said in her small voice. It would be more dignified to pass, but her need for alcohol easily outstripped her need to preserve any shred of dignity she might have left.

Zach handed her a glass of sherry, then poured a large scotch for himself. "Cheers."

Mildred acknowledged his toast with a minimal nod, then inclined her head in Cassidy's direction. "You're the therapist."

Cassidy nodded.

"I suppose you know this is trespassing. Or is it breaking and entering? Well, I'm sure the arresting officer will enlighten me."

"You want to call the police?" Zach asked. "This should make an amusing entry for police reports. Zachary Moran, son of Mildred Lawrence, arrested Monday for trespassing on his mother's property. The girls in the Nineteenth Century Club'll love it."

Cassidy trailed Zach over to the white marble fireplace. He propped himself against it and she tucked herself in next to him.

Mildred's voice hardened. "What are you doing here?"

Zach held her gaze. "Investigating Ryan's murder."

Mildred's angular chin went up a notch. "You're delusional, of course."

"Oh? You think this's simply more of little Zachary's usual madness?" Zach cocked his head. His voice got that laconic tone. "Then you shouldn't object to humoring me. Madmen are supposed to be humored, aren't they, Mother?"

"I have no intention of humoring either one of you. In case you didn't get the drift, Zachary, I gave up on you a long time ago."

Cassidy's lips compressed in a thin line. She fixed her attention on a three-foot high statue standing on a pedestal next to the fireplace. The marble figure, which looked like something out of an Indian temple, depicted a man with oversized genitals mounting a woman doggy-style.

"Since we're talking about the death of your number one son, I expect you'll go along with me. Cassidy and I have a few questions we'd like to pose. About Ryan's childhood." He took a swallow, rattling the ice cubes in his drink.

"I can't think of a single reason why I'd choose to discuss Ryan with you."

"I always thought you were cleverer than that, Mother. How's this for a reason? A front page story in Oak Park Review, headed something like this—'Brother of So-Called Suicide Victim Charges Murder.' "

"Why are you making all this trouble? Ryan was the best friend you ever had. Why in God's name do you want to sully his memory like this?"

"I'm sorry, I don't follow you. If I come up with evidence he was murdered, how's that sullying his memory?"

"I won't discuss him with you. I refuse to listen to your petty little jokes." Turning away from them, she faced the window. "He was a better man than you'll ever be and you've never forgiven him for it. And now that he's dead, you still can't leave him alone."

Cassidy glanced at Zach out of the corner of her eye. *Jealousy? I wonder.*

"That may be true." Zach pushed away from the fireplace and went to stand behind her. "But I think he was murdered and I intend to get the information to prove it.

Even if it means embarrassing you. You've got a choice. You can talk to me. Or you can read about my delusions in the newspaper."

Coming back around, Mildred lowered her brows angrily. "You want to believe he was murdered because you'd like to think someone hated him enough to kill him." She spat the words at Zach. "You're the only person that ever hated him."

"Think what you like. You still have to choose."

"Why is she here?" Mildred nodded at Cassidy. "What's going on between the two of you, anyway? I suppose she's passing along everything he said, violating his confidentiality. She's probably hoping you'll succeed in fabricating a murder so she can get out of her little malpractice suit."

"What'll it be?" Zach persisted. "You talk to us or we talk to the press."

"I have to think about it."

They got into the gray Datsun and closed the doors. Cassidy leaned back and let go with a long whooshing sigh.

"Oh God, I thought I'd die when I saw her standing there. I felt so . . . caught in the act."

"She can be a real fire-breather."

"So, what do you think she'll do?"

"Oh, she'll go along. She'll rant and rave, and bitch and moan, but she'll do it. You'll get to hear about Ryan's childhood. She'll get to feel vindicated that I'm a worthless shit. I'll get to fortify my sense of maternal rejection. What more could you want?"

23

OBSESSION

She was in the basement sorting laundry when she heard the phone. Counting rings, she raced toward the stairs, hoping to grab it before the machine cut in. Third ring at the landing. Fourth at the top of the stairs. Bolting through the doorway. she tripped over the cat. Halfway stumbling, she pulled the receiver off the kitchen wall just in time to hear the recording, "This is Cassidy McCabe."

"I'm here," she yelled over the sound of her recorded voice, which she hated. "Wait till it's done and we can talk."

Why do you get so compulsive? You should've let the machine take it.

Shifting from foot to foot as her message droned on, she watched the cat leap onto the counter and put on her wounded look. "We can talk now. So . . . what can I do for you?"

"At last, a voice that's not a recording." Her body went rigid. "I've been rather frustrated, you know, at your stubborn refusal to talk to me."

Oh shit. He hasn't called in so long I fell back into my old habit of answering the phone. Her throat closed. She had to swallow more than once before she could get words out—words that came out an octave too high. "It wasn't on purpose. You just happened to call at all the wrong times."

Public Radio Voice continued. "You may come to regret that you didn't find a way to make yourself more available. But now that I've finally got hold of you, you can clear this matter up quite easily. Just tell me how to locate your ex-husband."

She took a deep breath. "I can't. Even if I wanted to, which I really don't, I couldn't help you because he wouldn't be so stupid, you know, as to tell me—considering that he already realizes you're trying to get at him through me. So even though you saw us together, all that happened was, he picked me up and dropped me off and that's all there was to it. I have no idea where he's actually staying." *Stop babbling.*

"That's unfortunate." Voice emotionless, words measured. "The only recourse, then, is for you to make good on his debt. You'll have to deliver the sixty-five thousand. Or pay the penalty. Unless, of course, you want to reconsider and tell us where he is."

"I can't. Come up with sixty-five thousand, that is. Or tell you where he is."

"That's even more unfortunate. Also untrue. If it were

important enough, you'd get the money. I wonder what's preventing you? Could it be that I've foolishly allowed this little game to continue over such a long period of time I've lost credibility? Let me assure you, it would be most unwise to assume we won't follow through."

"Oh no, that's not the problem. I believe you all right. It's just that, I really don't have any way to get the money."

A long silence. The cat, deciding to forgive her for tripping, jumped down and began rubbing against her legs. Cassidy started to wonder if he might be gone, her unspecified penalty to become a frozen statue, one ear glued to the phone, her flesh rotting away. A cobwebby skeleton leaning against the kitchen wall, skeleton cat at its feet.

"This has gone on far too long," the voice resumed. "If you don't come up with the money by Friday, there will be consequences. Severe consequences." *Death or mutilation? Do I get a choice?*

"If I find a way . . . if I get the money . . . how will I let you know?"

"Call this number at two-thirty on Friday." He rattled off the number.

"Wait . . . I didn't get it . . . let me write it down." She grabbed a pen. "Tell me again."

He repeated the number slowly. "This pen isn't working. Wait a minute."

"It's on the machine. Twice." The phone clicked down.

Her hand, cold and so cramped she had difficulty getting her fingers to release their hold on the receiver. Her whole body, paralyzed, held in place by steel wires that had replaced the nerves. She raised and dropped her shoulders, rolled her head, took slow, deep breaths.

What to do? Give in and ask her grandmother for money? *I can't stand being pushed around by slime. Accept the consequences? What're they going to do? Kill me? Put me in the hospital?* Could she be stoic about it if they simply beat her up? Take the punishment and be done with it? *I hate pain.* If only they'd told her what the consequences were, she could decide. Death or mutilation, which would she prefer? *Neither. I can't tolerate either one.* That meant she'd have to get the money from her grandmother. *No, not that either.*

She snatched up the squirming cat and made a dash for the front door. Why didn't she have a Doberman instead of a cat? She stood in the middle of the porch, clutching the wriggling animal to her chest, and tried to think why she'd gone running out here. The cat broke loose, bounded onto the windowsill, then shot her a venomous look. The three small children were playing in their yard. A mild breeze sloughed through the trees and lightly jangled the chimes.

She'd been ignoring the threats because they seemed so unreal. Every time Public Radio Voice called, she'd spent a couple of hours crazed with fear, then put it out of her mind. *This time you won't get out of it so easily, kiddo. Proof that the call really happened is right upstairs on your answering machine.*

When clients were in crisis, she instructed them not to make decisions until they calmed down. Best choice would be to follow through on her plan for the day, then schlep out to Woodridge for supervision.

≈ ≈ ≈

"The black circles look like anger," Honor commented. "I'd say a very angry child. Over here, in the corner, it looks like the figure of a child. The red mark seems to be genitals. I'd guess the artist started off by drawing a representation of himself with an oversized penis, probably an erection, then expressed his sense of self-hatred by covering it up with heavy black lines."

Cassidy leaned forward in the sleek, black armchair. "Anything else?"

"The obvious interpretation is that the child who drew this was sexually abused."

"That's what I thought. But I needed an objective evaluation."

"Keep in mind, I said *the obvious interpretation*. An interpretation is only that. It's not at all the same thing as proof. Sometimes an interpretation can be pretty far off the mark." Clattering the chains she wore over her long, black and white sundress, Honor reached across to lay the drawing on the glass coffeetable between her sofa and Cassidy's chair.

"Well, maybe. But I'd take your interpretation any day. Weren't you an expert evaluator in child sexual abuse cases for several years?"

"That was almost ten years ago, when I was more of a zealot. Back then, there were times I went way out on a limb and testified that a kid had been the victim of abuse on the basis of a few drawings and the rambling statements of a four-year-old. I've gotten more cautious in my old age."

She's not old. Cassidy nibbled at her banana bread as she checked for signs of aging, noting the warm brown eyes which, now that she looked, seemed more tired than they used to; the speckled, toughened skin above her sundress; the flabbiness that had crept into her upper arms, even though overall Honor was not the least overweight. Cassidy felt the slight stiffening in her spine that signaled resistance. She didn't want to hear caution. She wanted zeal.

"You know," Honor continued, "back in the early eighties, when it seemed like we'd uncovered an epidemic of sex abuse, a lot of us got overzealous. We took it as an article of faith that children never lie about sex abuse. That we could identify an abused child on the basis of evidence such as the child's verbal responses, drawings, the use of anatomically correct dolls."

"That's pretty much what I've always believed."

"The problem is, it's so damned subjective." Honor's creased face livened. "There's simply no way to tell how much a kid has picked up from a mother who's out to get her ex. Or a social worker who smiles when the kid tells her what she wants to hear. I'm convinced there are some over-eager clinicians out there who've yelled fire on the basis of false alarms. I watched our movement turn into a witch hunt, and I regret getting so carried away that I sometimes overlooked the distinction between interpretation and proof."

"Well . . ." One corner of Cassidy's mouth twisted wryly downward. "I was really hoping you'd get carried away. I wanted you to say, *Ryan was abused, you can count on it.* But I guess I'll have to take what I can get. At least what you saw in the picture was the same thing I did, and you've got a lot of credibility with me."

"Especially when I tell you what you want to hear." Honor poured more tea, setting off a whispery rattle of chains. "Now, what's the rest of the story? I won't be put off any longer."

Cassidy brought her up to date on the disclosures by Kristi and Scott, the attic archeological dig, and the encounter with Mildred. She chose not to mention the threat from Public Radio Voice, the meeting with Kevin, or the passes from Zach—which she was not inclined to take seriously anyway.

"So you see," Cassidy continued, "We've gathered a lot of information. Unfortunately, everything supports the suicide theory. Ryan knew there was something wrong with him. He probably was sexually abused, beginning at the time of his fifth birthday. As Luke's birthday approached, his repressed memories started coming closer to the surface, causing the increased depression. All of this points to a scenario in which he experienced an abuse flashback that brought up so much pain he grabbed a gun and shot himself."

Honor nodded. "That could be it. It's the kind of thing that happens all too often." She picked up the drawing and examined it again. "Anything else?"

"Yeah, there is." Slumping back in her chair, Cassidy recounted her failure to diagnose Ryan properly as a borderline.

"Another forest and trees situation," Honor commented. "You were too close. You couldn't see it."

"Do you think borderlines are always abuse victims?"

Honor shrugged, handing the drawing back to Cassidy. "Who knows? All I can say for sure is that a high percent of borderlines have experienced abuse."

"I wish you weren't feeling so cautious today."

"Maybe you could do with a little more caution yourself. I seem to detect that gleam of fanaticism in your eye. Could you by any chance be getting obsessive?"

"Funny you should ask." Cassidy crossed her legs, jiggled her foot. "While I was on my way here, I got to thinking that in the beginning, Zach was the one pushing to do this thing. But lately, it seems like he's kind of lost his momentum and I'm the one feeling driven."

"*Driven.* That another word for obsessive?"

"I'd have to say, I've got that obsessive feeling again, and it worries me. When I'm obsessive, I get so single-minded I bulldoze my way through anything and everything. At least, that's how my mother sees it. I just can't let go until I've gotten what I'm after."

Honor regarded her with brown eyes that had brightened during the course of their discussion. "Do you think that's necessarily bad?"

"Well, yes. At least the way I do it. I'm not very considerate of others when I get this way." Cassidy was surprised to feel her throat thickening.

"What's your obsessiveness enabled you to accomplish?"

"Let's see. I got through graduate school. I earned enough money to keep Kevin out of bankruptcy when we were married. I've built up a private practice."

"What has your mother accomplished?"

"Not much. Her mission in life is to get other people to take care of her."

"Does your mother get obsessive?"

Cassidy gazed out the window at the green fields, the flat open land, a sky the same deep blue as the color of her tea cup. "I see your point."

"So," Honor continued, "what's that obsessiveness doing for you now?"

She tried to read the bemused expression on her supervisor's face. "I don't understand."

"That obsessive feeling. What's it trying to get you to accomplish this time?"

"That's a tough one," Cassidy sighed. "I feel like this whole rotten experience has some kind of lesson in it, and I can't quit until I've learned what it is. I think it has something to do with the way I screwed up Ryan's diagnosis. It also has to do with what you were saying earlier . . . about the way we tend to have such an investment in our own interpretation, our own way of seeing, that we forget a reality exists beyond our individual perceptions."

"That's a hard lesson to learn," Honor observed. "I think we spend our whole lives struggling with that one."

Cassidy set her cup on the glass table. "We try to make reality conform to our beliefs instead of the other way around. All I was hearing was Ryan's version. I lost track of the fact that there also is such a thing as the truth. And now I feel this compulsion to uncover it. Even if it's not what I want to hear. Even if it hurts."

ðə ðə ðə

The instant she walked in her door, the call from Public Radio Voice came rushing back. Better to play the message right away and get the phone number down. Hearing him on the tape would reinforce her sense of urgency. If she got urgent enough, maybe she could force herself to decide.

Upstairs the red light was blinking once, indicating only one message on the machine. Setting her jaw against the surge of anxiety his voice brought on, she pushed playback.

"This is Zach. We've been working too hard. Let's go out Friday night and listen to music. I know an intimate little piano bar with a torch singer who does great classics like *Smoke Gets In Your Eyes*—mush like that. One more thing. I propose we make a vow not to talk about Ryan—or the investigation—or my family. That'll answer the burning question . . . " a pause, his voice turning melodramatic, "will Cass and Zach sit in total silence all evening if they are forbidden to discuss," his voice dropped lower, " . . . the case."

Holy shit. It's gone. The message is gone.

She rewound the tape and played it again.

This is unreal. I must be the one who's delusional. I've had a psychotic break and I think I'm in my house with a cat who mysteriously appeared on my doorstep. But in reality I'm on a locked ward and the cat is my caretaker and none of this ever happened outside of my own schizoid nightmares.

The only bright spot was—she no longer had to decide.

24

A NIGHT OUT

"Moran here."

"Hi. It's Cass." *Should I tell him Public Radio Voice set a deadline?*

"So, how 'bout a night out?"

"Friday's not good—have to get an early start the next morning. Maybe Saturday instead?"

A long pause.

Her spirit drooped like the coleus in her office when she forgot to water it. "If you've got other plans, that's all right." *Don't tell him anything.*

"I think I can switch things around. Let's go with Saturday and if it doesn't work, I'll get back to you."

❧ ❧ ❧

Friday afternoon Carla settled into her usual place on the other side of the wicker table and proceeded to relate a complicated story about having seen Jim with another woman when he was supposed to be out of town. Daylight streamed through the expanse of glass on two sides. An open window let in brisk air and high decibel teenage voices aggressively yelling obscenities.

"Have you talked to him about it?"

"When I saw him, I just took off in the opposite direction. Since then, I've picked up the phone dozens of times, then hang up when he answers." She smoothed down a curling edge of black tape. "He only calls when no one else is available. I've got to get him out of my system."

The clock chimed. Cassidy's eyes flew to the dial. Two-thirty Friday. Her mouth went dry. *This is it. Death or mutilation. And I don't have to decide because no one's going to ask. It will simply happen. At some moment when I'm thinking about Ryan or cleaning out the cat box or asleep in my bed.*

"What's really frustrating is, one of my friends fixed me up with her brother. We went out Saturday night—I hate to admit it but I held him off till the last minute hoping Jim would call. This guy is really nice. I mean, he took me to the Italian Village. He listened to what I was saying. He didn't make any moves. He even asked me out for next weekend."

Cassidy could just barely pick up the refrain from the waiting room. A woman's voice singing, "There's got to be a morning after, if we can make it through the storm . . . " *No mornings after for you, kiddo. Not after the mob gets done.*

"We've talked and talked about how I keep choosing the wrong men because of my childhood . . . "

Unless, of course, I imagined the whole thing and I am right this minute sitting on a locked ward in a catatonic state.

"What I can't figure out is, how can I *make* myself feel attracted to men who're good for me?" Carla looked at her expectantly. It was her turn. She had to say something.

"So." Cassidy tried to steady her voice, "what do you see as your options?"

ะ ะ ะ

After the first drink she started to relax, melting back into the crook of Zach's arm, where she fit very nicely once the rigidity had gone out of her spine.

"That's a good girl," he murmured, sliding his hand around to rest against the bare skin above her breasts. Normally, she'd have taken offense at being called a good girl. But tonight she was feeling too mellow. Tonight it felt good to be his good girl.

The singer was a sultry black woman in her thirties who bore some small resemblance to Diana Ross. She wore a long, black, sprayed-on dress covered entirely with sequins. Cassidy floated in an easy, tranced-out state, watching the muted spotlight flash off sequins, listening to the undulating voice croon, "I'm gonna love you . . . like nobody's loved you . . . come rain or come shine."

What an interesting idea . . . wonder what a come-rain-or-come-shine kind of love would be like . . . not just I'm-broke-I-need-you-babe . . . Somebody ought to invent a way to keep love going regardless of the weather.

They were seated in a black leather booth encircling a blood red table. The black and red upholstered room felt like the inside of a dark, pulsating womb. Approaching their table was a luscious teenager. *She can't really be a teenager . . . it isn't legal.* Zach ordered two more Jack Daniels. Tonight, it even felt good to have him order her drinks. She watched the waitress move away, her buttocks twitching under the skirt of a short, red, not quite see-through costume, and wondered how she could walk around in spike heels all night.

The singer finished a set and Cassidy separated herself from Zach's arm to applaud. Zach gave her a contented smile, his bronze face under fine, dark hair smooth and boyish. She had initially regarded his face as ordinary—bland even; now it seemed solid and stable.

"My prediction's coming true." His hands rested quietly on the table.

"What's that?"

"We won't have anything to talk about if we don't discuss the case."

"We can talk if you like. You feel like talking?"

"Doesn't matter. Okay, let's talk. You tell me about your family. You know all about my history and I don't know anything about yours. That's another way of keeping score, you realize. The person who tells all loses. The person who gets to keep their secrets wins."

She wrinkled her nose. "Tit for tat?"

"So you don't like talking about your family either?"

"I have to say, that's a pretty swift manipulation." She

blotted a wet ring with her cocktail napkin. "Okay, I'll talk. Only child. Father walked out when I was five. Mother, the helpless type, couldn't manage on her own. Moved in with my grandmother, who was widowed before I was born. Three generations of women together in the same crazy household. Married a younger version of my father. Got walked out on twelve years later. That's it. My whole history, more than you bargained for."

"What was your father like?"

"Lousy husband."

"Lousy father too?"

Cassidy put her elbows on the table and looked off at the nubile teenager as she slithered through the crowd balancing her tray. There were many things her mother never taught her.

"Not so bad, really." She moved her eyes back to Zach's easy-going face. "When he happened to notice me. He made me feel like . . . one of those fluffy, little lap dogs rich women fawn over."

The waitress brought their second round of drinks. "Okay, now it's your turn." She felt like Zorro, rapier poised.

"Uh, uh. Can't talk about my family. Remember the rules."

"This is about you. You said you don't want to get serious, and what I want to know is, how do you manage that? What do you do? Date ten different women at once?"

"I told you, I like having a regular bed partner. What I do is, establish a relationship with one woman and see her pretty exclusively until the warning bells go off. Then I move on."

"That sounds awfully hard on the woman."

He shrugged. "I never mislead anyone, never make promises or say things I don't mean."

"But that doesn't keep the woman from getting hooked. I see women all the time who've been devastated when some guy evaporates on them. You wouldn't believe how torn up they get."

His face creased momentarily. "Talking about this is not fun. Stop acting like a shrink."

"Okay." She took a sip of her drink.

"Come on back over here."

"Not just yet. I was feeling all warm and fuzzy, and then we started talking and my head clicked on again. It's going to take me a while to regain my mindless state."

The singer returned, leading off with *Stormy Weather*. Allowing the music to take her, Cassidy exhaled slowly, leaned back, and focused on the scintillation of light reflecting off black sequins. "Since you and I ain't together . . . it's been raining all . . . the ti-ime." She sipped at her drink, listening to the smoky voice caress the words. Gradually, she was able to tune out all the irritating static in her head and slide into that unmoored, unanchored, floating-in-outer-space feeling.

"Make it one for my baby . . . and one more for the road."

She eased into the hollow beneath his shoulder, and his hand returned to its place just below the jet beads at her throat. She pictured Honor's leathery chest and felt grateful for the moist warmth of his fingers against her skin. The waitress stopped at their table and Zach ordered a third round. She could hear her proper behavior voice saying, *One more drink and it's all over for you,* but the voice seemed muffled and far away, easy to ignore. One song slid into another. "Body and soul, you are the one . . . only you and you alone . . . " The drinks arrived and she continued sipping. Zach's hand toyed with the top button of her sundress, creating a flush of heat throughout her body. After a long time passed, after their glasses were empty and their bodies glued together, Zach placed his free hand on her chin, turned her head so it was close to his face, and delivered a hot, lingering kiss, his fingers all the while grazing along the top of her sundress.

"You want to come up to my condo? The view from the balcony's pretty spectacular."

❧ ❧ ❧

When the elevator door shut, Zach gripped her in a tight clutch as if fearing she might run away. At the forty-first floor, he led her by the hand into his apartment and out onto the balcony, showing her the startling constellation of dia- mond- bright city lights against the night-washed sky.

"How about some Grand Marnier?" He left her standing on the balcony and disappeared into the kitchen.

As soon as he was gone, the proper behavior voice reasserted itself. *You're drunk. You don't know what you're doing. Make him take you home.*

I don't want to know what I'm doing.

You can't do this. What about birth control? What about AIDS?

I don't have to think about those things because I'm

drunk and I don't know what I'm doing. Besides, Public Radio Voice is going to kill me any minute now so I might as well grab what I can before it's too late. No point worrying about AIDS when your life expectancy is about a week.

What if it's only mutilation? Remember all the times you've gotten on your soapbox about AIDS? If you're determined to go through with this, you have *to insist on condoms.*

She pictured the two of them lying naked in bed, she demanding condoms.

It's too embarrassing.

Zach returned with a large, cut-glass snifter half filled with amber liquid. He stood behind her and put an arm around her chest, pulling her back against him. He handed her the glass.

She dipped her tongue in it. It reminded her of a honey-whiskey-lemon drink her mother used to make when she was sick.

"What's wrong?" he asked, picking up the tension in her body.

"Nothing."

They stood against the railing, taking turns sipping from the same glass, and gazed at the high-rise lights in the sky, the herky-jerky cars on the streets, the black river flowing directly beneath them reflecting black light like black sequins on a dress.

"This the first time since your divorce?"

"Uh huh."

"No wonder you're nervous."

Swiveling around, she tucked her fingers into his waist-band and bumped her head against his chest so she could talk down at his feet. "There's something else."

"Are you about to break the mood?"

"Um hmm." *Oh shit. He probably thinks I'm going to say I have herpes. Or ask if he loves me.*

"Okay, what is it?"

"Oh, this is awful. I feel so dumb. But I've got to say it because I'm always telling clients they have to."

"That all? I thought it was going to be some kind of problem. It's okay. I've got condoms."

He drew her close, cradled her, rubbed his cheek against the top of her head. "It's all right," he said. "Everything's going to be all right."

They made love on his waterbed, which surprised her with its bouncy waves and slurpy sounds. She was awkward at first, then forgot to think about the way she looked, how she smelled, what she was doing. The movements came back, more easily because the linkage between them was so good. He moved with her the way a dancer moves with a partner he's been dancing with for years. She wondered if he was like this with everyone or if what was happening between the two of them was different. She'd have to remember to ask.

Afterwards, they sat up in bed and cuddled.

"This is when I miss cigarettes the most," he said.

"It's been such a long time. I'd forgotten how good it is."

"Don't know how anybody could forget."

"Makes it easier if you have to do without."

"Why've you been depriving yourself?"

She shrugged. "Too busy. Scared. Nobody I wanted to do it with. All the usual."

After a while she said, "It's going to be hard to put on my clothes and go home."

"You don't have to."

Her stomach tightened. "Yeah, I do."

"Why?"

"Well," she thought fast. "My cat's never been left alone overnight before."

He laughed. "You claim the cat as yours, you'll have to come up with a name."

"I'll put it on my list of things to think about."

25

MAGGIE'S CLIENT

Waking next morning to crisp, clear light and a long absent sense of well-being, she called her mother to suggest the two of them pick up sandwiches at the deli and drop by her grandmother's house for Sunday supper.

As the day progressed, her contentment gradually eroded. She caught herself darting glances at the phone and trancing-out in front of the window. When the time came to get her mother, she was glad she'd made a commitment that forced her out of the house.

Stopping for a red light at Chicago and Forest on the way to her mother's, she noticed, a little thrill of pleasure zipping across her chest, that a hunched, elderly man was seated in a folding chair on the northwest corner, a huge bouquet of red, yellow, and blue balloons floating above his head. Here it was June already, and this was the first she'd seen him. Every year she worried he might not be back. A rusted-out beetle parked next to him and a middle-aged white man wearing shoulder-length hair and an African dashiki hopped out. When she was a kid, Gran had regularly stopped to buy balloons. The swarthy Italian balloonman, old even then, had told Gran he was the third generation in his family to sell balloons on that same corner, and it made him sad to think that when he was gone, there'd be no one to take his place.

After picking up her mother, they stopped at Erik's and filled a sack with salads and sandwiches, then drove to her grandmother's bungalow in southwest Oak Park. They came up the walk toward her grandmother's bungalow beneath a wide-branched sugar maple as shadows lengthened across the lawn. Just as they reached the porch, Gran threw open the door. "My two favorite girls."

Dashing up the steps, Cassidy folded her arms around the old woman's birdlike body. Although Gran weighed no more than a hundred pounds, she was not the least frail. Her small-boned frame seemed as strong as a steel cable and she hopped around with the vitality of a robin in nesting season.

"How do you like my new hair?" Gran fluffed her tousled, red curls. "I call this my Orphan Annie wig."

"I think I like Hedy Lamar better," Cassidy said.

"You're so silly with those wigs," Cassidy's mother said.

"Oh, come on, Helen. It's harmless. Makes me laugh to wear these things around the house. You should try it. Just think of the fun in being able to choose different hair for every mood."

They went into the remodeled, southwestern-style dining room with its one peach wall displaying five Georgia O'Keefe posters. Cassidy and her mother began removing books, newspapers, and CD's from the bleached white table.

"You know, Cass, I got the idea from you, when you were explaining multiple personalities. It seems to me we all have lots of different personalities inside of us. Multiples are just people who take a basically good idea and go too far with it."

Cassidy washed off the table, Gran spread out the food, and they all sat down. Cassidy's mother glanced fondly at the other two. "I wish we could do this more often."

"It's a shame," Gran said. "We live so close. But we're so busy and all. It's hard to find the time."

"I can't keep up with either one of you." Helen put down her chicken sandwich. "Sometimes I feel like I should've started buying wigs or gone to college years ago, instead of cooking dinners and trying to keep track of my family."

"What you do is important too," Cassidy said. "Somebody has to make the phone calls."

"More Pepsi, anybody?" Gran held up a two-litter bottle, then refilled her own glass. "Last week I signed up to volunteer at Community Response. You know, the group that does stuff for AIDS patients? It's amazing how many we've got right here in Oak Park. You should sign up too, Helen, then we could do it together."

"Mother," Helen shuddered slightly, "how can you get involved with those people? Why, you might end up drinking out of the same glass or . . . or using the same toilet."

Cassidy pressed thumb and forefinger against her forehead and ground her back teeth.

"Well," Gran grinned at Cassidy, "how's your love life?"

Cassidy felt her cheeks get hot.

"You're up to something, I can see it," Gran crowed.

"She's got a secret," Cassidy's mother chimed in. She turned to Cassidy, "Maybe I've been an old crab about men. But I get . . . jealous. I don't want to share you. Especially with somebody who's just going to hurt you like Kevin and your father did."

"Oh, Helen, leave her alone." Gran blew a straw wrapper at her daughter. "Just because you picked a lemon doesn't mean they all are. Personally, I like men. In fact, I've been thinking of placing one of those personal ads. What do you think of this one? Old lady fart with youthful hair, out to spend all her money before she dies, seeking man young enough to keep up with her on the dance floor."

Cassidy laughed. "I love it. Why don't you let me put it in the paper for you?"

Gran dropped the remains of her sandwich, jumped up and went to rummage at her desk in the next room. She returned with an envelope which she handed to Cassidy. "I clipped some more of those cartoons for your refrigerator. Sylvia's the best, but Calvin and Hobbes is pretty good too."

Cassidy thanked her, then said, "You know how you've related stories about families sometimes and it's helped me understand clients better? Even though I can't tell you who the client is."

"You must hear such interesting gossip. It's a shame

you can't pass it on." A sparkle came into the faded eyes nested in wrinkles. "You got some family you want to hear the low-down about?"

Cassidy draped a napkin over her half-eaten food, hoping her mother wouldn't nag about cleaning her plate. "Can you remember anything at all about the Lawrence family? Especially Mildred and Martin?"

"The Lawrences . . . " her eyes slipped off into the past. "They traveled in a different circle from us, of course. They were bigwigs in town. Your grandfather earned a nice chunk of change manufacturing machines in that little shop of his, but we weren't North Oak Park at all. Still, I did used to hear things. Seems like the parents were gone a lot, off traipsing around Europe or something. And the two kids kind of raised themselves. She was a wild one, as I recall. She had what we used to call round heels. And her brother was always trying to keep her out of trouble."

Cassidy waited. When her grandmother did not continue, she said, "Thanks for the scoop. It helps to get a sense of history."

Gran's eyes were still focused on the past. "Seems like there was something else but I just can't get it back."

🙞 🙞 🙞

Cassidy practically pushed her mother out of the car in her eagerness to get home, but as she walked in the back door, anticipation turned to dread.

The cat sat erect on the green countertop, ears pricked, listening closely.

Cassidy crossed her arms and glared. "Most of the time

you could care less about what I have to say. The only reason you're so interested now is because it's about Zach and you have a crush on him."

The cat hunkered down and switched her tail, a wild look in her amber eyes.

"This afternoon I couldn't wait to get away from the phone because it wasn't ringing. Soon as I was gone, I couldn't wait to get back to check the answering machine. This is nuts."

Upstairs the red light was blinking three times. Her hopes zoomed. The first message was a woman interested in therapy. The second, a hangup. The third, a reminder from Maggie about lunch on Monday.

Okay, kiddo, time to face reality here. This is your classic no-win situation. If he does call, you'll feel terrific in the present and miserable in the future—when his alarm goes off and he dumps you. If he doesn't call, you'll feel miserable in the present and back-to-normal in the future. So, how do you want your pain? Small dose now or large dose later?

Morosely, she faced reality: the best thing that could happen would be for Zach to evaporate.

🐾 🐾 🐾

Monday at noon she rode her bike through mild spring sunshine to Erik's, wondering if she'd see Public Radio Voice again, and also wondering if having seen him in the first place was a symptom of paranoid schizophrenia.

You just want to convince yourself you're nuts because mental illness looks good in comparison to death or mutila-

tion.

She walked into Erik's, a heavy feeling in her stomach, and looked around for Maggie, who waved from a corner table. She filled her plate at the salad bar, then said to herself, *what the hell*, and loaded on a chunk of chocolate cake and chocolate ice cream. Whenever that heavy feeling was with her, all she wanted was chocolate.

She emptied her tray at Maggie's table and sat across from her. "So, what's going on with you lately?" She aimed her fork at the cake, ignoring the salad.

"Up to your old tricks again, are you?" In beige cotton shirt and pants, Maggie was plainly dressed except for intricate silver earrings that dangled to her shoulders.

Cassidy frowned, shaking her head.

"You just want to get me babbling so you can sit back and make therapist noises and get out of explaining yourself. When you avoid people, it usually means you're in some kind of lousy mood, and I want to know what's going on."

Cassidy clinked her fork down on the plate. "I don't know why I avoid things so much. Especially considering I always feel better after I've talked."

"So tell me." Maggie's widely spaced eyes, the color of Lake Michigan on a cloudy day, became quietly attentive. The best thing about Maggie was her stillness, which always came as a surprise because of the way she joked around.

Cassidy launched into a partial story, focusing on her failure to diagnose Ryan as a borderline and the likelihood that this had contributed to his suicide. She left out Zach and the investigation but spared no details regarding her own culpability.

"Cass, honey, we all—"

"Don't say it," Cassidy interrupted sharply. "Don't tell me all therapists sometimes fall in love with their clients. Don't pat me on the head and say, 'There, there'. The only reason I told you is, I trusted you not to come back at me with any reassuring claptrap. A man *died*, Maggie. And it was my fault."

Maggie cocked her head, earrings jangling. "You want to wear a hairshirt, is that it?"

"Considering the consequences, I think a hairshirt's entirely appropriate." *That's it, wallow. Crank up the guilt. You should've been a Catholic, you enjoy penance so much.*

"I've talked enough." Cassidy picked up her fork. "Now it's your turn. You have to talk so I can eat." She dived into the lump of soggy cake sitting in its puddle of ice cream.

"All I ever do is bitch and moan about my love life."

"Susie still giving you trouble?" Cassidy asked, talking around her food.

"These things never get better. She's so blessed possessive, I feel like I can't breathe. Sometimes I think we ought to go for couple's counseling."

"Why don't you?"

"'Cause I think if I'm a therapist, I ought to be able to solve my own problems. I can see what we're doing. We're caught up in the distancer-pursuer routine. But I can't break out of it."

"You're too close. It's the forest and the trees."

"And you know what else is weird? As a therapist, I absolutely believe that when two people have a problem, both are equally responsible. But here it is, my own situation, and I absolutely believe that it's all her fault. That if she'd *only change*, everything would be all right."

Cassidy laughed. "So why not give up on it? Start over with somebody else."

"You wouldn't have said that before your divorce. Now you think divorce is the answer. Straight women usually think it must be easier to work things out with a woman. I think it'd be easier with a man."

Cassidy regarded the plate of bright green spinach, orange carrots and red tomatoes with distaste. "Well, you're wrong. Men are every bit as difficult."

"What *is that* bitter note?" Maggie lifted one eyebrow, a trick, as she confided once to Cassidy, that she'd practiced in front of the mirror for hours when she was twelve.

Cassidy pushed back a tangle of hair that had fallen across her cheek. "I'm just sick of talking about men, that's all. I prefer loftier topics."

"You know they finally passed the gay amendment to the human rights doctrine? What a fight—but at least we won."

"Will it make a difference?"

"Makes me feel better. I like living in a place that says I've got rights too."

"I've always clung to the fond delusion that Oak Parkers are the good guys," Cassidy said. "I'd like to believe the red-necks and gay-bashers, the muggers and abusers all live some place else."

"Hah! The bashers and abusers are everywhere. Look at how many women clients we've both got who were abused as kids."

"Not just women."

"You're right about that," Maggie said. "I had a case recently where I'm certain the little boy was getting molested. Whole thing gave me the creeps."

"What happened?"

"Woman came to see me about a relationship problem. Sort of reminded me of Goldilocks—I never would've guessed she had a four-year-old. Anyway, she was seeing this older guy who wouldn't commit. She'd tried dating other men, wanted to make him jealous, nothing worked. So then she comes in a couple of weeks ago all hysterical because her son tried to talk the neighbor boy into giving him a blow job. She must've realized her kid'd been abused, but she wouldn't admit it. Insisted it couldn't have happened. All she wanted to do was deny the abuse so she didn't have to feel guilty."

That's what I've been doing—denying the suicide so I don't have to feel guilty.

"Have you seen her since?" Cassidy asked.

"Nope. She didn't show for her next appointment and she won't return my calls. My guess is, I'll never see her again. And meantime, I know there's this kid out there who's being abused. And this bitch of a mother who's shutting her eyes so she won't have to give up her boyfriend or feel guilty."

"You reported it, didn't you?"

"Sure. But what good will that do? You know how it is with Protective Services. They go in, do a quick once over, and determine it unfounded."

26

WHAT IF'S

Cassidy parked in front and hustled upstairs to check the machine. One message. She felt a rush of hope.

"Hi, honey." Her grandmother's perky voice. "It just came back to me, what I was trying to remember—at least, part of it did. But the memory's so fuzzy. I can't for the life of me remember when it happened, or any of the details. I had this friend, you see, who had a little boy, and she used to get somebody from the Lawrence family to babysit. Then one day she told me she'd never let that kid in her house again, and when I tried to find out why, she just clammed up. The problem is, I can't pin down who the babysitter was. Seems like it was somebody connected to Martin—Martin's son or sister or something—but he didn't have a son so I guess it had to be Mildred. It probably doesn't mean anything but that's what I remember."

It's beginning to appear that the Lawrences are one messed up family.

She saw Zach cradling her in his arms, whispering into her hair, "It's all right. Everything's going to be all right."

Sure it is, asshole. Everything's all right for you.

She allowed the cat to lead her downstairs, all the while telling her in an aggrieved tone about the sorry state of her food bowl. Weaving clumsily in her attempt to avoid stepping on the cat, who did circle eights around her legs, she stepped into the kitchen and glared at muddy paw prints leading across gray linoleum, countertop, sink and stove. "What is this, some kind of comment on my housekeeping? How the hell do you come up with all this mud— you don't even go outside?"

As punishment, she made the cat wait for lunch while she wiped down the kitchen. The cat's patience running out, Cassidy received a nip on the knee, which prompted her to relent and put food in her bowl. When the cat's stomach was filled, she leapt onto the counter and began her ablutions.

"So, what do you think? You think he's an asshole?"

Licking one paw, the cat scrubbed her face.

"I gather you're reserving judgment." Cassidy rinsed the dishrag and scrubbed at a muddy print on a cupboard door. "You think maybe he left a message and the machine ate it?"

The cat stopped washing and gave her a cold stare.

"Okay, I get it. You think I'm doing denial again. Refusing to see the handwriting on the wall."

The cat twisted around to wash her rear end.

"Power of suggestion," Cassidy muttered. "You probably think I'm an idiot, that I deserve exactly what I got. As any therapist should know, a man who has such a fucked up relationship with his mother is hardly a good prospect." She threw the dishrag in the sink. "You think I should come to my senses and simply accept the fact he's a jerk."

She poured ice water, drank some, and set the glass on the counter. "No, that's my mother talking. It doesn't make him a jerk if he's not interested. *'Everything's going to be all right'* cannot be translated into *'I want to have a relationship with you.'* The man has a right to not be interested."

The cat lapped water out of Cassidy's glass.

"But why isn't he interested? What did I do wrong?"

The cat's eyes turned to slits, her head nodded.

"You're bored. You don't want to hear about Zach any more. If he doesn't love us, you're just going to forget about him, right? And I should do the same."

❧   ❧   ❧

Cassidy, seated in her beige director's chair, was doing group therapy in the middle of Erik's while the lunch crowd ate at surrounding tables. Maggie, Susie, Zach, Yvonne and her son were sitting in a semicircle around her. They were all talking at once, except for Zach, who wasn't talking at all. They all expected her to solve their problems.

"Tell Susie I've gotta have more space," Maggie said.

"He did it," Yvonne accused, pointing to Zach. "He's the one." The child, who was on the floor clinging to his mother's skirt, began to scream.

She woke suddenly, not in her usual groggy state but

wide awake and alert. She jumped out of bed, put on her robe, and went down to make coffee. Only eight o'clock and the sunlight flooding through her kitchen window was hot already.

Zach had said he'd dated Yvonne a short time, then learned she was only going out with him to make some other guy jealous, some older guy who didn't want to commit. Maggie'd described her client as a cross between Goldilocks and Marilyn Monroe and also mentioned jewelry, which certainly matched Yvonne's description. Yvonne's son, who appeared to be about four, seemed disturbed. Yvonne could easily be Maggie's client.

Cassidy leaned against the counter, arms folded across her midsection, right fingers dangling. The cat stood on hind legs and bapped at her fingers.

Coincidences like this happened all the time. So what if Yvonne was Maggie's client? She set her mug on the counter, got out the envelope from Gran, and started taping up new cartoons in the blank spaces left by the ones she'd ripped off.

But what about the fact that Yvonne'd known so much Lawrence family history and Zach did not think the information'd come from him. Who else in the family might she be connected with? And then there were the similarities displayed by three little boys—Yvonne's son Chucky, Luke, and the five-year-old Ryan? Just a coincidence that two out of three blonde, blue-eyed boys about the age of five had been abused? While dark haired Zach escaped? And what about Luke? Didn't Ryan tell Scott, just before he died, that he was doing it for Luke? Did Ryan fear that the person who'd abused him might also abuse his son? The memory of Ryan's dream, in which Luke was being threatened on his fifth birthday, came rushing back.

She dropped the tape. The cat pounced and began bapping it around the kitchen.

How could the same man—it didn't have to be a man, women were abusers too—have gotten away with abusing blonde, blue-eyed boys for thirty-eight years?

This is too far-fetched. Now that you've dropped the psychotic break idea, you're trying to concoct a whole new fantasy to distract yourself from the anxiety of waiting for the mob to spring.

But what if Ryan's molester and Chucky's molester were the same person? What was the harm in talking to Yvonne? It would give her something to do while she waited out the rest of her life.

She saw herself at Yvonne's door. *"I just stopped by to ask the name of your son's molester."*

She took the tape away from the cat and put up a Sylvia strip in which a cartoon feline whose owner refused to get up and play at three a.m. complained, "What do you expect me to do, read a book?"

She wouldn't have to deal with problem number two—getting Yvonne to talk—until she solved problem number one—finding her. She couldn't ask Maggie for her client's name without an explanation. And if she admitted she wanted to go knocking on the woman's door, Maggie would be justifiably reluctant to pass on her name. If she were in Maggie's place, she probably wouldn't do it.

It would be easier to ask Zach, but she didn't want to

be the first to pick up the phone. If she called to ask for Yvonne's name, it would look like she was making an excuse to talk to him. And if she explained what she had in mind, he might not like it either.

The cat dunked her nose in Cassidy's mug and came up spluttering. Cassidy looked at her in exasperation. "Why do I have anything to do with those of you who go around sticking your noses where they don't belong?"

How could she possibly locate someone when all she had to go on was a first name? Call Maggie or call Zach or give up. She'd think about it later. She and Hamlet would've made a swell pair.

❦ ❦ ❦

"So you were at Colettes the other night and you ran into Roger. And what a surprise—his wife was out of town. He go home with you?" Noticing a piece of tape that had curled around on itself, Cassidy made a mental note to replace it after the session.

Michelle turned her dark, curly head to look out the window. Her jiggling foot increased its tempo. "We were just joking around. Having fun. It seemed like a good idea at the time."

"What happened afterwards?" Cassidy asked.

"What do you mean? Nothing happened." Her throaty voice crackled with irritation.

"Did he call? Tell you when he'd see you again? Say he was going to divorce his wife?" Cassidy picked brown leaves off the coleus and dropped them into the yellow plastic basket at her feet.

"No, of course not. I know better than to expect any of those things." Michelle folded plump arms across sequined chest and slumped down to sit on her spine.

"You slept with him last Friday night and the sex was great. How did you feel after he left? How do you feel now?"

"Not so hot." The words mumbled.

"You made any progress toward letting go?"

"I know, you think I should just stay away from him. But it's fun to flirt. If we enjoy a little fooling around now and then, what's the harm? I don't see any reason not to take—"

Cassidy stared past Michelle's head at bright green leaves covering branches of the small tree she'd planted last fall. *This gets so boring. What's the matter with her? She's bright enough in other ways. But when it comes to Roger, she's such an airhead. Week after week, she just happens to bump into him at Colettes, they just happen to go home together, and then she's got no idea why she's depressed all the time. What a bimbo.*

"And besides, who says his marriage is gonna last forever? If he's so fond of his little wifey-poo, how come he shows up by himself at Colettes all the time?"

Colettes. Oak Park's only upscale bar. Everybody with a taste for classy bars makes an appearance from time to time. Yvonne's definitely the Colettes type.

"So I don't see anything wrong with dropping around Colettes on Friday night—and if Roger happens to be feeling lonesome, so much the better."

"If it feels good, do it. That the idea?"

ха ха ха

Parking the Toyota about half a block from the entrance to Colettes, she turned off the key and clutched the steering wheel. Although fully dark, the street and entrance lights were bright enough to allow a clear view of people coming and going from the bar. Cool night air blew in through the window.

You can do this. Characters in mystery novels do this kind of thing all the time.

She got out of the car and marched inside. It was after nine on Thursday night and the lounge was crowded. Men in suits or sports jackets and women in business or evening wear occupied most of the stools surrounding the circular bar. She located an empty seat, hopped up, and scanned the room. Some of the people around the bar were paired but most were singles, women in groups of two or more and men by themselves. She was the only solo woman at the bar.

The bartender serving her section was a young blonde man with a body builder's overdeveloped arms and chest attached to a slender frame. He bounced from person to person, his engine zooming in high gear.

"What'll it be?" His eyes landed briefly on her face, then skipped off.

"A glass of white wine. But there's something else— "

"Chardonnay, chablis, white zinfandel?"

"Uh, chardonnay, I think. But what I wanted to say—"

He took off again. She glued her eyes to his whirling figure, determined not to let him get away when he brought her wine.

"Well." The voice spoke right in her ear, so close she had to jerk away. "Haven't seen you here before." A cozy baritone with a slight crackle to it, oozing warmth.

27

THE TOE CHEWER

She turned toward the man on the stool next to her, who was leaning over to talk in her ear. Around forty, slightly underdressed in an open-necked plaid shirt, chiseled face and unnerving dark eyes. He gazed straight at her, his eyes grabbing hold of her, forcing her to pay attention.

"I never come here on my own. I mean, I'm only here now because I'm trying to locate somebody." *Don't be nice.* It was hard to be openly rude. She had no experience in it.

"I'm here a lot," he said. "Bars may not be the best place, but it beats sitting all alone in an apartment. Sometimes I meet nice people, and I've got a hunch tonight's gonna be one of those lucky nights."

"No, you don't understand. I'm only here because I need information."

The waiter pushed a glass of wine in her direction, placed her tab in a clip on his side of the bar, and darted away.

"Wait . . . "

Like a hummingbird, he never stopped moving. He skillfully took orders, zipped tabs through the cash register, and served drinks, without allowing anyone to flag him down.

"Well," the man next to her continued, "name's Ralph. Work for the government, administrator more or less, and I'll bet you're a . . . let's see, I'll bet you're a teacher and this is the first time since your divorce you've gotten up the nerve to walk in a bar alone. Am I right?"

"Look, Ralph, I'm trying to find someone, so if you're a regular you may be able to help. Have you seen a woman named Yvonne? Very attractive, petite blond, long loose curls, wears a lot of jewelry?"

"Oh, sure. She comes around every so often."

"I need her last name."

"Can't help you there. Never been able to get near her, myself. Just yearn from afar. But let's not talk about Yvonne. Let's talk about you."

"Ralph, I'm sorry. I'm not available."

"So, what's your name?" He chuckled. "Tell me your name and I'll let you buy me a drink."

The bartender slowed down long enough to glance at her glass and she grabbed his hand.

"I need some information." Talking rapidly, she asked if he could help her find Yvonne.

"I'm just a substitute. But I'll have Geri talk to you

when she gets a break."

"Why're you looking for her?" Ralph asked, his breath warm on her neck. "You into girls or what?"

No wonder Michelle keeps going back to Roger, if this is the alternative.

Cassidy looked him in the eye. "I am not here to pick up anyone," she said forcefully.

"Consider it a bonus. You found somebody, you didn't even have to try. Now like I was saying . . ." His voice rattled on. He kept edging closer, undismayed by her refusing to make eye contact or crossing her arms over her chest.

This is like trying to pry myself loose from an octopus. Now I understand why so many of my single clients've given up on meeting men.

Eventually a lanky bartender with short, fluffy hair and wide, toothy smile stopped in front of Cassidy.

"C'mon, Ralph. The woman'll suffocate. Stand back, give her air."

Ralph chuckled, a bad boy who enjoyed getting caught.

"You gotta knee this guy in the balls to get him off you. He gets all over newcomers like stink on shit."

"I could tell subtle hints weren't working." Cassidy leaned across the bar to shut Ralph out of the conversation and described Yvonne.

"Oh yeah, I know who you're talking about. Can't miss her. She walks in the place, every eye's on her. The women want to kill, the men just want to. So—why you trying to find her?"

"I met her here a couple of weeks ago, and I've got a kid the same age as hers, and we made plans to get together except I lost the piece of paper I'd written her number on and I was supposed to call her only I can't find the number and so . . . " *Shut up. You're overdoing it.*

"Didn't know she had a kid," Ralph said.

" 'Course not." The bartender grinned at Cassidy. "She's too experienced to let a creep like Ralph glom onto her."

"About Yvonne. Can you give me her last name so I can look her up?"

"Wish I could help," the woman shrugged. "Yvonne's all I know. Most I can tell you is, she shows up for Friday Night Happy Hour on a regular basis."

🐾 🐾 🐾

Later that night Cassidy put on the Springsteen tee shirt that hung down to her knees, assumed a lotus position on the threadbare bedroom carpet and began deep breathing. After half an hour of flexing and stretching, she was still too wired to sleep, so she made a cup of herbal tea and settled into bed with her long overdue library book. She reread the same paragraph three times, then wiggled her toes under the lightweight blanket. The cat pounced.

"Ouch!" She jerked her foot away, reminding herself not to tease if she didn't want to be bitten. The cat tunneled under the blanket, creeping up to the edge and peeking out, entirely hidden except for pink nose and amber eyes.

"So, why did Zach lose interest? If he likes having a regular bed partner, he's probably not one of those guys who always runs out after the big seduction scene."

Mrup.

"Maybe I'm not so hot in bed. It's tough to figure how I rate in that department, since there's no way to do comparison studies. So maybe I'm lousy in the sack and nobody's ever had the heart to tell me."

The cat crawled out from under the blanket and stretched, forepaws extended, rump in the air.

"The worst thing about Zach not calling isn't the not-calling—it's the not-knowing why."

The cat curled up on her chest, her eyes gradually transmuting from cold amber to moist green. She rumbled contentedly as Cassidy stroked her back and scratched her ears.

"How do you do that with your eyes? Clients go through this same demented thought process all the time. What I always tell them is, you can't know what goes on inside another person's head and it's a waste of time guessing. Why is it so damn hard to take my own advice?"

Around midnight the cat, sleeping at the foot of the bed, abruptly raised her head and stared with ears pricked toward the open doorway leading downstairs. Cassidy laid her book down and strained to listen. All she could detect were distant noises from the wind and the street. Her heart started pounding.

The cat leapt down and sidled toward the stairs, her back slightly arched. Cassidy rose and pulled on her robe over the Springsteen tee shirt. She crept out into the hall, following the cat, and peered down the darkened staircase toward the landing where the steps veered off at a ninety degree angle. She stood frozen a very long time, listening to creaks, wheezes, and rattles from down below. One particular sound seemed to occur at regular intervals like footsteps. *Nobody could spend that much time walking around the living room.* The longer she listened, the more impossible it became to guess what the noises were or where they were coming from.

When the tension got so bad she couldn't stand it a second longer, she flipped on the hall light and cried out, "I'm calling nine-one-one. The police'll be here any minute." Then she stomped over to the phone and yelled into the receiver that someone was in her house.

She slammed the phone down, tromped back to the head of the stairs, and listened again. The sounds had not changed, so she marched downstairs, making as much noise as possible, and turned on the living room light. She checked the lock on the front door, then walked through the living room. Turned on the light in the dining room, walked through the dining room. Turned on the light in the kitchen, walked through the kitchen. Opened the office door, turned on the light. Checked the lock on the back door. No sign of an intruder anywhere on the ground floor.

She trudged to the open basement door, switched on the light, and looked downstairs. Creeping down to the landing, she peered around the corner into the sparsely lit, unfinished basement. Beyond the dim circle of light at the foot of the stairs, all she could make out were hulking, unrecognizable shapes emerging out of blackness. "The police are coming any minute." She scampered back up the steps.

Standing at the kitchen sink, she looked through her window into the unlighted window of the house next door. Nobody in her neighbor's kitchen. Nobody in her house.

She'd over-reacted to the hallucinations of a lunatic cat.

She fished the last peanut butter cup out of her handbag and as she gazed into the dark kitchen next door, slowly consumed every crumb.

She went back to bed and tried to blank out her mind, but the image of Zach holding her on the balcony, the sound of his voice saying, *Everything's going to be all right*, kept intruding. Without conscious intention, her hand picked up the phone on the nightstand. One ring. Two. Zach answered on the third, his voice groggy, and she hung up.

ə ə ə

An octopus with fanged tentacles grabbed her foot. She kicked it away, but it instantly clutched her foot with its other tentacle and bit down on her toe.

Oh, shit. Not now. This whole night is a waste . . . I'll be a wreck tomorrow.

As she propped herself into a sitting position, the cat quite predictably disappeared into her favorite spot under the desk. Cassidy crawled after her, dragging her out and depositing her on the other side of the door. She stumbled back to bed, hoping to slide into a dream uninhabited by octopus tentacles.

She was just dozing off when the lament began.

Mrowr! A loud, aggrieved tone.

Oh shit.

Mrowr! Mrowr! Mrowr!

Fully awake now, she opened the bedroom door. As the cat sprang inside, one hand grabbed scruff, the other wrapped tightly around her body. Even having her pinned with both arms, the cat's wildly flailing claws drew blood.

"That's it. I've had it. It's off to the pound with you tomorrow. I knew I'd be sorry for not listening to my mother."

She marched into the kitchen, heading for the open doorway leading to the basement. Stopped suddenly. Something was wrong. Her arms loosened their hold. The cat clawed free, leapt down, and disappeared.

28

COULD OF BLOWN

Gas. Coming from the basement. Whirling around, she grabbed the phone on the kitchen wall and dialed nine-one-one. She told the officer her basement reeked of gas and gave him her address.

"Anyone there in the house with you?"

"No."

"Go outside immediately. Do not take time to pack or do anything else. Your house could explode any minute."

She raced to the closet, put a raincoat on over her tee shirt, grabbed her handbag—wishing she had not finished off the Reese's—and ran out the back door.

Oh my God. The cat.

She bolted back to the doorway. "Here, kitty, kitty." Dashing into the kitchen, she looked frantically around. She darted through the dining room and living room, then ran upstairs, shouting all the way. She tore through the bedroom, got down on her hands and knees and searched under the desk. No sign of the cat. A distant whine of sirens. Rushing down to the kitchen, she checked all the corners, then looked up.

The cat was gazing down at her from the top of a seven-foot cabinet. Dropping her handbag, she grabbed a chair from the dining room and climbed up to pull the cat down, getting her face scratched in the process. She jumped off the chair and raced for the door. As she threw the screen door open, she nearly collided with a huge, black-shrouded figure in a Darth Vader mask. He yanked her outside and a policeman dragged her away. The cat screeched and went flying out of her arms. A horde of looming, alien figures strode into her house like storm troopers.

When they reached the curb, the policeman let go of her. "You didn't stay inside just to save that damn cat, did you? You crazy or something?"

She tried to respond but all she could get out was a stutter.

"I don't know why people get so stupid over their animals. You're lucky to be in one piece, you know that? The house could of blown."

The cop glared and she shrank into her skin. Red lights pulsated around her. Police radios spit out static, electronic music gone mad. Cars were still arriving, tires screeching as drivers hurtled up to the curb and slammed on brakes. She felt overwhelmed with the jittery throb of lights and the staccato soundtrack, as though she'd suddenly landed in a disco from hell. *The house could of blown, the house could of blown, the house could of blown.* The words repeated themselves in her mind like a chant to ward off evil spirits. This was not the way she'd envisioned it. She'd imagined Tony Chiparo slipping into her room at night and cutting her throat or shooting her in the head through one of the windows. But not her whole house blowing up.

How long had she been standing here gaping wordlessly like a lobotomy case? She wanted to explain to the cop, make him understand, but she couldn't get the words to come out right. He gave her a disgusted look and turned aside, muttering something about the cat. *Don't go! Stay here and protect me. Let me explain about the cat.* She opened her mouth and tried to say the words but her teeth started chattering and she had to clamp them shut. Odd, that her teeth were behaving so badly when, for the most part, she just felt numb. Except for an internal crackle, like electricity, arcing through her body.

Hugging herself and bouncing up and down on the balls of her feet, she watched the sky behind her house gradually lighten. Neighbors wandered over and spoke to her. She responded but had no idea what she said. Cops and firemen clustered and reclustered on her lawn. A gas company van pulled up and a gray uniformed man went into her house. Cops drifted away, getting into cars, slamming doors. She watched it all happen but not from inside her body. The part that watched seemed to be somewhere overhead, a vantage from which she could look down and observe herself observing the scene.

Two cops and a fireman approached. The fireman,

divested of his long black coat, his mask and boots, looked like a teenager who'd been out partying all night. "Seemed like the leak was in a strange place."

The sound of his words, which struck her ears as unnaturally loud, jolted her back. She realized how utterly exhausted she was. All she could think about was finding a place to collapse.

"We're havin' trouble figurin' it out." One of the cops, a middle-aged black man with a bald head and round wrinkled face, rubbed his forehead.

"Can I go back in now?" Cassidy swayed on her feet, arms dangling at her sides.

"Soon as we're done," replied the other cop, who was long and gangly and probably played basketball in a previous life. "Thing is, the leak was coming from this flexible hose behind the dryer and those hoses usually don't break. You got any idea how this could've happened?" His face drooped over hers like a giant sunflower, squinting down from his seven-foot height. Cassidy felt child-like standing next to him.

"Can't imagine." *Tell them the mob's out to get you,* her proper behavior voice shrieked. But her body, an empty shell, was too drained and lifeless to comply.

"You been movin' the dryer around? Cleanin' behind it?"

Cleaning behind the dryer? What a strange idea "I really don't have any idea . . ."

"Thing is," the basketball player continued, "this is on the suspicious side. If you didn't do something to cause it, we're wonderin' if somebody might've cut it on purpose."

"We're thinkin' maybe we need to write up a report," the black cop said.

Tell them somebody's trying to kill you. "I'm sure that won't be necessary. It's an old machine. These things happen."

The two cops regarded each other uncertainly. "Well, if you're sure . . . "

"You don't know what a close call you had," the fireman said. "Next time the water heater would've ignited—kablooey."

"I appreciate the way you've handled things." She shifted her weight from one foot to the other. "But I'm totally wiped out. I've got to work tomorrow . . . I mean today . . . and all I can think about is grabbing an hour's sleep."

When everyone finally left, Cassidy went inside and started upstairs. Then she remembered having last seen the cat peering out from the bushes in front of the house. Dragging herself back down to the porch, she stood in the doorway and called. The cat raced up to the foot of the steps, then circled slowly. The message was clear—*I'm not sure if I want to come back to you or not.*

Cassidy closed the door, lay down on the couch for five minutes, then got up to open it again. The cat marched through, tail erect.

"Okay, so I won't send you to the pound. At least not today. But don't let it go to your head. A Doberman would've devoured Public Radio Voice before he ever got to the hose."

Early Friday evening, Cassidy sat in one of the booths lining the wall at Colettes. Nearly empty when she arrived, the bar was filling rapidly. The majority of people who walked in the door were members of the club. A handful were strays, people who sat alone and avoided eye contact.

When Ralph came swaggering in, Cassidy scrunched back in the corner of her booth. She watched him work the room, moving from person to person with his eager smile and raucous laugh. He appeared to delight in seeing how far he could go before people turned their backs on him. His eyes fastened on her from across the lounge and he came straight over.

"You're back," he boomed. She saw smirks on the faces of some of the women who'd undoubtedly undergone a similar hazing upon first joining the Colettes' Happy Hour Fraternity.

"Do not sit," she instructed as he plopped down across from her.

"Regretted the missed opportunity, did you?" he said, breaking out in his rich chuckle.

"C'mon Ralph, give me a break. I already went through this once."

"I don't get it. You women complain all the time there aren't any men around."

"You left out the qualifier. That's 'good' men. There aren't any *good* men around."

"That's the problem. You're all so picky."

She looked him coldly in the face. "Keep moving."

Being rude's not as hard as I thought.

When the waitress came around, Cassidy ordered a glass of chardonnay and sipped slowly. By the time Yvonne made her entrance, the glass had long been empty. Yvonne had on a cream-colored silk sheath, creating a subtle foil for her display of gold and diamonds. Seeing her waft into the room, Cassidy was reminded of Richard Cory, the man who glittered when he walked. Heads did not exactly turn, but that was the overall effect.

Unlike most of the regulars, Yvonne did not make the rounds. She went directly to an empty stool and sat down. After a short time, a man disengaged from the woman he was talking to and drifted over to take the stool next to hers. Another man made a similar progression, ending up in a hovering position behind her shoulder.

Cassidy observed Yvonne in operation for close to an hour, then slipped out and returned to her Toyota. She pulled a peanut butter cup out of her handbag and nibbled slowly.

Three candy wrappers had accumulated on the floor before Yvonne emerged from the bar, walking out with a man on each arm. Cassidy held her breath, waiting to see if either of the two would make off with her. The three-some stood and chatted in front of the entrance while Cassidy tapped her foot on the floor. At last the group broke up, each of them heading off in a different direction.

Cassidy put her hand on the ignition key. Yvonne strolled off toward a white Porsche parked on the opposite side of the street, about a block's distance from the Toyota. The Porsche engine turned over, and moments later Yvonne's car went zipping past. Cassidy pulled a fast U-turn just in time to see the Porsche turn left three blocks ahead of her. She followed Yvonne to a two-story frame house in south Oak Park, then waited as the blonde parked in the attached garage.

If Kevin could see me now. I never imagined the day would come that I'd wish I'd taken lessons. Where's the master of scam now that I need him?

Cassidy rang the bell. The door opened a crack, revealing a narrow sliver of Yvonne.

"Remember me?" Cassidy gushed, slurring the words slightly. "We met on Village Day. I was with Zach, remember? I saw you tonight at Colettes and I just had to talk to you. I won't make any trouble, I promise."

Slowly the door widened. Yvonne's face, creased in bewilderment, became visible in its entirety. "I don't think I . . ."

"The reason I followed you home is, Zach's driving me crazy. And I thought, well, it's obvious you two know each other pretty well. I figured you probably know him better than I do, and I just had to ask . . . Look, this is really hard. Could I come inside? I'm not dangerous—I'm just a girl who's going nuts because of a guy who's jerking her around."

"I guess we've all been there," Yvonne said, opening the door and allowing Cassidy to enter.

Yvonne's living room surprised her. It was oddly mismatched, the gold and gray not quite harmonizing, the furniture an incoherent mix of styles. Cassidy plopped down on a worn, low slung sofa and put a droop into her body.

"God, I feel so stupid. Look, I know I'm imposing but—

You have anything to drink?"

"Well . . . " Yvonne hesitated. "I guess we could have a glass of wine. Wait here, I'll be right back."

Yvonne returned with two glasses of blush wine, handed one to Cassidy and sat down across from her. "Now," she said briskly, "what's bothering you?"

"Zach and I—we've been seeing each other for awhile now. At first, everything was wonderful. I started thinking, this is it. And then, just about the time we bumped into you at Village Day, Zach started backing off. All of a sudden, I'm not seeing him Saturday nights any more, he isn't calling so much. I asked if there was someone else and he said there wasn't, but I couldn't help wondering . . . "

Yvonne gave her a bemused smile. "Don't worry, it isn't me."

"I wouldn't blame you if it was. He's the one I'd be pissed at, not you." Cassidy sat up straighter and pushed the hair back from her face.

"Believe me, I haven't talked to Zach since Village Day."

"I figured, if you were the one, it was all over for me. There's no way I could compete."

Yvonne nodded, acknowledging the validity of Cassidy's statement.

Cassidy stopped herself from clenching her jaw and made her face take on an admiring look. "It must be so different for you. You could have anybody you want. How do you ever choose?"

"It's not that different." Yvonne leaned back and crossed her sleek legs, providing a clear view of thigh under the short skirt. "It's the same for me as anybody else. When it clicks, that's the one."

"Know what you mean." Cassidy leaned back, mirroring her as she did with clients. "The problem is, when it clicks for me it never clicks for the guy. I keep getting hooked on jerks like Zach who make me crazy. I always figured somebody gorgeous like you wouldn't have that problem." She drained her glass and held it up. "I know I'm a terrible pest, but would it be possible . . . ?"

"Sure. I'll go get the bottle." Yvonne brought a half gallon of Almaden white zinfandel out of the kitchen and refilled both their glasses.

"So tell me," Cassidy said, "with your looks and all, do you really run into this kind of problem?"

"They're all the same animals, aren't they? They come on strong at first, panting down your neck, can't get enough. But once they've got you, you're day-old bread."

Cassidy laughed, moving in sync with Yvonne as she sipped her wine. "My problem is, I always get hooked. I know Zach's jerking me around. But when it comes right down to it, I can never walk away."

Yvonne twisted a long, blonde curl around her finger. "I'm feeling kind of stuck in the same place."

Cassidy set her glass on the scratched mahogany end table and laced her fingers across her stomach. "This guy you're hooked on, he must really be something if you can't just snap your fingers and get somebody better to come running."

"At first, he was all over me and I was only going along because I thought he could help me out. I've been trying to break into TV—commercials, you know—and this guy has connections. So at first, it was just a lark. It was exciting for Chucky and me to spend the weekend in the city with him. Then I started liking him more and more. And he sort of stopped with all the special little touches. Now I'm the one wants to make it permanent, he's running in the opposite direction." She shrugged. "They're all such jerks. The only way you ever win is to turn off your feelings and never let them get under your skin."

Cassidy raised her glass. "I'll drink to that. But at least it sounds like your guy is around on a regular basis. You and Chucky go to his place every weekend?"

A bitter look came over her tiny, perfect face. "Not any more. Lately, he's away on business all the time. But I don't think I believe it's really business."

"That sounds like what I'm going through. I've got a kid too, just a little older than yours. It's so damn hard to worry about the kid all the time and try to keep a relationship going at the same time."

"My guy doesn't mind kids." A muscle twitched next to Yvonne's eye. "He always tells me to bring him along."

Cassidy lowered her voice. "I dated this guy once. He was real friendly to my kid." One knee started up a slight, jittery dance. "And it turned out—this is hard to admit but I feel I can trust you—it turned out he was fooling around with my son."

Yvonne's face paled. "It's not like that with . . . I know this guy I'm seeing wouldn't do . . . " She took a large swallow of wine. Her voice dropped to a hush. "But you know something? This is really freaky . . . somebody actually turned in a report on me to DCFS and this social worker came out and investigated. It was so embarrassing."

"I'd die," Cassidy said.

"Well, it was unfounded, of course. I mean, I knew there couldn't be anything to it. He'd never do anything like that."

"How can you be sure?" Cassidy asked softly.

"Well, I just know . . . He's not that kind of person." A frightened look came over her face and when she spoke again, her voice was so low Cassidy wasn't sure she heard the words correctly.

"If he did do it, if he thought I knew about it, I think he might . . . "

Her large, darkly fringed eyes flew to Cassidy's face. She stood up suddenly. "Who are you, anyway? I don't know a thing about you. Why are you here, asking me these questions?"

Cassidy jumped up, raising her hands palms out. "I didn't mean to ask any questions. I was just telling you what happened to me." She grabbed her bag and started backing toward the door.

"I want you out of here. Get out right now."

"Yvonne, I'm sorry, I didn't mean . . . "

"Get out of my house."

29

CATNIP MOUSE

Cassidy opened the refrigerator, checked out the nearly empty jug of wine, and slammed the door. She reread a Bucket's cartoon in which the mother says, "I've shifted my parental role from giving my kids a perfect childhood to limiting the stuff they're going to tell a therapist." The cat appeared in the kitchen, but instead of jumping on the counter to talk, zoomed to the door and demanded to get out, as she had several times now since her escape on the night of the gas leak. Cassidy tried to ignore her but the yowls grated on already twitchy nerves, forcing her to relent.

She stood at the back door for a moment, watching the cat chase fireflies in the dusky yard. After ten on Saturday night and nothing she wanted to do. She got out an unopened bag of Reese's and went to sit on the front porch. The family across from her had come out to enjoy the windless, cooler than usual mid June weather. Not a whisper from the chimes, nothing but high-pitched shrieks and giggles, touching off a pang of loneliness inside her chest.

Who abused Ryan? Same person who's abusing Chucky? What's the connection between the abused boys and Ryan's death?

She unwrapped her first peanut butter cup.

She could not think of a single way to find answers. She'd followed every possible lead, had no place to go from here.

So what? You've already exceeded your life expectancy. Just because he didn't get you with the gas leak is no reason to think Public Radio Voice is going to quietly slink away.

She nibbled another peanut butter cup. Sirens wailed down Austin Boulevard.

The way she was feeling over Zach, what difference did it make? When Kevin left, she thought she'd hit the all-time bottom. And here she was, right back in the sub-basement again.

Images started popping into her head. Her father packing to leave. Kevin demanding a divorce. Zach holding her, saying everything would be all right. A hard knot formed in her stomach.

She went upstairs and dialed Zach's number. She counted rings, picturing him in bed with another woman. His machine clicked on.

"This is Cassidy. We have to talk."

🙟 🙟 🙟

The phone rang around noon the next day and she picked up at her desk. Zach came on the line, voice unusually subdued.

"Where were you last night?" *Oh shit. That was not cool.* "Wait, scratch that. That's not what I intended to say." A pause. "But . . . where were you?"

Another long pause. She took a pen out of the pink flowered mug and scribbled dark circles on a client insurance form.

"I was out." He waited a beat. "Listen, I know it's stupid to say this now, but . . . I really was going to call."

"You just didn't get around to it."

"Yeah, I know. I've been acting like a jerk, but I do want to talk. After you understand what's been going on with me, maybe we can try again."

Remember Kevin? All those times you were 'understanding'? All those second chances?

"What did you have in mind?"

"Thought maybe I'd come over tonight. I've been missing your cat."

"I probably shouldn't let you near me."

"Probably. But you're going to have to make that decision for yourself."

A long silence. She drummed fingers on the wine bottle, not yet half filled. At this rate, even McDonald's would be out of her price range. "What time?"

"Eight o'clock?"

🙟 🙟 🙟

Zach arrived with bottle of champagne, bag of peanut butter cups and catnip mouse. They settled on the porch with ice bucket and glasses. The cat, demonic gleam in her eye, rolled over on her back, clutched the mouse with her front paws, and kicked it to death.

Zach popped the champagne, the cork shooting to the far end of the porch. Dropping the mouse, the cat captured the cork and scooted into the house. He filled glasses, clinked his against hers. "Here's to working something out." Kevin's voice echoed in her mind—*To love, money and the good life.*

"That's vague enough to cover almost anything."

He put his hand on her bare knee. "I want you to understand why I didn't call."

She removed his hand. "*Understand's* a code word for *sucker.*"

He rubbed his jaw. "Must've reached for the phone a dozen times, then I'd realize I didn't know what to say."

"You could've called and told me that."

"I'm not as good at this as you are. Last time I tried to tell anybody what was going on in my head was when Mildred forced me to see a shrink. And then I didn't really try, just bullshitted my way through."

It had turned hot again, but a breeze from the windows kept air moving on the porch. The rustling of trees and clinking of wind chimes merged, a pleasant background murmur.

"So what is it that's too hard for you to tell me."

"The way I feel about you. I've never felt this way before and I don't know what to do with it. Sometimes I think I should just dive in, just go with it. Then I remember what happened with Lisa. I felt really crummy walking out on her like that, and I'm afraid I'd end up doing the same with you."

The cat landed in his lap, carrying the mouse in her teeth. Wagging her head furiously, she shook it to death.

"Did you feel the same about Lisa as you do about me?"

"I just told you, I've never felt this way before."

"How is it different?"

"God, I hate those therapist questions. I feel like I'm sitting in your office." He shifted away from her on the couch, disrupting the cat who dropped her mouse and flew across to the plastic chair, knocking the magazines to the floor. "How is it different? With Lisa, it was fun. We liked doing the same things. The sex was great. But she wasn't important to me. When she wasn't around, I didn't think about her. When I'm with you, half the time I'm aggravated as hell. It's too soon to tell about the sex. And you ask the most irritating questions of any woman I've ever known. But you make me think about things. You stir things up. And when I go for days without talking to you, I don't feel right."

"It must be love," she said wryly, picking up his hand and putting it back on her knee.

"So, the reason I've been fighting with myself is, I want to say—let's see if we can make this thing work."

She sat very still, holding her breath.

"But I don't know whether I can stick it out. When I look into the future, all I can see is me leaving. And if that happened, I'd feel twice as bad as before and it'd also be hard on you. I want to find out if I could change enough to stay in a committed relationship. But I've got this voice inside me saying it's impossible, I'll never be able to do it." Shrugging, he took his hand off her knee and refilled both their glasses. The last tint of rose above the trees was darkening into bluish haze.

The cat hid the mouse under a magazine lying face down on the floor, then raced around the porch, zooming from one side to the other. Screeching to a halt, she dug the mouse out, held it down with her paws, and tore at it with her teeth, biting it to death.

Cassidy's neck tightened. "You haven't even asked whether or not I give a damn."

"Do you?"

"Yes. But I prefer to be asked."

"I know, I'm arrogant and cocky. A presumptuous sonuvabitch. But I'm sure you'll be able to straighten me out."

She grinned. "Just watch me."

"Does that mean you want to take a chance on this thing?"

"No. At least, I'm not ready to sign on the dotted line just yet. I still find *this thing* a bit vague. I believe it's safe to assume you're not proposing marriage. You also don't seem to be telling me to get lost. But there're a lot of possibilities in between."

"I wish I had a nice clear picture." He thought for a moment. "Okay, how does this sound? I'd like to try having a relationship, with the understanding it's going to take some time to find out whether I can get comfortable with the idea of commitment. I'll do my best, but until I know for certain, there won't be any guarantees."

No guarantees. Never any guarantees. I'll do it as long as it feels good, and when it doesn't, I'm outta here. Wasn't there ever going to be a come-rain-or-come-shine kind of offer?

She watched the cat rolling around on the floor with her mouse.

"Where were you last night?"

He looked embarrassed. "I went out with someone I met a few weeks ago. I did not go to bed with her. I think I was testing myself to see whether I could go back to dating other women and be satisfied."

Her back stiffened. "I need some time."

"Sure." He put his arm around her shoulders and leaned his head over so it was touching hers. "Come up with a name for her yet?"

"Finding a name for the cat's at the bottom of my list."

"Look how seductive she is when she rolls around. How about Jezebel? Zsa Zsa?"

"She is not just a sex object."

They finished the champagne. Zach kissed her and said, "Why don't I stay tonight?"

The heat was coursing through her body. She wanted to say yes. "I've got to think, and if you stay I won't be able to."

"Okay." He stood and pulled her to her feet and held her in a comforting hug. "I almost forgot to mention— Mildred called the other day and invited the two of us over for a chat. Acted like it was her idea. What night sounds good?"

She suddenly remembered that severe consequences were overdue. Maybe she ought to let him stay. *Don't make it too easy. Better to hold out.*

"Set it up with Mildred for tomorrow."

ka ka ka

She awoke the next morning with a warm dreamy feeling. She went downstairs and fed the cat, who gobbled her food, then bounded up on top of the refrigerator to stare down with cool amber eyes.

She remembered the dream in which the cat was perched on the mantle, advising her to run for her life. "This is not a telepathic message from the cat. This is my subconscious warning me about Zach. It's telling me to run like hell. But what does my subconscious know?"

The cat flattened her ears, swished her tail.

"I thought you were in love with him too. You certainly acted like you were in the throes of love or some other form of mental illness last night, the way you were rolling around showing your tummy."

Your cat has better sense than you do. Zach told you straight out that when he looks into the future he sees himself leaving. But you—you're off and running again, hearing only what you want to hear, ignoring reality.

She drove down to the lake and sat on a boulder. Stabbing glints of light reflected off the surface, a cool breeze blew in her face. Gradually the slosh of water and roll of waves quieted the debate in her head.

ka ka ka

She pulled up by her gate around noon, glanced out the

car window and saw the cat sitting on the mat outside the back door, looking much the same as the night she'd first appeared. *Who let her out?* Cassidy sat behind the wheel and tried to think. No sign of the gray Datsun. No green Mercedes or black sedan. Was someone waiting in her house? How could she avoid walking in and having Public Radio Voice or Tony Chiparo knock her over the head? Her mind totally locked up, refusing to provide a single escape. So, lacking a better alternative, she got out and plodded up to the porch, where she was greeted enthusiastically by the cat.

The door was unlocked. She inched it open. She could hear a familiar male voice booming from the kitchen. Throwing the door wide, she raced around the room divider to see Kevin and Phil lounging in her kitchen. *First Zach, now Kevin. Next thing you know, you'll walk in and find your father asleep on the couch.*

"What in God's name are you doing here?"

"Waiting for you, darlin'." Kevin leaned against the worn countertop piled with dishes from the past two days, a thick sandwich and glass of milk close at hand. The smell of tuna fish was in the air. "Looks like you haven't improved your culinary skills one bit. How do you expect to catch yourself another husband with such a poorly stocked larder?"

"Are you nuts? Have you gone totally psychotic?"

Kevin, raising his brows quizzically, exchanged looks with Phil. "She always was a tad on the hysterical side."

"Will you tell me what's going on here?" she demanded.

"We came to thank you." Phil ducked his head and

looked at her from under his brows like a kid expecting a scolding. He was leaning against the counter on the other side of the sink with a sandwich and milk at his elbow.

Kevin beamed his most radiant smile, raising her blood temperature by a couple of degrees. "You bonny girl— you've always been my one true love. I knew you'd never allow the vultures to peck old Kevin's bones."

"Are you telling me I don't have to be in a panic that a hit man is any minute going to pick off all three of us right here in my kitchen?"

"Why bother to kill us now they've got their money?" Phil asked.

"They've got their money?"

Kevin wagged his head. "Poor girl, the excitement's too much for her."

"You paid them?" she asked.

"No, darlin'. You did."

"This is crazy. Why would I want to save your sleazy hide?"

Kevin turned his lopsided grin on Phil. "Now I get it. She doesn't want me to figure out she's still carrying the torch."

Let him think you did it. Let him think he owes you.

"Spell it out," she said slowly. "How did you find out? How reliable is your source?"

"This guy I know dispenses information. Last time I checked in with him, he told me the bounty'd been removed from my head."

"And your informant said I bought them off?"

"You got it, babe."

"So you just dropped by to express your gratitude?" She cocked her head in disbelief. "You're not here to hit me up?"

"Au contraire." He shook his head. "You should be ashamed, thinking such nasty thoughts. Just to prove I know when I'm beholden', I brought you this small token of appreciation."

She planted herself in the middle of the kitchen, about a yard from Kevin, mouth compressed, arms crossed.

From his pocket he withdrew a diamond pendant on a long gold chain. Holding it up dramatically, he lowered it around her neck and fastened the clasp.

"You ripped this off from your girlfriend, I presume. The one who provided you with a hideout—unbeknownst to her."

"It's not nice to ask where presents come from."

She touched the diamond, which was finer than any piece of jewelry she'd ever owned. "You figured I'd refuse to accept, then you could take it and sell it. But you'd still win points for making the offer."

"You've got a nasty suspicious mind, love."

"Thank you, Kevin, for the lovely present." She stood on tiptoes, brushing her lips against his. "I'll treasure it always."

Phil chortled. "Looks like you guessed wrong this time, guy." He picked up his sandwich, gave it a loving look, and stuffed the remainder in his mouth. Cassidy, who'd always considered watching him eat slightly obscene, averted her eyes.

"Can't win 'em all," Kevin responded cheerfully. "Oh, and by the way," he continued, trying to sound casual, "I hear you've been hanging out with some new guy. Zach something-or-other."

"Oh? How'd you hear that?" She kept her face neutral, although an interior smile was warming her insides.

Phil thunked his plate down on the counter and wiped a pudgy hand across his mouth. "Some guy named Zach left a message on your machine. Said he'd pick you up at eight tonight."

Cassidy disciplined her face to appear shocked. "You listened to my messages? You leave me for some bimbo and then you've got the nerve to come back here and ... " *He's actually jealous. Sometimes fantasies do come true.* If she'd been alone, she would've done a little tap dance.

Kevin gave her a sidelong look. "So who is this character, anyway? He had a taste of your moralizing yet?"

Smiling coyly, she fluttered her lashes.

"Well, Phil me boy, it's time for us to be moving. There are other, more appreciative lasses. Womenfolk who know how to show a man a good time and would be willing to cook a meal on occasion."

Phil shoved his floppy yellow shirt down into his pants and hitched up his belt.

Kevin stopped in front of her, just inches away. "Well, darlin', it's been interesting but it's time for us to split. Give us a kiss for luck?"

"Ummm . . . not this time."

As they started for the door, she remembered that there was one more piece of information she needed.

"Kevin?"

He turned around.

"When did you hear about it—that the mob got paid off?"

"Last week. Thursday afternoon."

"You're sure about that?"

He thought for a moment. "Yeah, it was Thursday. I remember taking out the calendar and counting up the days we'd been holed up and the last one was a Thursday."

30

GOOD NEWS, BAD NEWS

"The gas leak happened after the payoff to the mob." Cassidy filled the dishpan with hot soapy water and reached for Kevin's milk glass. The cat, having instantly come out of hiding when the men left, had taken up her favorite spot on the counter and now was trying to cajole Cassidy into throwing out her barely-touched food and replacing it with something better.

"Either Public Radio Voice has lost his grip—or someone else cut the hose." A creepy feeling started in her stomach. She remembered the whispery voice on her machine after Chiparo's session.

The cat nuzzled her hand.

"You're just sweet-talking me so I'll feed you. But this is important. If I don't get this figured out, you might have to go live with my mother. How'd you like that?"

Sticking a paw in her dishwater, the cat jerked it out, splattering drops of water.

Cassidy inserted a can into the electric opener, her hands shaking so badly it took two tries to get the lid off. "So who is it? Who besides the mob could possibly want to kill me?" She set the cat food on the counter and stared out the window. "The answer is obvious." The cat nibbled around the edges of the can. "And it's good news, bad news, just like everything else. Good news Zach wants a relationship, bad news it's a no-strings, no-guarantees kind of deal. Good news the mob's no longer trying to kill me, bad news someone else is. Good news we were right in thinking Ryan was murdered, bad news the murderer's now after me."

The cat nudged the can off the counter onto the floor, then hopped down to lick up the spilled food. Cassidy wiped cat food off her legs and went upstairs, leaving the cat to clean up.

She sat at her desk fingering the chipped corner. She had to find out what happened on Ryan's fifth birthday. She knew of three adults who'd attended his party. If she could question all three, would their stories match? She could track down Jerry Moran through the phone book. Later tonight she'd get a crack at Mildred. The toughest would be Martin, neither weird enough to talk to strangers nor subject to blackmail.

How to get to Martin? As she doodled on unopened envelopes, a number of wild schemes came and went in her head, until finally an idea surfaced that wasn't totally crazy. Not more than fifty percent. She called in a favor from Kristi, persuading her to phone Martin at his office and check on the time he'd be home tonight. Kristi agreed to do it, no questions asked, reporting back promptly that Martin expected to arrive at his condo around six.

Cassidy's plan also required one prop, which she carefully prepared and stowed in her handbag. Although her usual M.O. did not include dressing for success, she decided that in this instance the situation warranted it. *Martin's sharp. I won't be able to pull this off if he thinks I'm a flake.* She picked a simple black dress and purple jacket, even going so far as to brush off the white cat hair. Then she headed across Chicago toward the address listed for Jerry Moran. Jerry first, then Martin.

   ~ ~ ~

Cassidy studied the square plate beside the heavy wooden door. Two of the buttons were labeled with printed names; a third had a scrap of paper with a handwritten name taped up next to it. The remaining two were unidentified. Since none of the names on the buzzer was Jerry Moran, one of the mystery buttons had to be his. She knew he was home. She'd phoned, hanging up when she heard his Hello.

She punched one of the unlabeled buttons. Her palms were damp, more from nerves than the late afternoon sun, tempered here in the city by a brisk lake breeze. A McDonald's bag skittered past her feet. She pressed the other unlabeled button.

"Who is it?" Even with the staticy distortion of the

inter-com, she recognized Jerry's mumbly voice.

"Cassidy McCabe. We met at Ryan's wake."

"What do you want?"

"I'm a friend of Zach's." A skin-headed twenty-year-old wearing a vest with no shirt and cowboy boots paused on the sidewalk to give her a long, menacing stare.

The door buzzed and she pushed it open. She crossed a gloomy foyer smelling faintly of urine, then started up a narrow flight of stairs. *What're you doing? It's crazy to go up there all alone.* She forced herself to keep moving, although the air was so heavy she could barely fill her lungs. When she reached the top of the second flight, Jerry was standing in a doorway adjacent to the landing, leaning against the frame. His heavily lidded eyes flicked across her face, then dropped to her feet. "What's Zach got to do with anything?"

She took a step closer, hoping he would back up and let her inside. He smelled of cigarettes and unwashed clothes. "Zach and I are trying to piece together Ryan's childhood. We think it has some bearing on his death, which, by the way, we're not convinced was suicide."

He looked surprised. "Who knows, maybe not. A lot of guys were just as happy to see him blown away."

"And your name's at the top of the list. Now why don't you let me come inside so we can talk?"

He dropped his bony chin onto his chest. "Why should I?" he mumbled sulkily.

"You may not know it, but somebody tried to kill me. And if that's not enough, then because Ryan and Zach both had pretty shitty childhoods. You were the parent—it was your job to take care of them and you didn't do it. And even though it's too late for Ryan, if we can piece together what happened, it'll help Zach deal with it."

When logic fails, there's always guilt and confusion.

"All right," he sighed, turning to retreat into the cave-like interior of his apartment. She followed into a room containing a ratty sofa and chair, an ancient console television. Covering most of the threadbare rug were piles of newspapers and brown paper sacks overflowing with junk. Heavy drapes dimmed the light and closed out the rest of the world.

"Go ahead. Sit down."

Wishing she were not wearing her best black dress, she lowered herself onto the grubby seat of the chair, leaving a half-empty bag of potato chips undisturbed behind her tailbone. She placed her handbag on her knees.

"Wanna beer?" He slouched off toward the kitchen.

"No thanks." She brushed at the potato chip crumbs on the arm of the chair.

Jerry returned with a can of Bud and flopped down on the sofa. "So," he said, "I don't know why I'm talking to you, but go ahead."

It beats a one-way conversation with Oprah. She pushed shaggy hair back from her face. "What was your marriage to Mildred like?"

One side of his face wrinkled in disgust; the other mocked his reaction. "Miserable."

She folded her arms over her handbag and waited.

Jerry fidgeted on the sofa, then continued. "When we were first married, I adored her. She was so pretty and smart and high spirited. I always knew she was too good for me. Problem was, she knew it too. We'd barely finished unwrapping the wedding presents when she started treating me like I was her pet, her lap dog. She wanted to keep me on a leash and bring me out for social occasions, so everything would look right. I was supposed to wear what she told me to wear, keep my mouth shut in public, and stay out of her hair."

"What was Martin's role in the family?"

"To come between us. Martin and Ryan, they were all she ever cared about. I was nobody." He briefly made eye contact. "I used to think if Martin wasn't always around doing what I should've been doing, we might've had a chance. But that was wishful thinking."

"Did you fight a lot?"

"Not at first. In the beginning I gave in to her all the time. But then I got sick of it and we started fighting. Would you believe she had Ryan sleeping in bed with her for years after wc wcrc married, and she expected me to sleep in the other room?"

"How did you fight? Did you yell? Hit her?"

A look of embarrassment crossed his face. "Sometimes I hit her. Not often, only a couple of times. She'd cut me up with her tongue, and I'd feel like I couldn't compete with words and then I'd hit her."

"What about Ryan? You hit him too?"

"Little bastard said I did but it wasn't true. Never laid a hand on him. But he was determined to get rid of me from day one."

"What happened on his fifth birthday?"

One half of Jerry's face looked bewildered, the other

amused. "How the hell should I know? It was all so long ago."

She straightened her head, pinned him with her eyes.

"Let's see . . . " Jerry continued, "Ryan was four when Zach was born, so that means Zach would've been not quite one. What do I remember . . . ? Seems like, I was pissed because everyone was acting like Zach and I didn't exist. I was really irked—here the whole family was fawning over this tyrannical little five-year-old, didn't matter he had a mean streak a mile wide. His fifth birthday . . . " He cracked his knuckles. "I think that's the time he opened this huge pile of presents, then threw a tantrum 'cause there weren't any more." A muscle rippled in his cheek. "Mildred took him off somewhere and they were gone a long time . . . That's what I think happened but I couldn't swear to it. It was too long ago."

She let out a long breath. "Just a couple more things." She stopped to think. "What was your relationship with Zach like?"

His face softened briefly, then the guard went up again. "Not much to it, but not because I didn't try. Nobody else gave a shit about either of us, so I figured, at least we had each other. But I never had a chance. Ryan got to him first." Both sides of his face twisted. "From the time Zach was old enough to talk, Ryan started poisoning his mind against me. I never blamed Zach, but I could see it in his eyes he was ashamed of me." He finished his beer and tossed the can into the corner, a gesture that set her teeth on edge it so reminded her of Zach.

She slid forward, suddenly in a hurry to get away. "Last

question. Where were you the night Ryan died?"

"What night was that?"

"May twenty-third, a Thursday night."

His eyes rolled upward; his mouth contorted in his effort to remember. "With a friend. We hit the bars. You can ask him about it if you like."

ﻙ   ﻙ   ﻙ

She parked on Lake Street at five-fifteen, a time when people were returning from work, and headed down the walkway toward the setback entrance to the recently constructed, Frank Lloyd Wright-style building where Martin's condo was located. After passing a decorative pool, she stopped near the glass door at the far end of the courtyard. Standing off to the side, she rummaged in her bag, waiting until a middle-aged couple opened the outer door and walked past her into the foyer. She pulled out her keyring and followed close behind. The man unlocked the inner door and held it for his companion, then continued to hold it for Cassidy, who nodded her thanks as she walked through the door, the keyring held conspicuously in hand.

She crossed the vast, high-ceilinged lobby to the elevators at the rear, disembarked on the second floor and followed a long corridor past two left turns to apartment two-fifty-three. She punched the bell. No answer. *So far, so good.* She removed an audio tape from her bag and leaned against the wall to wait, hands behind her back so the tape was out of sight. Her breath was coming too fast, her fingers were twitchy. *Never been a good liar. Don't know if I can pull this off.*

Fifteen minutes later Martin came around the corner of the hall, saw her standing there, and proceeded toward his condo, neither body nor face betraying the least reaction. "He was a gentleman from toe to crown" ran through her mind as she watched him approach, backlit by the evening sun so that a faint aura seemed to surround his figure. He exactly matched her image of a proper family patriarch: thick, white hair; kindly, aquiline face; immaculate business suit.

"Ms. McCabe." Courteous but distant. "What can I do for you?"

"I need your help to solve a problem. Serious problem. Concerning Ryan's reputation and the malpractice suit."

"These are matters best discussed with your own attorney." He turned his back, thrust his key in the lock. Case closed, his tone said. Court adjourned.

"You don't understand." She held up the tape. "This is a tape of Ryan's last session." He regarded her sadly, as if she were too stupid to understand she'd been dismissed. "Ryan's confession that he sexually abused his son."

He looked at her again, face unchanged except for a slight pallor.

Have to give him credit. He hides his emotions as well as any therapist.

"This allegation strikes me as highly improbable," he said slowly.

"It's on the tape."

"I don't believe I fully grasp your purpose here, young lady. Surely you don't expect the suit to simply be dropped because of your tape."

"We have a problem," she repeated. "You and I are the only ones who can solve it."

He opened the door and ushered her into his condo. She stepped into an impeccable Victorian room, replete with polished mahogany tables, claw-footed sofa, wing-backed chairs, a deep-toned Oriental. She eased onto the burgundy velvet sofa, crossed one leg over the other, tugged her short black skirt down over her thigh. Martin sat across from her, his blue-veined hands arranging the creases in his trousers.

He gazed through owlish glasses. "May I assume this to be some sort of clumsy attempt at blackmail?"

"Blackmail never entered my mind." She'd desperately hoped to sidestep the topic of blackmail. Her chest tightened at the thought of confrontation. In a legalistic shootout with Martin, she could never hope to win. "All I want is to keep the whole thing quiet. I routinely tape sessions—all my clients know about it. During the last few weeks of therapy, Ryan'd been hinting that there was something he felt very bad, very guilty about." She put a hand to her throat. "In this final session he told me he'd been molesting Luke for almost a year. He knew he was being taped, knew I'd have to file a report. He asked me to hold off for twenty-four hours—said he wanted to prepare the family." Her voice dropped a pitch. "He talked about getting treatment, denied any thought of suicide."

"I'm sorry, my dear, if I misunderstood." His voice softened. "If your sole purpose is to prove your innocence, I fail to see why you haven't taken the tape to your own attorney."

Her eyes dropped. "Ryan was my client. Even if he did

molest his son, he wasn't a bad person. I don't want to destroy his reputation or see Kristi and Luke hurt. I just want the whole thing dropped." She met his eyes. "And you're the only one who can make that happen."

He nodded, the courtly nod that reminded her so of Ryan. "As much as I'd prefer not to eavesdrop on my nephew's therapy, it will be necessary for me to review the tape."

"I'd rather you play it after I leave." She hunched her shoulders, as if warding off a blow. "This is a duplicate. I have the original in a safe place."

"Of course." He held his hand out for the tape.

"Before I give it to you, there's one more thing I want." His face shifted slightly, became more closed. "I want you to answer some questions about Ryan's childhood. He had almost no memories from the early years, and I need to know what could've happened to cause this." She held up the tape. "As a therapist, it's been tearing me apart, not understanding. Ryan saw you as a father figure. I think you're probably the only person who could give me an objective picture of his childhood."

Martin removed his wire-rimmed glasses, took a monogrammed handkerchief out of his pants pocket and polished the lens. He replaced the glasses and sent her a forthright look. "I think perhaps I can understand your need for some kind of explanation. But I must confess, that was a difficult time—one I prefer not to dredge up."

"I wouldn't ask if it wasn't really important. But I just don't think I'll ever be able to put this behind me unless I can fill in some of the missing pieces." She lowered her head, clenched her hands tightly in her lap, her body automatically taking on a supplicant pose. She instinctively knew that Martin would be more vulnerable to pleading than threats.

His clear blue eyes, magnified by the thick lens, looked her up and down. "I suppose working as a therapist engenders this kind of curiosity." His tone made it sound as if he considered mucking around in other people's secrets a dirty business, one step up from selling porn. "All right," he said rather tartly, "I won't refuse."

She raised her head, smiling weakly. "I really appreciate this."

"What do you want to know?"

"I got the impression Ryan was troubled by his mother's remarrying and I'd like to understand more about the second marriage. What would you say it was like?"

His face took on a melancholy cast. "A mistake from the beginning. I tried to tell her, but it's impossible to dissuade a young person in love. He severely lacked confidence, and her attempts at improving him simply made him more insecure." He steepled his fingers. "You know, to some extent I blame myself for their disastrous union."

"How's that?" Cassidy leaned back in the sofa. *Once people start talking, they'll usually say most anything.*

"When we were young, I took on the role of parent with my sister. I more or less talked her into marrying Ryan's father. I thought he'd be a good influence. But I'm afraid she was bored. Then, when he died and she got a taste of freedom, her pent-up frustration caused her to swing too far in the opposite direction."

"You think your efforts at getting her to be more responsible may've backlashed?"

"I've always feared that was the case." His voice dropped and she could hear the regret in it.

"What do you know about violence in the second marriage? Did Ryan's stepfather batter either Ryan or his mother?"

He sighed. "I feel quite uncomfortable with this. I realize it's today's fashion to broadcast one's dirty little secrets on Oprah, but when I was growing up, we took a different attitude toward our soiled laundry."

"Okay, we'll skip that one. To what extent were you involved with Ryan and his mother after his father died?"

"It's a tradition in our family for men to take care of women, and since I'd always felt responsible for Mildred, it seemed natural to step in during that difficult time. If Mildred's second husband had been a different sort, I could've removed myself more easily. But it was apparent from an early point that he was unable to provide Mildred with the stability she needed, and so it seemed necessary for me to maintain my involvement even after she remarried."

"I can understand your feeling obligated."

He sent her a pointed look, reminding her that it was not a good idea to start talking like a therapist. She quickly moved on to the next question. "Why was the second son treated so differently from the first?"

"As a matter of fact, I've always had mixed feelings about little Zachary. I felt sorry for him, but at the same time was frustrated by his obstreperousness. Now, as I think about Ryan," he took off his glasses and rubbed his face, "I wonder if Zachary may not have been the lucky one after all. He got off to a bad start because Mildred was so disenchanted with her marriage. As he grew older, the difficulty was exacerbated, primarily because Zachary was so like his mother. We all hoped he'd come around as he matured, but he's persisted in cutting himself off from the family—except, of course, when he wants something."

"Wants something?" She thought she detected a slight, avuncular twinkle. *Maybe underneath that lawyerly facade, he sort of likes me.*

"I probably shouldn't tell you this—although I suppose there's not too much Ryan hasn't already divulged about the family—but Zach came to me recently for a rather large loan." Martin's voice turned ironic. "Apparently, he wants to indulge his taste in exotic careers without having to discipline himself to live on the meager salary that goes with it." He looked up with his sad smile. "But you aren't here to listen to an old man's grumblings."

"I also wanted to ask what you remember about Ryan's fifth birthday."

He cocked his head inquisitively.

"Ryan had the feeling something happened to him on his birthday but he couldn't retrieve the memory."

Martin's eyes moved off into the distance; a faraway look came over his face. "After all this time I can't be positive, but I'll tell you what I can. I believe there was a family party early in the day. Mildred had her hands full, considering Zach was less than a year old and Ryan such an active little boy. He was overstimulated by the party and, as the day wore on, became loud and demanding. Mildred tried her best but there was nothing she could do. Her husband, it seems, had passed out on the couch by then." Martin paused and blinked slowly. Cassidy thought his pale skin had deepened slightly but she couldn't be sure. "So I suggested we take Ryan for a drive, hoping he'd fall asleep in the car as he often did. We drove around for awhile, then put him down for a nap at our parents' house. After that we may have taken him to the zoo—I'm not sure."

Cassidy noticed that her foot had started jiggling. She made it stop, made herself sit calmly. "You have a remarkable memory."

"As one grows older, they say, remembering what happened twenty years ago becomes easier than holding on to yesterday."

Cassidy grinned. "You can't fool me. You're an old fox and you never forget a thing."

He nodded, the small, courtly bow she'd seen before.

One more question. How're you going to pull this one off? Cassidy rearranged her face, the grin fading into sadness. "Sometimes you wish you could forget." She dropped her eyes. "There's something I'd like to ask. In confidence. You see, the night Ryan died, he put in a call to me. I got the message, but I was tired and postponed calling him back. And it keeps haunting me, that I'll never know what he wanted." *You're sticking your head in the opposing attorney's noose.* "So what I'm wondering is, did he call you too?"

"I'm sorry, I can't help you. I did not receive a call, nor do I know anyone else who did. Evidently, you're the only one Ryan tried to reach." He stood up. "I think I need to warn you. You seem to be assuming that once I play your tape, the suit will magically disappear. At this point, I can't make any promises."

"I understand. I just wanted to find out if he called anyone else. Were you home at the time? Are you sure he didn't call?"

"I was in New York. I flew out that afternoon and didn't hear about his . . . about Ryan until late in the day on Friday. I was sitting in an auditorium listening to a speaker when I got the page from Mildred."

Cassidy stood up also. "Thank you so much. You've been very gracious."

"You said blackmail never entered your mind and I'm willing to accept that you aren't after money. However, it's quite clear you were determined to exact a certain price. Now I think I've provided more than enough information in exchange for a tape, the contents of which I have only your word for." He extended his hand.

She gave over the tape, which was clearly labeled "R.H.-5/23," and quickly got herself out the door. As she drove away, she envisioned Martin's face—she indulged herself by picturing an actual display of emotion—as he pushed *play* and heard the lyric voice of Barbara Streisand: "Memories . . . like the corners of your mind . . . " She'd given him a copy of her favorite cassette. It was the least she could do.

31

THE ROYAL FAVORITE

She got back from Martin's and realized she was hungry. Looking for something to eat always depressed her. It forced her to notice how broke and disorganized she was, how lax about shopping, meal planning, and cleaning out the refrigerator. *Kevin's right. When Zach finds out the truth about me, he'll run the other way.*

Her current foray into the big white box revealed a number of plastic containers she did not feel up to opening, the remains of a head a lettuce, some fruit and vegetables that were past their prime, and an empty milk carton that Kevin had put back. A chunk of cheese looked promising. The delicate lace of mold around the outside was still in its early stages.

She filled a tray with snacks and headed for the front porch, assisted by the cat who bobbed along beside her, chirping encouragement. She sliced moldy edges off the cheese and piled them on the rough wooden picnic bench. The cat pounced, finishing off every crumb before Cassidy was done arranging her own plate of cheese, crackers and fruit. The cat extended her nose and sniffed Cassidy's cheese.

"Cheese is a special treat. You do not get to stuff yourself on it."

The cat inched closer, her eyes never wavering from the yellow slices on Cassidy's plate.

Cassidy broke off another bite and handed it to the cat. "Now that Zach's back on the scene, we have this one slight problem."

The cat oozed in her direction, gazing intently at each piece of cheese as it moved from the plate to Cassidy's mouth.

"You see, there're a few details I've neglected to mention. The drawing I found in the attic. The consultation with Honor. The gas leak. My little chat with Yvonne. And of course the tidbits I picked up from Jerry and Martin." She sighed. "This is going to require a lot of explaining."

The cat reached out, tentatively touching her plate.

"Get your paw off my food. Cheese costs as much as steak. At least it did when I used to buy steak. Anyway, the problem is, I do not look forward to telling him all this."

The cat made a swipe at one of the slices. Cassidy barely succeeded in snatching it out of her reach.

"This is important. Why can't you get your mind off your stomach long enough to hold a decent conversation?" She popped the last piece of cheese in her mouth. The cat turned her back and swished her tail. "The reason I'm dreading it is, he's going to stick pins in all my theories and then I'm going to start doubting myself, and all this confidence I've finally built up will slip away again."

❧ ❧ ❧

"This should be interesting." Zach turned off Hazel onto Chicago Avenue. "In all our past encounters, it was Mildred demanding answers and I was the one trying to weasel out. This is a real reversal."

Tell him now. Get it over with.

"How honest do you think she'll be?"

"Good question. She's always had this self-righteous attitude so she never felt any need to lie. But when it comes to embarrassing disclosures about her number one son, who knows?"

I'll do it later, when we go to Clancy's. Why trust him, anyway? For all I know, he'll be gone again tomorrow.

Zach pulled up in front of Mildred's white colonial. Cassidy reached for his hand and gave it a squeeze. "This is even worse for you than for me," she said.

"Let's get it over with." He pulled his hand away and opened the door.

They rang the doorbell, then waited on the porch a long time.

"Maybe she's changed her mind," Cassidy said.

"She's just showing us who's boss." He rang again.

"Oh, one more thing. She's slightly deaf but too vain to wear a hearing aide so be sure to look right at her when you talk."

Eventually Mildred opened the door. She was wearing an understated fawn suede lounging outfit that made Cassidy see her own hot pink blouse and blue skirt as flashy and cheap in comparison.

"I'm surprised you bothered to wait. Instead of breaking in." She turned abruptly and led them into the sunken living room.

"When adult children return to their family home and admit themselves with a key, it's not usually considered breaking and entering," Zach said.

Mildred seated herself in an off-white sofa facing the white marble fireplace. Cassidy and Zach sat across from each other in matching loveseats on either side of the fireplace. Cassidy stared at the Kama Sutra style statue, then pulled her eyes away to watch the interaction between Zach and his mother.

"Mothers usually don't have to change their locks to protect themselves from adult children ransacking their houses."

Zach stood up. "I'd like a drink. How about you two?"

"You may pour me some DuBonnet," Mildred responded.

"Me too," Cassidy echoed.

They waited in uncomfortable silence while Zach stood in front of the gold and white liquor cabinet pouring drinks. When he had taken his place again, Mildred looked pointedly at the glass of scotch in his hand and said, "I see you've inherited your father's taste in alcohol."

"You think there might be a reason we both tend to drink when we're around you?"

She raised her brows. "And not otherwise?"

"All right, Mother. Now that you've drawn first blood, let's proceed to the main event. I'd like to begin by hearing about your marriage to my father. Why was it such a failure?"

Mildred directed a look of distaste toward Cassidy. "I can't talk in front of her. We're suing. She's the one responsible for our having lost Ryan, you know."

Cassidy compressed her lips to keep defensive words from pouring out. Her training in when to keep her mouth shut came in handy sometimes.

Zach laid an arm across the back of the loveseat and stretched his feet out in front. "If we leave here with unanswered questions, we're driving straight to the *Oak Park Review* office. The editor's a friend of mine. And, as I'm sure you know, Cassidy had access to a lot of information that might prove titillating to anyone interested in the real poop about the upstanding Lawrences."

"I can't see how questions about my marriage could have anything to do with Ryan."

"No censoring. We get to pick the questions, you have to answer."

Her brow creased; her mouth turned sour. "It was a dreadful mistake, that's all. I never should have married that foolish little man."

"What made it so bad?" Cassidy asked.

"I tried to overlook his boorishness because I so hated having to admit that all those people who said it was a mistake were right after all. But there was nothing I could do. He'd be sullen for days, then blow up and become abusive. No matter what I did, the marriage became more and more intolerable."

"Was he physically violent?" Cassidy asked.

"Why don't you ask him?" She inclined her head toward Zach.

"We'd like to hear it from your point of view," he said.

She looked down at the floor. "All right, the answer is yes. He used to hit me. A lot."

"Ryan too?" Zach asked.

"Ryan said he did and I believed him."

"It's apparent Ryan and Zach were treated very differently." Cassidy searched for nonblaming words. "And I'd like to understand what caused you to have such dissimilar responses to the two boys."

Mildred shot Zach a poisonous look. "You were nothing but trouble from the day you were born. Cranky baby, constantly out of control when you were little, sneak and conniver as you got older. I wanted to like you—but you made it impossible. Ryan, on the other hand, was every mother's dream. I was so ashamed of the mistake I'd made in marrying your father. I couldn't confide in anyone except Ryan and Martin, and Ryan always listened and did whatever he could to make my life easier. Which included taking on far too much responsibility for you."

"Well, Mother," Zach said, his face impassive, "I'm happy for you at least one of your sons was flawless."

"I wish that were true. I wish you *were* honestly capable of feeling for others. But you don't care about anybody but yourself."

Cassidy's shoulders tightened. *I'd like to throttle her. Can he really be as nonchalant as he looks?* "Moving on, I'd like to hear everything you can tell me about Ryan's fifth birthday."

Mildred demanded to know why and Cassidy gave the standard blocked memory explanation. Mildred insisted nothing could have happened, then said she had something to show them and left the room.

Zach added more scotch to his glass. "We'll never get her to acknowledge that the royal favorite could've been anything but perfect. The only way she can bring herself to accept the suicide theory is by casting all the blame on you. Poor little Ryan, hypnotized by the evil therapist."

The phone rang and Zach answered. He was still talking when Mildred walked back in the room carrying a gold framed photograph. "It's for you," he said, handing the receiver to his mother.

"That was Kristi." He sat down next to Cassidy while his mother talked on the phone.

"What's up with her?"

"More trouble. Scott's taken off again, which doesn't surprise me. I figured his miraculous recovery was too good to be true."

"Taken off where?"

"Southern Illinois. He drove down in Kristi's car—without permission, of course. Probably with the idea of peddling drugs to college kids. But whatever his intention, it got cut short when they picked him up for driving under the influence. They're holding him in jail until Mommy bails him out."

"It'd be better if she left him in jail."

"I agree. But Kristi's been running to the rescue all his life. She's not likely to change now."

"What's she going to do?"

"If Mildred agrees to babysit, she'll rent a car and drive down first thing in the morning."

Finishing her conversation, Mildred rejoined them.

"You're babysitting Luke?" Zach asked.

"Martin had a little dinner planned with one of the relatives but that can be postponed," she said, thinking aloud. "Yes, I'm going to babysit." She gave Zach a direct look. "Scott's a lost cause, but Luke's another story. He's got potential."

"I see that gleam in your eye. Are you by any chance thinking of grooming him as Ryan's replacement?" Zach inquired.

"What I choose to think is none of your business." She resumed her place on the sofa and held up a photo of a golden haired boy in a sailor suit. "This was taken on his fifth birthday." Her sharp eyes softened as she regarded the picture. "He was so beautiful. I tried to talk him into wearing one of his nice new outfits but he told me he was going to be a sailor and that's that. The family came to our house for the party—the little house on Forest Avenue. Our parents were still living here, you know."

She handed the picture to Cassidy, who gazed into an innocent, soft focus face that easily could have been Luke's.

"After we finished eating, Ryan got restless. It's hard for a five-year-old to spend the day with a houseful of grownups, you know. Anyway, I remember that Ryan kept saying he wanted to go to the zoo for his birthday. Then somebody offered to take him and he was gone a long time. I remember waiting for him to get back ... Martin was there with me, and Jerry was gone or drunk or something. And I got to talking to Martin and that was the first time I admitted that Jerry'd started hitting me. Martin urged me to leave, but I insisted I could handle it. And that's all I remember."

Cassidy leaned forward. "Who took Ryan to the zoo?"

Mildred stared into space for a moment, then shook her head. "I can't remember."

Cassidy sighed. "You're sure? Try again."

Mildred shot her a look of irritation.

"Okay," Cassidy continued. "So, what do you think caused the changes in Ryan after the party?"

Mildred looked at her curiously. "What changes?"

"Mrs. Kowalski said Ryan had problems at school that she discussed with you," Zach replied. "He was acting out in some way she found too embarrassing to talk about."

Mildred shifted in her chair. "She shouldn't have said anything," she snapped.

"What was it, Mother?" Leaning back, Zach lay his arm behind Cassidy's shoulders.

"I refuse to talk about it." She pursed her lips.

A long silence. Mildred crossed her legs. The toe of a fawn pump twitched.

"You're making too much out of it. It was nothing, really, Just some little incidents ... some things that occurred in the bathroom."

"With other little boys?" Cassidy prompted.

Mildred nodded, her face flushing.

"I was told," Cassidy said slowly, "that when you were a teenager, you used to babysit for some woman. Something happened while you were babysitting and the woman said she'd never have you in her house again."

"That's ridiculous. I never babysat. Why would I want to babysit? I had all the money I wanted."

"Okay, last question," Cassidy said. "Where were you the night Ryan died?"

"I can't believe you're asking me that," Mildred said in disgust.

"Believe it," Zach said.

Narrowing her eyes, she tilted her head back and sighted him down the line of her nose. "I was home. I went to bed at ten o'clock, as I always do. Alone."

Cassidy and Zach finished quickly. The minute they were out of the house, the door slammed and the lock clicked. When they were safely in the car, Cassidy said, "That was downright brutal. What she said to you, I mean."

"Just about what I expected."

"But doesn't it make you furious to hear her rave about Ryan in one breath and tear you down in the next?"

"That's just how she is."

"I wish you'd stop being so damned impervious and feel something."

"I'd rather be impervious."

Stop playing therapist and deal with your own issue. Tell him what you've been up to.

Wait till we get to Clancy's. I'll do it then.

Zach surprised her by driving straight to her house. He parked, pulled her over next to him and gave her a long kiss, which started her blood racing.

This time when he asks if he can stay, I'll say yes. I'll tell him everything after we make love.

He took hold of her chin and moved her face a few inches away from his. "We have some catching up to do. How's Friday night?"

"Friday?" she said in dismay.

"That's right, Fridays are bad. Saturday then? If you're ready, maybe you could spend the night. You can bring your cat if you think leaving her alone'd traumatize her."

32

THE BABYSITTER

She looked at the clock again. Ten-thirty. Probably too late for Zach to call. Probably she wouldn't hear from him again until . . . when? Later in the week? Saturday? Never?

The cat pounced on the bulge in the blanket, sinking teeth into Cassidy's toe.

"Ow!" She pulled the cat off and covered both feet with the burgundy comforter, too hot but better than having her flesh punctured.

"Stop picking on me. I feel bad enough already."

Here you are, trying to get the attention of a cat who won't even sit still and listen, when it's Zach you should be talking to. You blew it. You should've told him everything last night.

I hate it when you lecture me.

Crawling up on Cassidy's chest, the cat settled in with a rumbling purr. Her slitted eyes turned a warm, glistening green.

"You wouldn't tell Zach anything, would you? You'd act mysterious and keep your own counsel and never let him know you gave a damn. And you'd never ever let anybody hurt you."

Stop distracting yourself and do it. Pick up the phone and tell him everything. If you can stop your game playing, you and Zach might have a chance. She put her hand on the phone.

"What if he isn't home?" she asked the cat. "You have any idea what it'll do to me? I'll spend the rest of the night imagining he's with somebody else."

Mrowr.

"Or, what if he's home and screening his calls? What if he doesn't want to talk to me?"

The cat turned around and flicked a tail in her face.

"I suppose you think that's silly. I mean, why wouldn't he want to talk to me? That's what I'd say to a client. But if I were talking to a client, I'd be objective. All I am now is insecure."

She scratched the cat's face, trying to coax her into continuing the conversation.

"I called first when he disappeared after sex. It's his turn. He's got to prove he's really interested before I pick up the phone again."

To get her mind off Zach, she turned on the television and tried to make sense of an old movie that was half over. The phone rang and she grabbed for it, noticing it was now after eleven.

"Hi, this is Kristi. Hope it's not too late."

A heavy, dropping sensation in her stomach. "No, it's fine. Something wrong?"

"I'm not sure . . . That is, everything's probably all right. It's probably just an overreaction on . . . so many things have happened . . . I'm feeling spooked and so it's probably . . ."

"What is it?"

"Well, the problem is, I can't get hold of Mildred. I'm stuck down here in Springfield, and Mildred's babysitting at my house, and I've been calling and calling and . . . I keep telling myself she's probably just fallen asleep or something but . . ."

"Maybe she took Luke over to her place."

"I tried there. I know she doesn't hear well—sometimes she doesn't hear the phone and so . . . well, anyway, I've been trying to forget about it but . . . "

"Why don't you call the police?"

"Oh no, I couldn't do that." Her voice got shrill. "Mildred'd kill me if the police showed up at the door and it was all a mistake."

"Is there something you'd like me to do?"

"I know this is a terrible . . . I hate to be such a bother but . . . well, I mean, I was thinking that if you'd be willing to go over and peek inside the house and make sure everything's okay . . . well, it would mean the world to me. I'd appreciate it so much."

Why me? Tell her no.

"I'd like to help out but . . . I'm just wondering why me instead of Zach."

"It'd take Zach an hour to drive back and forth, and you're so . . . Even though we haven't known each other very long, you already know more about me than any of my other friends. I guess I'd be embarrassed . . ."

"Well . . . I suppose I could. You want me to ring the bell and see if Mildred answers? If she's sleeping through the phone, she'll probably sleep through the doorbell too."

"Actually, what I thought you could do . . . I have a key hidden in a flower pot next to the . . . if you just slipped inside with a flashlight and made sure they were both all . . . I mean, that way Mildred wouldn't have to know about it and she couldn't get upset with either one of us."

She saw a policeman hauling her off to jail with Mildred in the background commenting, "She has a habit of breaking and entering, you know." *I don't want to do this.*

"Okay," Cassidy sighed. "Give me your number and I'll give you a call when I get back. Now tell me exactly where I can find the key."

As she hung up the phone, a chill started up her backbone. Two out of three blonde, blue-eyed boys had been abused. What if the reason nobody answered was . . .

She did not allow herself to finish the thought. Jumping out of bed, she threw on some clothes, found a flashlight and hurried toward the back door. She had her hand on the doorknob when a voice inside her head screamed at her to stop.

You're doing it again. Racing off on your own without telling Zach. This time, do it right. Call and tell him what you're up to.

She trudged upstairs, got Zach's number out of her

Rolodex, and dialed. When his machine clicked on, she slammed down the receiver.

What the hell is he doing out at this time of night? Last night, he couldn't be bothered to stay over with me, but here it is eleven-thirty and he's not home. What's going on, anyway?

She rushed back downstairs, but by the time she got to the kitchen, the other voice had kicked in.

If you're going to try for a relationship, you've got to give the man a chance.

I'm sick of giving men chances.

This could be dangerous. You've got to tell somebody. If you can't trust Zach now, you never will.

She picked up the phone in the kitchen. When his machine clicked on, she said, "This is Cassidy. I'm going to Kristi's to check on Luke because no one's answering the phone. I'm a little nervous because I've learned that Ryan was sexually abused, the same person is still abusing little boys—at least I think he is—and someone tried to kill me last Thursday night, which means I'm very close to figuring out who the murderer is. So, if you don't hear back from me, it's possible I'm in trouble."

≈ ≈ ≈

She pulled up in front of Kristi's at eleven-forty. No cars in the driveway. Mildred probably would've parked in the garage. The house was dark except for the living room on the ground floor and one room upstairs. She got out of the car and crept around to the back, where she found the key in an urn on the corner of the porch. She turned on the flashlight, opened the screen, and unlocked the door.

As she inched the door open, moving in slow motion, she could hear her heart thudding. Holding the flashlight out in front with her right hand, she clutched her handbag straps in her left. She crossed the threshold, then, with her left hand twisted around behind her, attempted to ease the screen door closed. As she beamed the light around the room, the straps slipped out of her hand and she lost her grip on both the door and her bag. All at once, her bag dropped to the floor and the screen banged shut on her heels, slamming with the retort of a gun fired close to her head. Her whole body twitched, hair-trigger reflexes firing off wildly.

After several moments of agonized listening, she decided no one was coming to investigate. She took a deep breath, picked up her bag, and focused the flash on the door at the other end of the small utility room. She passed through the door, which led into a large, dark kitchen, and tiptoed across to a doorway opening onto a palely lit dining room. On the other side of the dining room was an archway leading to the hall, and across the hall was the living room, where two table lamps burned, sending dim light filtering through the ground floor.

When she reached the arch, she stopped to look past the hall into the living room. From where she stood she could not see anyone in the room, but since one of the sofas faced away from her, she could not be sure it was unoccupied. Slipping across to stand behind the leather sofa, she peered. Mildred, fully dressed except for her shoes, was sprawled out on the seat. Her mouth was slack. Her closed eyes showed tiny crescents of white. A liqueur glass and a

DuBonnet bottle were on the end table next to the sofa. She felt a twinge of smugness. The high and mighty Mildred drunk on the job.

This one of the family secrets? She didn't hear the phone 'cause she's passed out? If that's it, then there's nothing to worry about.

Finding Mildred should've reassured her, but her nerves were still strung tight, she still had to check on Luke. She could not simply assume all was well and go on her way. She watched Mildred snore gently, making sure the Dragon Lady would have nothing worse to fear than a hangover, then started up the oak staircase.

When she reached the top she had to stop and catch her breath because of the constriction in her chest. The door to Luke's room at the end of the hall was outlined with light. She tiptoed up to it and listened intently. She could just make out the shrill sound of Luke's high-pitched voice. Was he talking to himself? Somebody in there with him? Hard to figure what to do next. Open the door surreptitiously and peek inside? Throw it wide? Knock?

She gingerly twisted the knob, easing the door inward until a thread of light was visible at the edge. Peering through the crack, she glimpsed a narrow sliver of the room. Pushing slightly, she widened the sliver to include one end of Luke's bed. Another push and she could see Luke standing naked on top.

"Forget the comic opera, why don't you? Just open the door and come in." The sharp voice sliced through her concentration.

The muscles in her legs jerked convulsively. *Oh shit.*

This can't be who I think it is.

She stepped inside. Tony Chiparo, in a polo tee shirt and slacks, was sitting on the other end of the bed. He stood up as she came into the room, his metallic eyes glinting sparks of light.

Cassidy took a deep breath. "I'm sorry, I didn't mean to interrupt. I was just . . . that is, Kristi called and she asked . . . uh, what I mean is . . . "

"It's Cassidy," Luke jumped off the bed and took Chiparo's hand.

He pulled himself up straight, looked Cassidy in the eye and said, in a grown up voice, "This's Cousin Frank. He's in our family 'cause Uncle Martin married his mother. so now he's Martin's son. Frank went off to live with his other father for a long time, but now he's back." He beamed with pride at his ability to keep track of family relationships, then giggled and dived under the covers. "I'm not s'posed to run around in front of girls without any clothes on." He pulled the sheet over his head.

"Well, isn't this a surprise," Chiparo's words dropped into the room like icicles falling from a roof.

"Now that I see everything's under control, I'll be on my way." She edged backward.

Chiparo moved rapidly to block the doorway. "What's the hurry?" He took hold of her upper arm, his long fingers digging into her skin. She gritted her teeth, trying to ignore the pain. Tentacles of fear wrapped around her stomach.

33

CANDY WRAPPER

Maintaining his grip on her arm, Chiparo said, "If you insist on leaving, I'll have to walk you to the door. My duty as host, you know." He looked back over his shoulder at Luke. "I've just decided—we're going to the Lake House."

Luke's head popped out. "The Lake House!" he said, clapping his hands.

"You can get dressed while I'm gone but be sure to stay in your room. Understand?"

Escorting her out of the bedroom, Chiparo shut the door and continued down the dark hall toward the stairs.

He can't let you go. You've got to get away before he figures out what to do with you. Run. Scream. Bite. Kick. Push him downstairs.

Her mind whirled, flipping rapidly from one possibility

to another. Too many choices. She could not stop racing around in her head and pick one.

When they reached the top of the stairs, he backed her up against the wall and grabbed both her arms, knocking the flashlight out of her hand. She clutched at her handbag, barely managing to hold onto the straps. She made a feeble attempt at resistance, but he was much too strong for her. He moved in close, looming over her, making her feel suffocated. She could see the cords standing out on his neck and smell the mix of sweat and sex leaking from his pores. "Have to hand it to you—you almost caught me in the act. Now I've got to stow you some place while I regroup. I suppose it's possible you might find some way of escaping, but if you disappear on me, I'm taking off with the kid. Nobody'll ever see him again."

He walked her downstairs and through the hallway, stopping in front of a bathroom. "Better use the facilities. It'll be a long time before you get another chance." He shoved her into the bathroom and closed the door. Something banged against the other side, the knob rattled, then it was quiet. She felt around and found the light switch. When the light came on, she was standing in front of a solid oak door. Knowing it was hopeless, she pushed against it with her shoulder, pounded on it till her fists ached, then lunged into it from the far end of the room.

Stop all this flailing. Take some deep breaths. Think.

She threw cold water on her face, put the lid down on the toilet and made herself sit quietly. *A note for Zach.* She rummaged through her handbag and pulled out one bite-sized peanut butter cup and a working pen. She popped the candy into her mouth and laid the wrapper out flat on the vanity. On the white square of cardboard inside the wrapper, she wrote: Martin's stepson. Lake House. After folding the wrapper around the cardboard, she looked for a place to stash it. Somewhere obscure enough that Chiparo wouldn't find it, obvious enough that Zach would. If it occurred to him to look. No, she couldn't think about that.

Where to hide it? Under the soap dish? Beneath the counter? Behind the toilet? Remembering that she'd once made a crack about his going through her medicine cabinet, she decided to put it there.

Would Zach think to look for a note? It all depended on how alert he was when he arrived, which in turn depended on where he was and what he was doing. What *could* he be doing out late on a Tuesday night? He could be in a bar, which did not bode well for clear thinking. He could be with another woman, which did not bode well for getting here in time. *Do not think about this. This is not helping.*

A thump on the other side of the door. The door opened and Chiparo stepped inside, gun in hand.

"Okay, Ms. Therapist, let's get going. We've got a lot of loose ends to tie up yet." His full-lipped mouth widened into a smirk, revealing the sharp edges of his small white teeth.

He took possession of her handbag, then directed her to walk down the hall and into the living room, making her stop behind the sofa where Mildred was sleeping.

She's not drunk after all. She's got to be drugged. Otherwise he wouldn't take the chance of waking her.

"Lie down and put your hands behind your back."

She dropped onto her knees, then stretched out with her hands behind her. Chiparo knelt beside her and jammed one knee between her shoulder blades, pressing her body into the floor.

"Stop. You're hurting me." She started to kick and squirm in an effort to throw him off. He shoved down on the back of her head, grinding her face into the floor. She bit her cheek sharply, got dust in her nose, couldn't breath. Gasping, she stopped fighting and let him tie her wrists behind her back.

He stood her up and guided her through the kitchen and on into the lighted garage, where a yellow Cutlass was parked. She halted beside the rear door.

"You think you're riding in the back seat? You and me and Luke, the three of us chugging on over to Michigan together?" His feline eyes laughed. "I've got something else in mind." He motioned in the direction of the open trunk.

A convulsive shiver ran through her. "Oh no. Oh my God. Please, don't make me get in the trunk. Oh please, I won't tell anybody, I promise. Please don't."

Stop groveling. It won't do any good. Can't you hang onto some tiny pretense of self respect?

She clenched her teeth to stem the babbling and shuffled toward the rear of the car. "I can't get in with my hands tied."

"Happy to assist." He grabbed her arm and yanked her into position squarely in front of the trunk. "Move it. We don't have that much time."

"We don't? Why not? What's going to happen?"

He struck the side of her head with the gun to let her know he'd had enough of her talk, then spun her around to face him and gave her a shove. The back of her head cracked the lid and her butt landed in the trunk. With legs splayed over the edge, she felt a flash of embarrassment at how undignified and wide open she was. An amused expression flitted across his face, then he swung her legs inside like tossing in a sack of laundry and threw her bag in after her. He stared down for a moment, his hand on the lid. Although his brassy, opaque eyes shut her out, she got the distinct impression that here was a man who loved his work.

As the lid of the trunk came slamming down, she shut her eyes and yipped like a frightened puppy. Hearing his footsteps recede, she opened her eyes on smothering blackness. The candy wrapper was her only hope. She lay in a crumpled heap on her side. The rough carpet felt like steel wool against her cheek. Her head hurt in back where she'd banged it and on the side where he'd hit her and her tongue kept poking into the hole in her cheek where she'd bitten herself. Tears dribbled down her face. Her nose ran, and not being able to wipe it, having it drip and clog her breathing began to seem worse than being locked in a trunk and about to die.

Rolling over on her back, she twisted her head around so she could rub her nose against her shirt. She gasped for air and whimpered, finding some comfort in the sound. As time passed she calmed down enough to try pushing against the trunk lid with her legs, but the lock held fast.

She heard a muffled voice—Chiparo. Then a squeal from Luke. The house door closed. The car bounced, Chiparo and Luke getting in. Car doors slammed. The engine turned over. Two red rims of light, bloody-eyed monsters leering from opposite corners of the trunk, blinked on. The car backed out of the garage and down the driveway, then turned and started forward. The trunk lid rattled. Now and then she could hear the faint slosh of gasoline from somewhere below. The heat was oppressive. There was not enough air. She could smell a trace of fumes and the stink of her own sweat pouring out of her body, leaving her wet and slimy. Occasionally the car lurched sharply, throwing her against the wall of the trunk. When they picked up speed, she figured they'd left Oak Park and hit the expressway headed toward Michigan.

She went to work on her hands. From the feel of the fabric, she guessed he'd tied her with a pantyhose. When she pulled on her wrists, the knot loosened. After tugging at it for some time, she succeeded in wriggling one hand free. Putting her hands behind her head, she worked out her plan, then went through it again and again, mentally rehearsing the same way an athlete visualized a play.

The car came to an abrupt stop. Cassidy's eyes flew open. The opposite corner red lights flicked off. She wriggled her toes and squirmed around, easing her muscles. The car doors on both sides opened and closed. The silent darkness settled in around her. She stared into a blackness like the inside of a coffin until her eyes started playing tricks and black-on-black images began forming and dissolving.

Was he simply going to leave her here? She'd heard stories of people found alive in trunks after days, even weeks. Just as she'd started thinking maybe she could survive until somebody found her, she heard footsteps. The key scraped in the lock. She stuffed her hands behind her back as the lid sprang up and a searing light blazed on, forcing her eyes to blink shut.

"Hope you made good use of your time. You come up with a diagnosis for me yet?"

Cautiously, she opened her eyes. Chiparo was leering down at her.

"That's an easy one." *Sociopath. No doubt about it.*

"Tell me about it later. Right now, you've got a choice. You can either make it easy for me to get you out, or you can just lay there and let me manhandle you." He placed a hand roughly on her left breast. "Personally, I'd prefer the later."

She raised herself into a sitting position and he leaned into the trunk and grasped both her arms. He pulled her forward and she maneuvered herself into a crouch with her feet under her. She had to concentrate on holding her hands behind her back, deliberately inhibiting the urge to use them for balance. She positioned her body so that her feet were beneath her, her torso upright. Then she lunged into him, pushing off with her feet.

Having caught him off balance she was able to topple him, even though he weighed almost twice as much as she did. He went over backwards and she came down on top of him. As she scrambled to her feet, he grabbed for her, clamping a hand around her ankle. She stomped frantically. His grip loosened and she took off, heading straight for a thicket of trees about fifteen yards away. She heard yelling and the explosion of gunfire behind her as she plunged into the woods.

She tore ahead through the underbrush, her lungs ready

to burst, until she was deep enough to be swallowed up. She gulped in air as quietly as possible and peered through the trees. Chiparo was advancing rapidly toward the thicket, gun in hand. Further back, the car was parked next to a house spotlighted by security lights, and way in the distance, patches of moonlight glimmered on water.

It was pitch black inside the woods. She took refuge behind a tree several yards in from the edge. She could see Chiparo silhouetted against the light from the house but he could not see her. If she stood absolutely still and leaned up against the tree, he would not be able to find her. Not unless he went back to the house for a flashlight, which would give her an opportunity to get away.

She stood hugging the tree. Chiparo stalked back and forth, halting from time to time to stare into the thicket. A long time passed.

Chiparo said, "Luke's asleep in the house. Walk out now and he'll remain among the living. Stay where you are and the next sound you hear will be a bullet going into his brain." He struck off in the other direction.

This is your punishment for not doing all those things you should've done.

Bullshit!

For not taking Ryan's call. Not telling Zach. You're always talking about how irresponsible men are. You're the one who's irresponsible and this is your punishment.

That's garbage. I don't believe one word of it. But it doesn't matter, I still have to stop him.

She released her hold on the tree and walked noisily out of the woods. "All right, you win."

He retied her hands with rope and marched her down to the lake front where a small motorboat was tied to a wooden dock. The boat's exterior lights were on, indicating that Chiparo was ready to take off.

After depositing her on the bench in the stern, he stood in front of her, legs spread apart, one hand in his pocket. There was enough visibility from the boat lights to make out the familiar sneer.

"I found something you may be interested in." He pulled a closed fist out of his pocket and shoved it in her face. He slowly opened his fingers, revealing a folded candy wrapper in the palm of his hand.

34

THE LAKE

The wind from the lake bore a sharp chill. A bout of shivers overcame her. "What are you going to do?" she asked through teeth clenched against the chattering.

"Why don't we just let that be a surprise," he said over his shoulder as he untied the boat and took his place in the revolving captain's chair.

"No, please, tell me," she wailed. "I hate surprises."

Starting the engine, Chiparo yelled back at her. "That's not all you're gonna hate."

He took the boat a few yards out into the lake at low speed, then accelerated. The motor roared and the boat lunged forward. An icy mist sprayed up from the sides, drenching her tee shirt and shorts. Her skin was covered with goosebumps, and fits of shivering rattled her teeth. Off in the distance she could see the orange glow of Chicago and directly behind them along the curve of the shore a sprinkling of white lights not much bigger than stars.

A gradual numbness came over her and she lost all sense of time. She wondered how long it would be before he stopped the engine. Probably he wanted to get far enough out so her body would never wash ashore. As her eyes grew accustomed to the faint light, she was able to distinguish the outline of two cinder blocks in the bottom of the boat. She imagined them tied to her ankles—pulling her down—her lungs burning. Scooting over to the edge, she looked down into the waves slapping the side of the boat.

That twitchy, panicky feeling started up again. She forced her eyes away from the water and tried to think of a plan. Perhaps she could establish rapport and coax him into shooting her first. She stared at diamond pinpricks of light overhead and blanked out her mind.

The boat skipped ahead, lurching from one crest to the next. She swung her feet onto the seat and pulled her knees up tight against her chest, withdrawing into the smallest possible bundle to escape the clammy air. As she squirmed around, she discovered she could wriggle her whole body through her arms and bring her tied wrists around in front.

She'd been riding along in a tranced-out state for some time when Chiparo cut the engine back to idle and swung his seat around to face her.

"Well, therapist-lady, any final words of wisdom? You want to tell me about my treatment plan or anything?" The cutting edge of his voice jerked her back into focus.

Death penalty's the only treatment that'd do this creep

any good.

Chiparo stood and stretched, then dropped back into the chair. "I see you managed to get your hands out in front instead of keeping them where you were supposed to. You really have been an enormous pain in the ass, you know that?" He drawled the words out as if bored.

"You love having someone to torment."

"Unfortunately, the opportunity's about to come to an end." ·

A prickly feeling of tension, like an electric current, ran down her arms. She squinted in his direction, watching for the first sign that he was ready to make his move. His seated figure stood out more clearly now against a horizon that had begun to pale.

"What happened on Ryan's fifth birthday?"

"What?"

"I've been asking all the wrong people. You're the only one who can tell me what I want to know."

"How clever of you to appeal to my natural sense of superiority." The amusement was back in his voice. "I was fifteen at the time and I'd had my eye on him for quite awhile. On the day of his party, I begged off. Last thing I wanted to do was hang around with a houseful of stuffy adults. I figured the whole family'd be over at Mildred's, so I took the opportunity to scope out the big house. That's where the old farts—excuse me, the grandparents—lived." He laced his hands behind his head. "I was in the middle of doing an inventory when Mildred and Martin walked in with Ryan. They put him to bed upstairs—I think they told him he could go to the zoo or something if he took his nap. They, of course, had no idea I was in the next room checking out the old broad's jewelry. Once they went back downstairs, I took Ryan up into the attic to teach him some games I know. None of the grown-ups ever realized I was in the house."

Her legs were cramped, her feet numb. She swung her sneakers down to the floor, forcing cold, knotted muscles to straighten. "I heard your mother committed suicide and you went to live with your biological father."

"She caught me with Ryan. It pushed her over the edge." His voice sounded bored again.

"It was you at the restaurant, wasn't it? Talking to Zach."

His full lips spread in a self-congratulatory smile. "I thought that an especially nice touch, if I do say so myself. I'd followed you to the restaurant, and when you went to pee, I ad libbed a little. Thought maybe I could create a soupcon of divisiveness between you two bumbling detectives." He leaned forward, hands on knees. "That do it? I know what an incorrigible little ferret you are and I'd hate to have you go out with any unanswered questions. But the sun's about up and I've got things to do."

"One more?" she begged. He nodded lazily, his glinting yellow eyes beneath invisible lashes looking particularly cat-like in the predawn light.

"What happened the night Ryan died?"

He glanced over his shoulder at the glow on the horizon, then settled back, arms crossed over his chest. "We'll have to make this quick. When I got home that Thursday night, I had a message on the machine from Ryan telling me to get my tail over to his study right away. I inferred from his tone that the subject was not going to be Dear Old Uncle Martin's seventieth birthday party. So I brought along my little persuader." He patted the gun tucked into his waistband.

Shivering uncontrollably, she tensed her jaw to keep from releasing the slightest sound.

"When I showed up, he shoved this picture in my face—picture of himself when he was five—and told me I'd ruined his life. Said I'd taken this innocent little kid and filled him with anger and shame. Whole lot of bullshit psychobabble." His mouth twisted downward in a loose sneer.

"Seems he'd read a newstory that night about a five-year-old molested by his babysitter, and suddenly he remembered all those good old times in the attic." He shook his head, face looking genuinely perplexed. "Way I remember it, he enjoyed 'em every bit as much as me. Anyway, Ryan's problem was, he let his feelings get out of hand. All happened so long ago—he should've put it behind him. But he was out of control, ranting about how I'd be lucky to get a job sweeping streets after Martin found out."

He jerked around to check out the radiance where the sun was about to rise on the horizon. "Long story short, I couldn't let him talk to Martin. Martin would've cut me off at the knees in Chicago, as well as costing me my piece of the inheritance pie. So I stuck my gun in his face and said I had a new game for him: shootout at the Hollister corral. One-way shootout. Gave him two choices. He could write the note I dictated and go out alone, or refuse to write it and take Luke with him. I would've made it look like a home invasion—shot the two of them in bed, ripped off the computer and television. Nobody'd ever've known."

"That's it? You just shot him?" The words popped out before she could stop them, her voice sounding shrill and accusatory.

"When he realized he was going to die, he got very calm. Said he didn't mind getting whacked because he knew, sooner or later, I'd get mine. Then he told me in this smug voice that he'd already spilled everything to you."

"Jesus," she whispered.

"That's why I added that bit in the note about therapy pushing him over the edge. Hoped it'd discredit you. Problem was, I couldn't figure whether you knew but weren't talking because of the confidentiality law—no disclosure if the victim's over eighteen—or if you didn't know and Ryan just made it up to see me squirm."

"So that's why you went through my file and set up that phony session." Her jaw was so tense her voice came out stiff. "But who left the message while you were in my office?"

"I did." He laughed with all the good humor of a knife blade chipping ice. "Programmed my computer to do it."

"And you cut the hose to my dryer and picked up messages off my machine."

"I take credit for all of the above—except stealing messages. You must have a secret admirer."

His eyes swept out across the water, which was flat and still except for little ruffles on the surface. "Shit! We've been drifting toward shore. That's what I get for being so damned accommodating."

He swiveled around to rev the motor, which roared

briefly, then sputtered and coughed. He leaned in toward the controls. The motor spluttered a few moments longer, coughed one more time, and died.

You've got to do something. Doesn't matter if he blows your head off. Shooting's better than drowning anyway.

Two steps across the gently rocking boat moved her into position directly behind his seat. She threw her bound wrists over his head and jerked backwards so that the rope between her wrists cut into his throat. Adrenalin pulsed through her system. He yelled, his hands flying to her arms. She shoved a knee behind his seat for leverage and pulled back hard as he fought to remove her wrists from his neck.

His torso lunged sideways, knocking her off balance. Her fingers grabbed at air as he thrust himself out of his seat. In pulling her down, he was able to slide out of her stranglehold. They both landed on the bottom of the boat, Cassidy on top, her tied-up hands scrabbling to get hold of something. She thrashed wildly, trying to stay on top. He bucked and rolled under her, his hands fumbling for the gun tucked into his waistband. *Oh shit. I can't hold on.*

He grasped the gun but she managed to knock it out of his hand and into the bottom of the boat. Every cell in her body was focused on getting to the gun before he did. Swinging her tied arms around, she grabbed it. He slammed his fist into her arm. The jolt loosened her fingers. Tightening her grip, she closed her right hand over the butt, and threw herself out of reach. Rolling away from him, she scrambled to her feet.

She leaned back against the railing and extended her arms straight out, holding the gun in her right hand and pointing it directly at him.

He sprang up, gripping the rail with one hand and brushing his hair back with the other. "Quite the little spitfire." She assumed his patronizing tone was meant to rattle her. "But not bright enough to realize it won't do you any good."

Why isn't the gun stopping him? I have to do something—what is it Kevin showed me?

He took another step.

The safety. Searching frantically for something that might unlock or undo or release, she discovered a black button on the handle. She pushed it, and the gun responded with a satisfying click that brought Chiparo to an instant halt.

She held the gun in his face, her forefinger on the trigger, and said, "Go back and sit down." He retreated to the captain's seat.

Keeping the gun trained on him, she returned to her place in the stern. As they sat watching each other, brightness grew on the horizon behind him.

Chiparo relaxed back into his swivel chair. "You're better than I thought. Pity this exciting little interlude won't make any difference to the final outcome."

When she didn't respond, he continued. "How long do you think you can sit there holding your arms out? How long can you go without sleep? Or taking a pee?"

"Long as I have to."

"You've got a distinct disadvantage—no killer instinct. Oh, you might be able to pull the trigger in self defense, if I rushed you. But as long as I just sit here, you're helpless. There's not a fucking thing you can do."

His eyes flickered. Something overhead momentarily distracted him. She heard the distant sound of a motor. What was going on behind her?

"All I have to do is outwait you. I don't have to keep my concentration up. I can take a nap or watch the clouds," his eyes flicked up again.

The sound of the motor grew louder.

"How long do you think it'll be before I get the gun back?" His eyes flipped up. His muscles tensed. He lunged.

She aimed at his groin and pulled the trigger.

A thundering helicopter achieved a hovering position overhead. A sliver of sun had emerged in a burst of light. She stood in the rocking boat and numbly stared up at the metallic bird looming just a few yards above.

"This is the U.S. Coast Guard. Prepare to be boarded."

      🙈 🙈 🙈

A Coast Guard officer strapped her into the harness and signaled the pilot to pull her up. Moments later Zach was unbuckling her.

"What're you doing here?" she demanded. "You shouldn't be here. Chiparo took the wrapper and I was sure you'd never find me because there wasn't any other way you could figure out where we were."

"I found you." He pushed the straps aside, drew her into his arms and cradled her.

"You should've seen him," the pilot yelled over the sound of the engine. "He was like a maniac, calling the police and the politicians, even that columnist, what's his name. He pulled every string in the book to get us out here."

Zach spoke to the pilot standing behind her. "What about the creepo she shot? Dead, I hope?"

"Naw," the pilot shouted, "She hit him in the knee."

Thank God!

Zach took a step back, his arms resting on her shoulders, and grinned. "I planned to arrive at the next to the last moment—like the old time cavalry. But I missed my chance. You got your licks in ahead of me."

Feeling weak as a blade of grass, she leaned her whole weight against him. Then she remembered getting his machine at eleven-thirty and spending all those hours with Chiparo thinking it was hopeless and he'd never find her.

Her spine stiffened and she pushed away. "Where were you when I called? Why weren't you home?"

Her hands turned into fists and she beat on his chest and sobbed. "Why can't you ever be where you're supposed to be when I need you?"

35

GOOD MORNING STARSHINE

They made love quietly in the late afternoon. Afterwards, as they sat up in bed, Zach pulled her into the crook of his arm and called her attention to the cat, who gazed down at them from the top of the television.

"You think we're seeing voyeuristic tendencies here?" Cassidy asked.

Diving onto the bed, the cat nestled into a crevice between them, establishing contact with both their bodies through the sheet they'd pulled up.

Cassidy stroked her back. "She's not bad for a cat. If you like cats, that is."

"We ought to name her. Right now, to celebrate the fact

that it's over and we survived."

She sighed. "I still don't think I've got it all straight. I know you explained things when we were driving home, but I was in shock or something. Did you say you were able to track me down because Luke drew a picture?"

Disentangling his body, he twisted around to pick up a folded sheet of paper that was laying on the nightstand. Luke had drawn a square house next to a large oblong with squiggly lines representing waves. "You know how Luke's been drawing everything since I started him on Pictionary? Well, he left this on that little table in his room and since it was all I had to go on, I made the assumption Ryan's killer had taken the two of you to the Lake House. When I arrived to find Luke drugged and the boat gone, I knew I had to get the Coast Guard out." He put the picture back on the night-stand and rubbed his foot against hers under the sheet.

Leaning forward, she scratched the cat's face. "I re-member you phoned Martin after we got in—last night or this morning or whenever it was—but I was so tired I didn't even want to hear about it."

He laced his fingers on top of his head. "Seems Chi-paro—or Frank Farrel, his real name—left Oak Park after his mother's suicide and wasn't heard of again until a couple of years ago, when he appeared on Martin's doorstep with some sob story about being down on his luck and needing a little help to start over in Chicago."

"Didn't Martin check him out or anything?"

"He's got a blind spot when it comes to family. Also, he was particularly susceptible because he'd always felt guilty about the kid's mother. Blamed himself for being so wrapped up with Mildred and Ryan he hadn't noticed how depressed she was."

"So Martin subsidized Chiparo or something?" The cat nipped at her finger and she jerked it away.

"Chiparo wanted to do voiceovers, so Martin hooked him up with Ryan, whose secretary, by the way, was the lovely Yvonne." He tried pulling her back under his arm but she resisted.

"Wait," she said, "there's something bothering me." She thought for a moment. "Chiparo didn't look like he had the kind of money it would take to ply Yvonne with diamonds and gold."

Zach's mouth twisted wryly. "Ryan'd had an affair with her. It was over before Chiparo came on the scene."

Cassidy felt a ripple of sadness. "He sure didn't tell me everything, did he? Speaking of not telling, how come you were, as they say, out of the loop?"

"I guess they all had the attitude—if I couldn't pick up a phone I didn't deserve my copy of the family newsletter. Oh, and one more thing," he pulled harder and this time she slid into place against his shoulder. "Remember Mildred mentioning she'd have to cancel out on Martin's dinner plans? Well, the other guest was Chiparo, so he knew she was babysitting at Kristi's, which made it easy for him to drop over with a bottle of DuBonnet."

She laid her hand on top of his. "With all these changes, you have any urge to get your name on the list for the family newsletter?"

An Are-you-nuts? look came over his face. "I already told you what I think about family togetherness. The only difference now is that the secrets are out in the open. All my life there've been these currents going on around me, and now I know why."

Removing her hand from his, she wiggled a finger in front of the cat's nose. "Family secrets," she sighed. The cat opened one eye and whipped out a paw. Cassidy snatched her finger away, but the claw pierced the sheet and dug into her thigh.

"So, what'll we name her?"

"You were the one picking up my messages, weren't you?

Embarrassment flickered in his gray eyes. "I couldn't just stand around and let some thug take you out."

"And you borrowed money from Martin to pay off the mob."

He grinned broadly. "Was Martin ever pissed after you fobbed him with that tape, then he found out he'd donated money to the Save-Cassidy-from-Herself fund." He draped an arm behind her neck and squeezed her shoulder. "As far as the money goes, you're worth every penny."

"I'd call that an expensive lay."

"C'mon, quit stalling. What do you want to name her?"

"So, do you really mean it that you want to have a relationship with us? The cat and me, that is?"

"I said so, didn't I?"

"What does that mean? Does it mean you want to move in or what?"

"It means, let's give it a try and see what happens. Okay, if you refuse to cooperate, I'll do it myself. I'll name her—Juliette. I like that, Juliette."

"No, Juliette's wrong. She died young, remember? You know, there's a song that keeps going through my head—*There's got to be a morning after, if we can make it through the storm.* I kept singing that song in my head when I was out in the boat."

"So, what are you saying? You want to name her *Morning After*?

"No, that doesn't sound right. Something else."

The cat raised her triangle face and rumbled contentedly, gazing at them out of moist green eyes.

"Good Morning Starshine," Cassidy murmured.

"You want to name her *Good Morning Starshine?*" Zach said, his voice dubious.

"That's it."

The cat stretched, then climbed up onto Cassidy's chest and touched her pink nose to Cassidy's lips.

"So," Zach said. "Starshine it is."